Second Print Edition 2026.

Front Cover, Artist Niah J. Stone

Chief Editor, L. A. Stone

Line/Proof Editor, J. Stone

Published By: Magnolia Xen, LLC Publishing

magnoliaxen@hotmail.com

https://www.magnoliaxen.com

https://www.facebook.com/@magnoliaxenauthor

https://www.tiktok.com/@magnoliaxen

https://www.instagram.com/@iammagnoliaxen

Contents

The Alpha Queen's Mate
Book ~ Two

A Jaidan's Prophecy Duology

Magnolia Xen

To my husband who is my biggest fan and motivator and believes I can do anything I put my mind to. He continues to push me to pursue all my passions and has been saying for years I should write my book, I finally heard You! To my oldest son who used his film education and production expertise to pull all the self-publishing parts together into a masterful novel. To my youngest son who is the best sounding board and brain stormer an author can have, especially during those writing block moments. Finally, to my baby girl, who is not only the artist who materialized the original cover for my debut novel but is the motivational strength behind my main character.

Prologue

THE PROPHECY

After Five Hundred Years the "Golden Wolf" will be born and years of fighting and regional separation will end. The truth of the Ruler will shine through their eyes, the mark of the Ruler will be born on their neck, and "The future Ruler of all wolves will unite the packs". The continued existence of our kind requires the Alpha born be taught how to rule with Knowledge and Kindness, be trained to Defend, Protect and Serve, and will know how to Love and in return will be Loved by many. This is the Prophecy!

Jaidan Emerald Scott was born and raised to be the Ruling Alpha Queen of all wolves and is on the journey of her life to solidify the Prophecy she now wants more than Ever!

TRIGGER CONTENT WARNINGS: BLOOD, GORE, SEXUAL-LY EXPLICIT SCENES, HEAVY PROFANITY, ANXIETY, AND DEATH of CHARACTERS.

Chapter 1

BETA JAY

*M*innesota

My head is pounding, my heart is racing, I can't think of anything else to do. I start feeling like I'm going to faint, and immediately think I should have asked for help sooner. I try to focus, to mentally concentrate on reaching out to the people I trust the most hoping they hear me. I hope this isn't the way I die as I scream "HELP. HELP ME, PLEASE."

I jump awake from my nightmare before I realize it's a memory. I wipe the tears from my face and look around before my eyes land on Olivia sleeping. I can tell she's still in pain, but she's alive, and that's what's important. I'm glad me having a nightmare didn't wake her. I look over to see Jane watching me with concerned eyes, I shake my head, letting her know I'm ok as I settle back in my seat. Jewel. *"Yes, Jay, I know, but you are strong, and you are going to be ok."*

Alright, Jewel. I close my eyes hoping I can get some uninterrupted sleep for the rest of the flight. My plane finally lands and when the doors open, standing there at the bottom of the stairs is Samuel. He wasn't what I was expecting but he is a good sight for sore eyes.

I quickly start descending the steps and he reaches up grabbing me in a tight hug. I let him because it's what I need most at this moment, still being really shaken up.

"I can see you're well, Jay."

"I am, Samuel."

"How about Olivia?"

"She's not as well, but she's alive. I was able to get as much of the wolfs-bane out of her as best I could without taking too much into myself. She needs to be under a doctor's care and fast. How long is the chopper ride to the lodge?"

"Not long, less than forty minutes."

"Good." As we talk, men are unloading the plane and moving our belongings to the chopper, as well as assisting getting Olivia moved. I make the introductions between Beta Jamison and Alpha Samuel Jacobs and then we get on the chopper. As we take off, I inquire about how he came to be here. He says he was in the area, but I'm sure he's hiding something, and I'm too mind wary to push him on it now. He knows we can't talk right now with Jane and Olivia here, but I can see he needs assurances.

I speak into his mind saying, "I received another power while in New York City, and yes, it helped me help Olivia. I think I could have done more, but not knowing what it would have done to me more than knock me on my ass, I didn't push it." He nods his head to let me know he heard and agreed. "I've missed you, Samuel." He smiles. I understand that to mean he's missed me as well. We settle in for the flight, I'm arriving early, so Alpha Peterson is not expecting me, as well as I'll be interrupting his ski season. But it could not be helped, and this mountain seems like the best place to be at the moment.

As the chopper lands, I don't see anyone, I imagine Tony wasn't able to get through to the Alpha. We exit the chopper and the men that were traveling with Samuel help us get unloaded and head to the front of the lodge. Finally, people come running out to assist us. The lodge is beautiful, but I don't really have the time to appreciate it, having to get Olivia settled and make sure we're welcomed at this time. We enter the front doors, and immediately I see Alpha Richard standing there staring dumb founded at me.

It's like a bolt of lightning shoots through me, I don't understand this reaction to him, but I don't have time for this right now. Jewel get it together. Olivia, remember."*Ok, Jay.*" I step forward and reach my hand out to him, "I'm Beta Jay Scott, the Ruler's Regent. I apologize for arriving early and unannounced, but for reasons I can't reveal in this location, it could not be helped. I hope that Alpha Mathews was able to get through to you."

"Uuhh, no, I saw that I had a missed call, but was not able to return it before I was notified I had an unannounced chopper landing. But I'm happy to receive you, my mother Luna isn't available at this moment because we weren't expecting you for over a week."

"That's of no concern, Alpha Peterson, I'm fine to settle myself in. But I request, please a doctor for my friend who is injured."

"Of course, Beta Scott."

He turns and speaks to someone standing at the desk that I hadn't noticed. I also drop my hand that he never reached out to shake; I don't know what that's about. I turn to him. "I would like to introduce my business associate from New York, Beta Jane Jamison. She comes with me from Alpha Mathews, pack. He would have told you about her accompanying me as well if you were able to receive his call. And I'm sure you know Alpha Samuel Jacobs, as you all were in Alpha training together."

"Yes, of course."

They shake hands, and then a group of people come and take Olivia to the pack hospital. I let her know that I'll be over to her soon, I just need to make sure we are settled into the lodge here and get things explained to the Alpha. "Is there a chance we can speak in private some where, Alpha Peterson?"

"Of course, Beta Scott, follow me this way."

I then turn to Jane, "If you don't mind, can you please accompany Olivia and ensure she's taken care of?"

"And what about you, Jay?"

"I'm fine. Samuel is here, he was the Alpha of our pack on the island. He will not let anything happen to me, plus, remember Alpha Mathews agreed this was the next best location for us to go." She reluctantly went with them to take Olivia. I then follow behind Alpha Peterson with Samuel following behind me. We walk down a hallway that eventually comes to what looks like a library. What is it with Alphas liking libraries? This one is very nice though. As I enter, I notice a very beautiful woman sitting with her feet tucked under herself on the couch reading a book.

She looks very comfortable, a lot more comfortable than I was in seeing her there. She has long black hair, curly but not as curly as mine, well built, brown eyes that are friendly when she looks our way, but for some reason I'm still not happy about her comfortable position in Alpha Peterson's library. He walks over to his desks and gestures for us to have a seat. The female who I can sense is an

Alpha, stands up and walks closer to us, asking Richard who do we have here? So, they're on a first name basis as well, what the hell.

But before he can say a word I start talking. I step closer to her and reach out my hand. "I'm Beta Jay Scott, the Ruler's Regent, and you are?" She blinks surprised by my bluntness I'm sure, but reaches her hand out and responds.

"I'm Alpha Lisa Small, a long time friend of Alpha Peterson. A close friend and long time repeat guest to the lodge for the ski season. It's nice to meet you and glad you arrived early so I had the opportunity."

I release her hand and now that I have I feel better about her, I turn saying. "With me here is Alpha Samuel Jacobs." He reaches forward to shake her hand and I notice he's reluctant to do so and so is she. They both look past each other like they're uncomfortable, making me wonder if they know each other.

"Well, it's nice to meet you, and hopefully I'll get to speak with you once you get settled."

She walks over and retrieves the book she was reading. She looks over at Alpha Peterson with a look I don't fully understand before she leaves the room. As the door closes, I hear Samuel clearing his throat behind me. What's up with him. I look over to Alpha Peterson, who's still looking at me all weird. Jewel, what's up with him? "*His wolf recognizes me as his mate and he's told him who you are. It's freaking him out because he can't smell you like he usually would. He does feel a connection he can't understand because of his wolf and he's on unsure footing. Plus, he knows you've gotten under the skin of both Alpha Jarrod and Alpha Tony.*" So why is that a problem? "*Jay, they're not only Alphas, they're friends. Just something to consider.*" Alright, but he can stop being weird about it. I walk to the seat opposite his desk asking if we can sit.

"Yes, of course, I apologize, it's just, you took me by surprise."

"I did? Why?"

"You know, your early arrival, that's all."

"You're an Alpha, so I'm sure you're adept at handling unforeseen circumstances and adjusting accordingly without totally falling apart, am I right?"

"What?"

I hear Samuel snickering to my right. "Alpha Peterson, you seem to have lost all ability to talk, to function, to be cordial to guests." I can see this statement got a rise out of him.

"Wow, Beta Scott, you show up unannounced on private property and then insult my response to not being prepared."

"No, Alpha Peterson, not your response to not being prepared, the time it's taken you to overcome not being prepared. It's not like I dropped a bomb on your pack house. I arrived with six people to a lodge, I might add, that's supposed to be accustomed to hosting guests and you seem to have checked out. You didn't even say goodbye to the guest you had in your library when she left the room. I wonder if the rumor of your lodge's hospitality has been overstated. We'll have to see. So tell me, are you going to contact Alpha Mathews or do you want me to explain the situation to get you caught up?

I do know that some Alphas don't take instruction from females very well." Through my whole statement I keep looking at Samuel wondering about his not so quiet snickering as he keeps avoiding my looks. I then look Alpha Peterson square in the eye. He closes his eyes, pinching the bridge of his nose, and takes a deep breath before he finally speaks.

"I think, Beta Scott, its best that I contact Alpha Mathews about what's going on. Even though I would like to go on record that I don't have a problem taking instruction from a female. I think it best you get settled into your suite that we've had ready for you and your assistant. I wasn't expecting as many but as you say we're a lodge and can make arrangements as needed. Plus, I'm sure you'll want to check on your friend."

"Very good, Alpha Peterson, I'm glad you've recovered your voice, at least." He reaches for the phone and then a few minutes later a pack member arrives.

"Martha will take you to your suite and then to the pack hospital. Martha is assigned to your suite, if you need anything she's the one you can ask."

"Thank you, Alpha Peterson. I look forward to speaking to you later once you've had your conversation with Alpha Mathews." I rise and follow Martha from the room leaving Samuel in his seat. As the door closes, I hear him burst out laughing. He must've been holding that in for quite some time, but I wonder about what.

A _lpha Richard_

I close my eyes as Beta Scott leaves my office and wait for Samuel to stop laughing. I look over, waiting for the laugher to stop,"Anytime you finish would be fine with me."

"Just give me a second, Alpha Richard. I've been away from Jay for some months, so I have missed how well she knows how to work a room."

"That was crazy, Alpha Samuel. What the hell did I do wrong?"

"Where do you want me to start?"

"How about from the beginning before I call Tony."

"Let me see if I can explain it to you, Richard. First, you didn't take the call from Tony, and she now assumes that's because you were entertaining the Alpha female that was sitting in your office, whether true or not. This means you were not there to meet her and her hurt friend, who has become very dear to her. Then, you didn't shake her hand when she reached out her hand, like she was not worth you doing so. Yet then, you reached out and shook my hand and Beta Jamison's hand.

Then, you didn't offer to get them checked in and just stood there starring like an idiot. Then, you didn't offer to have her friend taken to the pack clinic, giving her the impression you didn't care whether she was taken care of or not. Next, you lead us to this room and didn't introduce her to the very beautiful, comfortable Alpha female sitting curled up on your couch in your office referring to you as Richard. After that, you didn't even bother to introduce yourself to her, should I go on."

"Damn, I did all that?"

"Yes, you did it in less than twenty minutes. You must be faster than what you displayed this morning if you are going to keep up with Jay over the next couple of months that is for sure."

"Why are you laughing, Alpha Samuel?"

"Well, Jarrod and I like to say that you just got Jay'd. It's our way of saying she used you against yourself to her best advantage, and you had no idea it was happening at that moment. I have been a victim of it over the years, and there is no escaping it, even when you're aware of the power of it."

"I see your point, Samuel, thank you for explaining."

"Alpha Richard? Who was the Alpha female again? Alpha Lisa Small? She looks familiar."

"Yes, she's Alpha Andrew Small's sister, he was with us at Alpha training. Her mate died a couple of years ago and she comes every season. We're close friends, but you don't have a chance. Yes, Alpha Samuel, I noticed your interest even though I also noticed your interest in Beta Scott."

"It's a confusing situation in my head and my heart, but why do I not have a chance with Alpha Small?"

"Because she will not get involved with an Alpha that might challenge her twin sons' claim to their father's Alpha-Hood. That's why she has her maiden name, that way they're the only ones holding the Alpha title of Alpha Monte for their pack."

"Except for with you, though, right, Alpha Richard?"

"We're longtime friends, and she knows I'll always protect her and do what's best for her twins. They'll be Alphas of their packs no matter what. That's her wish and I'll ensure she gets it. She knows she'll never be my Luna because of it. Now that I think more on it, I know you and your integrity and your wish to not be a ruling Alpha, so she might be an option. But what do you do about your feelings for Beta Scott? I hear tell she has others falling heavy for her and I have competition for her, if what I know is true."

"You do, and that's my dilemma as well, but only time will tell. However, you need to get on the phone with Tony, then we can find out what the hell happened that sent Jay here early."

I hit the speaker on the phone and pressed his name to ring Tony, he answers on the first ring.

"Hey Rich, did Jay make it there safely?"

"Yes, she did, I missed your call because I was taking care of something for one of my guests. What happened, Tony, why did she arrive early?"

"You mean to tell me she's there and didn't tell you what's happening?"

Samuel starts snickering. "No, Tony, she didn't get the chance to tell me."

"Tony, just so you know, Jay is upset with Alpha Richard and went to get settled into her suite and then to check and make sure that Olivia is being taken care of."

"What the hell did you do this soon, Rich? She literally just arrived in your region barely an hour and you upset her already? That's a record, man. And you all say I'm the fuck up of the group! At least she was here longer before she got baby out of me. But man, you must've put your foot in it to have pissed her off already. I can't even imagine."

"You're right, Tony. I was here and couldn't believe it was happening right in front of my eyes, and didn't know how to stop it while it was happening. Also, not sure I wanted to, considering I wasn't the one that was going to be on the receiving end of her ire in the end, but it was something to see."

"Excuse me, if you both are finished, I would like to move onto the reason the angry little she wolf is here early, I might add, throwing me off my game."

"Yes, Tony, he was definitely off his game, which was part of the problem, I might add, according to Jay."

I stare at Alpha Samuel who is still laughing uncontrollably. "Enough already, I'm sure we have more important things to discuss than what I did to make Beta Scott upset with me."

"Oh, Alpha Richard, we're calling her Beta Scott."

"That's her name, Samuel, is it not?" Before Samuel could answer, due to his continuous and might I add annoying laughing, Tony answers.

"Yes, that's her name, Rich, especially when you're on the outs with her."

Before I can respond, Samuel gets hisself together to add his two cents.

"More importantly, Tony, since he failed to even introduce himself to her when she arrived, and when she reached her hand out to shake his, he didn't return the favor."

"WHAT? Richard, why are you treating my girl like that? You will show her the respect she is due, it's a wonder she didn't put you on your ass for the disrespect. You know she's the Ruler's Regent, by the way."

"Yes, yes, yes, it's just that I was surprised by her. I wasn't expecting to feel this overwhelmed by seeing her. By smelling something, I don't even know what and Bryce was going all crazy in my head I couldn't concentrate. Can we move on, please?"

"What do you mean about Bryce, why was he going crazy?"

"It's a long story, we will go into it later. Can we get back to why Beta Scott is here early?" Tony gets quiet on the line. "Tony, are you there?"

"Yes, it's just that my wolf was the same way, and I don't think I like how this is turning out. I love you guys, but how could this work with us and Jay?"

"Not discussing this now, we've more important things to worry about than whose mate she's going to be. If it's up to our wolves, she belongs to all of us." Alpha Samuel clears his throat.

"I think you both should table this conversation until later. We need to figure out who's threatening or potentially trying to kill Jay or Olivia or both, and why. More importantly, we must determine if it has anything to do with the Ruler."

Both Tony and I agree with Samuel. I listen as Tony begins to tell us about what happened a night ago that he was still confused about. How it could happen on his pack grounds was still a mystery he was trying to understand. Before he could voice his pack's security concerns, there's a loud noise coming from upstairs and I hand up the phone.

B *eta Jay*

As I follow Martha towards my suite, I'm not even paying attention to the direction we're going, too busy trying to settle my nerves over the treatment I've received from Alpha Peterson. How dare he be so dismissive of me. *"Jay, calm down, I don't think that was his intention. I just think he was caught off guard. I was getting a lot of feelings from his wolf who was trying to connect with me, but I was ignoring him. That didn't help your Alpha in that moment, so give him some slack".*

I get it, Jewel, but I'm going to need him to be better than that if he plans on keeping up with me."*Yes, I know that is right, because you're a handful.* "What ever, Jewel. I finally took a deep breath and with it came a smell from the room Martha was heading too. One that I'm sure that I don't want to deal with, even though I'm curious as to why she would be in a room assigned to me. I know we're not in a room together because I'll kick said slack mouth Alpha's ass if he was that insensitive as to put me in a room with his bed partner. Especially after knowing his wolf thinks I might be his mate.

"Jay, calm yourself, all I feel from Alpha Small is curiosity. What do you feel?" I take a moment and realize Jewel is correct, but I don't plan on making it easy for her. Jewel, can you make sure we're the Beta with a little Alpha we need to be? Can't let her cause us to come out of character unless we need to. *"Absolutely, Jay."* I finally enter the room. "Thank you, Martha. if I need anything I'll give you a ring." I close the door, noticing Alpha Small sitting in one of the chairs to the left of the entry in the living area. She has her hands crossed in her lap obviously waiting for me to acknowledge her presence.

I walk towards the dining area, placing my bag down on the table. I kick my shoes off, pulling my coat off, and putting it over the back of the chair. I release the pin that's holding my hair up letting my curls fall loose and releases some of the pressure in my head and neck. After a few seconds, I say, "I wasn't aware of a meeting between us that mandates you being in my suite before I even had a chance to get myself settled. Am I right, Alpha Small?" She rises from her seat, approaching around to the front of me on the opposite side of the table. I imagine this is her 'I'm an Alpha, and I don't have to have a reason, and I go where I want when I want to' stance, but instead she says,

"I knew you wouldn't give me an audience if I requested it at this time. I thought I would rather beg forgiveness for my forwardness than ask permission of the Ruler's Regent."

I'm appreciative of the recognition and immediately let my hackles down so to say. "Please have a seat, I've had a long day. I imagine I'll have many more ahead. You're correct, I probably would not have the time to socialize during the time you would still be here. However, considering if I wouldn't have arrived early, we wouldn't have had the opportunity to meet. I can't imagine what you would want a meeting with me about." She looks me in the eye as if she's trying to figure me out.

"This might not be what I think it is, but Richard, I mean Alpha Peterson, we've been friends for over fifteen years, and I want to clear the air."

I interrupt her, "Let me stop you, Alpha Small."

"Please call me, Lisa."

"Alright, Alpha Lisa, you don't need to explain your relationship with Alpha Peterson to me. You do understand we just met less than an hour ago, right before I met you, actually."

"Yes I do, Beta Scott, however, I'm aware his wolf informed him that his mate was coming. His response when he came in the office was very much off from the calm, confident, controlled Alpha I know him to be. I assume it was because he was thrown for a loop. With this knowledge and your unexpected arrival, as well as your not very happy response to seeing me in the library, I put two and two together."

"Let me stop you, again. I've not reached my twenty fifth born day, so if I'm Alpha Peterson's mate, I would not be able to confirm or deny that claim, nor would I think it any of your business. I also wouldn't care about any previous relationships he had prior to me becoming his mate. Only after our mating would that matter to me. I assure you, there's nothing for you to be explaining about. If that's all, I thank you for coming to do whatever you're here to do but there is no need.

I do commend you on being a good friend to Alpha Peterson, for any other person finding you cuddled up in the library of the man she just realized was her mate might have found it very disturbing and possibly hurtful." She looks at me with a blank stare saying nothing. Me thinking this means our conversation is over, I turn and head towards the suite door to escort her out. Suddenly I get this feeling that I'm no longer safe and I feel her moving quickly up behind me. I immediately step to the side, grab her around the neck, spinning her around and pushing her away from me.

I'm now confused because that came out of fucking nowhere. "What the hell was that about?" She looks into my eyes, steps towards me in a non-threatening way; she's maybe a few inches taller than me, especially since I kicked my shoes off. My senses go crazy, and at that exact moment, she punches out at me. As she keeps coming at me, I keep blocking, trying to stay in character.

She kicks out and I block and duck, swiping my leg to bring her down.

She jumps to avoid it, I jump back up and punch her in the face as she steps back and snarls at me. "What the hell lady, if you don't get out of here, you're going to get in a lot of trouble. It's a crime to attack the Ruler's Regent." Really, she says and comes at me again, we tussle back and forth for another five minutes before I'm done with this game of give and take. I kick her hard in the stomach, probably a little bit harder than I should have. When she hits the wall a huge crack forms spreading in numerous directions. Between that and the crashing of her hitting the floor I sure the noise is heard through out the lodge.

I immediately regret it and walk over to assist her up. She accepts my hand, but I stay on alert, Samuel taught me well, never let my guard down. But I had nothing to worry about as she is done for the day. As I help her rise, she limps over to the seat she was originally sitting in while holding her stomach. We both had small cuts and bruises but nothing that wouldn't heal quickly. "So are we done here, Alpha Lisa?" She looks at me with a smirk on her face.

"Yes we are, but do you want to know why, Beta Scott?"

"Not really, I've had a long day."

"I'm going to tell you anyway."

"I thought so."

"I know you've been training with the ruler for most of your life, and under the training of a very strong Alpha as well. But I'm Alpha born, and today when you walked into the library, do you know what my wolf, Rae, wanted me to do?"

"Of course I don't, but I'm sure you are going to tell me."

"Bend the neck, Beta Scott."

Immediately my head shoots up to look her straight in the eye. I say nothing, because what do I say to that? She smiles.

"Oh, I'm not here for you to say anything, but my Rae has never wanted to bend the neck to anyone, not even our mate. I had to know if it was just a fluke. And try as I might, she wouldn't let me harm you, and trust me I was trying to give you my hardest, though she was a little tempted with that last kick you just gave us. Rae assures me you've been holding back as well, which is why you're forgiven."

"Thank you I think, Alpha Lisa."

"No, it's good, Beta Scott. Whatever is going on. I just ask that you don't hurt Alpha Peterson. He's a good man, and if it wasn't for my twin Alpha sons, I would fight to be his Luna. Now that I've met you, I think that would've been a losing battle."

Chapter 2

BETA JAY

I'm still thinking about her previous statement while Alpha Lisa continues speaking.

"I will stay the rest of the season, even though I was going to leave early. But now that we've had this little talk, I want to see how things go."

She rises to leave finally.

"Beta Scott, I also felt some kind of vibe between you and Alpha Jacobs. Do you mind if I ask what's up with that? Again, I would really like Alpha Richard to not get hurt. He's been waiting for his mate for along time, and he deserves to be happy."

"Alpha Samuel was the Alpha of our pack on the island. Things are funny with us, but I don't know why. I'm sure there's no future there. He's a good man as well and I wish him to find his mate. What about you, Alpha Lisa?"

"I found my mate and lost him. I've vowed to not take a mate that would try to take the place of my twin Alphas. They're my life, and until they take their place as the Alphas of our pack, I will not take a chosen mate. I only date or get involved with Betas, that way I have the upper hand and can handle them if things get rough."

"Except, of course, when it comes to Alpha Peterson, right?"

"Yes, he's the only exception, but that has ended."

"Really, why is that?"

"Because as of about an hour ago, you showed up, and I know the importance of mates. Regardless of if you are or not, I'll not interfere with that, just in case."

"I respect you for that, and I hope we can be friends in the future when all this is settled. Can I count on you to keep whatever it is you think you know about me to yourself?"

"Yes, Beta Scott, if you promise to not hurt my friend as best you can."

"We have a deal, " I say and we shake on it. "Again, I'm sorry for the kick, but you were getting on my nerves, and I've had a long day."

"It's all good. I'll be all healed in a couple of hours, or I can just go for a run and let my wolf heal me, or just phase in my suite and take a nap. You did just give me some workout."

"Well, Alpha Lisa, I hope to see you at dinner if you feel well enough to join us."

"Maybe, Beta Scott."

"After all of this you can call me, Jay." As I close the door, I decide I'll follow her and take a nap, I text Jane to see how Olivia is doing. She responds that her vitals were improving when she left her. She's in her room getting ready to rest now, and will see me at dinner. I thanked her for looking after Olivia for me and put the phone down. I head towards what I hope is the bedroom for this suite and I'm right. I see where my belongings were left and peel off my clothes.

I grab a night shirt, pulling it over my head as I crawl under the covers. I can feel the coolness in the air, being so high up in the mountains, but the down covers are very cozy. I settle in, and sleep overtaks me.

A<u>lpha Lisa Small</u>

As I approach my suite, I hear someone running up the stairs. Whoever it is must have heard the commotion. I'm about two suites down from Beta Scott, but we both know that she is more than a Beta, don't we, Rae?*"Yes, we do, Lisa, but we'll keep that to ourselves. I felt nothing but good from her."* But will she be good for our Richard? *"That, Lisa, I think will be up to them, but for our kind, she has only good intentions."* I put up my hand to slow Richard down. "She's alright, I think she's resting and you should let her." I'm not sure how I feel knowing he was running to make sure she wasn't hurt and not me, but he knows I can take care of myself.

I was not prepared to see Alpha Samuel on his heels and he was looking me over, inspecting me, but for what? Injuries? That's curious. I look at him closer and I notice he takes a breath of relief, because he knows. Whatever she is, he knows and there was concern for me. That's sweet. He finally looks up into my face, surprised to see me watching him, he then turns his eyes to avoid mine, asking if Beta Scott was ok and should he go check on her?

"No, Alpha, let her rest. She's exhausted from her travels and we just had a very heated conversation that I'm sure didn't help." He shakes his head in my direction saying he will leave us to it then. He turns to go, telling Richard he'll meet him back in his study and they can continue their conversation they were having until they thought the pack lodge was under attack. I smile after him as he leaves. I move heading to my room with Richard following close behind.

"Lisa, what's happening? What was all that noise? It sounded like you guys were trying to kill each other. Are you sure she doesn't need someone to check on her? What's wrong with you? She's a Beta and you're an Alpha, you could have really hurt her."

"Relax yourself, Richard. Do you think I would do anything to really harm your future Luna?" This made him pause. "Yes, I think it's her, but until she has her next born day, we won't know for sure."

"What happened, Lisa?"

"Like I said, we had a conversation about her intentions for you. I needed to make sure she had the best of them, and after our conversation, I'm convinced she does. All things are settled, and I'm sure Beta Scott and I will be best of friends."

"That's all you're going to tell me, Lisa?"

"Yes, Richard, but I'm glad to hear how concerned you are about my well-being. Don't you see my bruises and how bad I'm limping? Your little Beta did a good job of holding her own, that's for sure."

"I'm sorry, Lisa, it's just that you're an Alpha and a very strong one, at that."

"Yes, yes I know, let me be so I can get cleaned up and rest before dinner." He moves in close, giving me a hug, I hug him back tight, sad that this is our relationship now. We're just friends, but surprisingly, I feel good with it. He leans in and plants a kiss on my cheek.

"I'll see you at dinner, if you're sore you know how to fix it."

"Yes, I know." I push him towards the door and as he exits, I close and lock it, I don't want any more interruptions today. I was going to phase to heal my injuries, but I think I'm going to wear these with a badge of honor for the next couple of hours. I peel off my clothes, tossing them toward the chair in the corner, promising myself I'll put them away when I wake. With just my thong on I crawl under the covers, planning to fall fast asleep, but my thoughts travel to a very tall handsome, gray eyed Alpha.

What do you think of him, Rea? "*I like what I see, but he's an Alpha and we have the twins to consider. Would he be a risk to them? Also, he looks to be harboring feelings for Beta Scott.*" Yeah, there is that, but I'm harboring feelings for Richard. Maybe we can help each other heal. Maybe we take this week to see if he can be our new Alpha protector. He is the brother to our regional Alpha, and he would be closer to us than Richard if we need assistance. "*There's that. You get some sleep, I'm going to go check on our pups.*"

Why? I spoke to them while we were waiting for Beta Scott, is something up? "*No, it's just, you talk to the boys, I want to see how the pups are developing. They are still sleeping, but I like to look in on them every now and then.*" Oh, that's nice. I drift off to sleep, feeling excited for my future, in a different way, for the first time in a long time.

A *lpha Samuel*

I know Alpha Small said Jay was fine, but I still want to check in to see for myself. I approach her suite listening to see if I hear anything that sounds like distress, but all is quiet. I agree she's well, then I hear quietly in my head as I turn to leave,

"I'm good, Samuel, just tired from the day."

"Alright, I just wanted to make sure you don't need me."

"Thank you for checking on me. I've learned not to scream in your head in my moment of distress."

"Very good. I'll see you at dinner, have a good sleep, Jay."

I head back towards Richard's library where we can get back on the call with Tony. We were about to learn what happened in New York City that sent Jay fleeing in the middle of the night a week ahead of schedule, which also interrupted my search for the individual who is behind all the attempts against Jay. I followed the trail to the eastern region, but it was a dead end for me. Then, I got this overwhelming feeling that Jay needed help, right before I hear Jay in my head screaming. I contacted Tony and he said he heard Jay screaming for help, as well, but he didn't sound like he knew it came from within him. He said he would get back to me when he had more to tell me. Four hours later, he contacted me via text, telling me Jay was traveling to Lutsen and would land in a couple of hours.

He didn't want to reveal anything until she was safely to her destination. I wondered how that was, and he said he wasn't sure that Jay had it covered. Since I was already in Grand Rapids, Minnesota, I quickly checked out of my hotel and jumped in my rental, hoping I would arrive at the airport before she did. I had no idea what flight she was arriving on, however when I got to the very small airport, I see a plane will be landing in the name of Jewel Scott. I know that's Jay's wolf's name, so I do some inquiring and find out she owns this plane. Not sure how it came to be without me knowing or how she commissioned a whole plane right under my nose, but she's never short of surprises.

I've been traveling commercial to hide what I'm up to, just in case those I'm tracking realize I'm looking for them. The funny thing is I still don't know who I'm looking for. All I know is that they have a connection at my pack and that shit is not acceptable. They also have a connection at Tony and Richards' pack and that's unusual. Lastly, they want to harm Jay and that's dangerous for them.

As I turn the corner heading down the next flight of stairs, I run into Richard. "Hey, Alpha, will Alpha Small be alright?"

"Yes, she's fine. She's an Alpha and can definitely hold her own against a Beta, even though she did say Beta Scott gave her a run for her money. Hats off to you for training her exceptionally well. How is she by the way?"

"I didn't see her, but all was quiet from her room, I chose not to disturb her."

"Lisa is going to get some rest and see us at dinner. She'll be here for the rest of the week. This will give you the chance to talk to her if you want to find out what the scuffle was all about."

"No, I'm sure it was about you, considering how comfortable she was in your library."

"Yes, that's what I think. We're long time friends and I care more about her than just a fling, I care about her safety and the future of her twin Alphas. She knows I will always be her protector."

"I understand, but can I ask why are your telling me this?"

"Because for the first time, my friend asked about you and your relationship with Beta Scott. I also would like her to have a protector that's trustworthy. Besides, she's in your region, and since you're no longer on the island and not the ruling Alpha of your region, you could be that Alpha. I trust you, not only because you're Jarrod's brother, but because I remember in Alpha training that you took your responsibility very serious. You were the best choice for the new Ruler and that connection would ensure Lisa and her twins would be protected."

"I have a question for you, Richard. Are you going to be unable to protect her?"

"My wolf informs me our mate is coming. "Don't ask me how he knows, it's crazy. I will not be as free as I've been in the past. And who better than the actual Alpha who trained and practically raised the new Ruler and a Beta that can hold her own with an Alpha in a scuffle. Who better to help raise and protect Lisa's twin Alphas?"

"How do you know Alpha Small would be open to this protection?"

"I told you she asked about you, but if you're against it I'll understand."

"No, it's just, I think it's a bad idea to make decisions for women, especially Alpha women without their knowledge. I've dealt with a Beta woman and it has gone badly for me over the years."

"This won't be without her knowledge or consent. Just spend the rest of the time Lisa's here to see how you both get along, and then you and she can determine if you want to continue this friendship beyond here. If not, I still hope you'll be a confidant Lisa will be able to call on if she ever needs it."

"I agree to at least that as we come to the library, ready to get back on the phone with Tony so we can find out what resulted in my arrival in Lutsen in the first place. As we enter the library, the phone is ringing and it's Tony.

"What happened guys, how is Jay?"

"She's fine and so is my friend. The word is they had a little conversation that got out of control."

"Alright hold on, I want to get Jarrod on the phone, I don't want to have to repeat myself."

He set up the conference.

"Hello fellas, how is our girl doing?"

"She's resting now, Jarrod, but not very happy with Richard."

"What the hell Richard, what did you do?"

"Wait, Tony, can we please go over what happened to Jay before we go down this rabbit hole again?"

"Sure. But you only say that, Rich, because it's you that's in trouble! If it was me, you would be having a vote to kick me out of the musketeers."

"We still might, Tony, but tell us what happened?"

Tony spends the next thirty to forty minutes telling us what precipitated Jay's untimely departure from his pack and the early arrival at Rich's. Were all silent, then Jarrod asks me how I was able to get to Jay and if I met up with her in New York City.

"No, Jarrod, I was in Grand Rapids when I got the call from Tony. I met her at the airport here and flew over with her on the helicopter. I've been on the trail of whoever is behind this. What I can tell you is the arrow is the same as the one that was shot at her when she was at our pack, minus the wolfs-bane. Whoever this is, they have a connection to all three packs. This is either by family or friend and they've tried to kill Jay three times. What I also know, Tony, is we need to figure this out and fast. We have a little over three months before Jay goes to Haven."

"They should be safe here, as this isn't an easy mountain to climb."

"Sure, Rich, but how do you know whoever it is isn't already up on the mountain? Likely they were already on each of the other pack lands, so we'll have to be diligent."

"I will, Jarrod, then I'm closing down the lodge for the season. I have a couple of new wolves here now."

Richard rises and leaves after letting us know only a select few will be allowed to stay.

My brother, Jarrod, says, "Now that he's gone, can someone tell me what he did to piss Jay off already?" and I start howling in laughter.

A*lpha Richard*

I'm glad I left the room as I refuse to hear what I did and listen to them laugh at me again, in such a short time too. I go to my mother's suite to inform her of Beta Scott's arrival, and that due to the situation, we're going to have to close the season early. She is too excited about Beta Scott being here to care about the guests leaving early. She says, it'll only be a problem for Alpha Holmes and Lucinda, and they're going to put up a fuss thinking they're special, but I know you're Alpha enough to handle it.

She then ushers me out of her suite to take care of things while she starts planning her day. I head down to the front desk to get the list of the guests that are still in residence. We have twelve including the Holmes. I inform the front guest what's about to happen and Mark arrives behind me, asking why we're closing our season early. I completely forgot to inform him. "Beta Scott arrived early this morning due to a situation in New York City. We can't discuss it right now and she's resting in her suite, but we need to get all guests checked out and off the mountain before dinner. I'm going to contact the twelve remaining guests and personally refund them for half of their trip."

"What reason are you telling them they have to leave, Alpha?"

"I was thinking something like the mountain isn't safe."

"We're wolves, Alpha, that's not a good enough reason."

"What would you say, Mark?"

"I don't know. You're the Alpha, it's your job. Think man."

Before I can respond to Mark, I hear footsteps approaching behind me and turn to see Beta Jamison, who smartly says.

"How about you inform them the Ruler's Regent is in residence a week early and they don't have clearance to be in her presence, so they have to leave the facility. Which, by the way, is actually the truth."

"You're a genius."

"That, Alpha Peterson, is true, but I've been running checks on the guests and quite a few of them shouldn't be in residence with Jay here. Or even you for that matter, but you're not my concern, Jay is. Now let's get to making those calls and getting those guests off this mountain as quick as possible."

Some of the guests weren't happy, but with half of their money being refunded and knowing they were leaving because someone that was close to the next Ruler, made them feel honored to go. Of course there was the Holmes', who put up such a fuss my Alpha father had to practically threaten them to get on the helicopter. We accomplished our tasks with the help of everyone including Alpha Jacobs. His presence added another authority of someone close to the Ruler that lent credibility to our request.

I was hoping we would have everyone gone before the sun went down, but I wasn't realistic about how many things people packed when they're traveling for three months. I only have two helicopters, which held things up. It was fine, because Jay went straight to the clinic to have dinner with Olivia who's recovering well, and Lisa decided to have her dinner in her room. It was just us guys once Mark came back from checking on Jay and her friends.

Beta Jamison is something, she put fear in quite a few requests that were Alphas and she's only a Beta, a strong one, but still, I hope to never be on her bad side, ever. Dinner that night was quiet, and I was glad for it because I had a feeling it was going to be a long couple of months.

"Richard, I noticed Alpha Lisa is still here even though she isn't cleared to be around Beta Scott."

"I vouch for her, Samuel, plus you vouch for her even if you don't know it yet, right?"

"I guess I do, Richard."

"Take the week, Samuel, and see how you both feel and let me know. Honestly, I would love to know she has more than me looking out for her."

"I will do as you request, but I will not push myself onto a woman that doesn't want me to."

B*eta Jay*

Olivia opens her eyes and looks at me, then says that I'm always saving her life, and when will she be the one who saves mine? "Well considering I was supposed to be the one who landed on the left side of the downed tree, you probably did save my life, so we're even. Besides, werewolves are strong, we can survive a lot, and you'll survive this as well."

"I feel like I was run over by a very big truck, Jay. What was in that arrow?"

"It was wolfs-bane."

"Wow, that shit needs to be found and destroyed for good. How long do I have to be in this clinic? I hope I have a softer bed than this at the lodge."

"You do, one of the best, I've been told. But you're here for evaluation until the morning, then you will be released, Alpha's orders."

"Well, this isn't my Alpha, does that mean I have to listen to him?"

"Those orders came from Jarrod, so yes you do have to listen to them."

"You told him?"

"Of course I did, Olivia, we can't have him mad at me for you getting hurt on my watch."

"You're right, thanks for being there to help me."

"You wouldn't have been there if it wasn't for me, so no thanks necessary. How about you get some rest, you were pretty out of it on the flight here."

"The doctor says the meds they're giving me makes me sleepy and it's good for my wolf to rest."

"I wanted to make sure you were better I'm going to head to bed and do my best to avoid Alpha Peterson and Alpha Small."

"I feel like there is a story there, Jay. I will get all the juicy details over breakfast."

"Sure thing, girl." I kiss her on her forehead, "Goodnight my musketeer."

"Night, Jay."

I head out of the clinic and run into Jane. "She's good."

"I know, I spoke to the nurse. How are you?"

"Relieved, considering the arrow was the same from California. I think I was the intended target."

"That might not be the case, Jay. Those are training arrows, all packs get the same ones. The only thing that differentiates them is the strip on the bottom, it tells what pack it belongs to. That one is not from our pack, but I don't know where the other one is to check to see if it's from California."

"It was exactly like the one from California. I didn't realize that the strip along the bottom was significant."

"It's not well known. Usually you don't leave your pack region, and you definitely don't take your training arrows from the training facility, meaning you wouldn't know. But I'm in charge of ordering supplies for our training, and after I saw the one that shot at Olivia was different from ours, I did some research, and that's what I discovered."

"This means we now know whoever had access to the California training facility also had access to the New York pack lands, Jane. So tell me what am I not seeing?"

"I thought the same thing, Jay, so I went and checked all the video surveillance while you were at the clinic. I saw nothing or no one that shouldn't be there. I have been reviewing footage since I've been here and still, I've seen nothing. But there is one place on our lands were we don't have cameras."

I look at Jane. "The east cliffs."

"Yes, but I don't know many wolves who would want to venture that cliff. It's damn near impossible to climb from the other side and there is no way to land a plane. Nor is there another way I can think of that anyone could be dropped off on top without us seeing it. The question is whoever shot that arrow wanted to hurt one of you bad enough to venture over that cliff. More serious thought is that they knew you would be in that region of the pack grounds and when. For them to make that shot, they had to be very good, so I'll go with the idea that they hit their target."

"Olivia? But we were about to switch places, as it's what we do to try to keep the advantage over each other while racing back to the pack lands."

"Yes, but how would the person know that, Jay?"

"If they've been watching us, they would have known, Jane, we had done it a couple of times that day. It was our routine the same each time." I thought about this and then I remembered something. "Jane, I usually go to the right, but I was going to fake Olivia out and stay on the left. Then when I thought she was going to go to the right to cut me off she stayed on the left as well. Which made me slow to keep from running into her, especially going over a tree log. Which, now that you have me thinking about it, wasn't down the last time we ran through there. I remember wondering if we would be able to clear it."

"Maybe, Jay, the person put the huge tree there, thinking you would both choose to be careful going over the tree and shot in the spot where you each started out. This means Olivia was the intended target, not you. I think we need to start looking at Curtis in a new light, because each time you were attacked, Olivia was there or in the vicinity, and that might be important. We're not thinking it is because you're the Ruler's Regent."

"Why would he want to kill Olivia?"

"Maybe she knows something she doesn't realize and he's afraid she eventually will. It will be a bad thing for whoever is behind all of this. We'll look at this through different eyes, but not until tomorrow. I know we're both tired and sleep is calling."

"I'll meet you here for breakfast to discuss this with Olivia," I say as we turn and head back to the lodge. As soon as we approach the front desk, I see Alpha Peterson standing with his back to me, talking to someone I hadn't yet met. I feel Jane grab my arm to stop my progress, I slow down and I notice whoever is talking to Alpha Peterson tenses as well. I see him sniff and begin looking around, basically ignoring whatever his Alpha is talking about.

"Pete, are you even listening to me?"

"Yes, Alpha, forgive me, but I smell something."

"What do you smell?"

At that moment, Jane turns and runs towards the front door and out, no coat, nothing. "Jane!" I yell. "Don't go out there, its freezing!" But she doesn't stop.

"Beta Pete, this is Beta Scott. Is this who you were smelling?"

He sniffs and I say no. "I think he was smelling Beta Jamison; she ran like a bat out of hell out the front door, with no coat, I might add. She is going to freeze."

"Good."

I look at Alpha Peterson. "Why is it good that my friend will freeze? You're unbelievable, I can't with you. I'm going to find her coat."

"No, Beta Scott, let me."

Before Alpha Richard could continue the person he was speaking with interrupts him.

"By the way, I'm Beta Pete James, nice to meet you, Beta Scott. And please forgive my Alpha, he's usually not this stupid. I'm not sure what is wrong with him. I'll grab a coat for your friend."

"Thank you, Beta James. Her name is Beta Jane Jamison, she's from the Anneleot-Skyline Pack in New York."

"Thank you for that. Jane, I like that, I'll take her a coat now and make sure she gets safely back in the lodge."

When he turns to leave, I turn to head up the stairs.

"Beta Scott, I apologize, but I didn't mean that it was good your friend freezes."

I stop, turning around to look him in the face. "You know, twice today you have disappointed me for whatever reason, and twice today friends of yours have defended you. I'm too tired for whatever you're about to say, so just save it. Goodnight, Alpha Peterson."

"Goodnight, Beta Scott."

A lpha Richard

I slap my hand to my forehead and then my head begins to pound from the inside. What the hell? I turn towards my office, trying to determine what is causing this banging. I can barely see straight as I stumble, grabbing the walls and barely making it to my desk before falling into my chair. I grab my head pinching the bridge of my nose. What the hell is happening? I pull open my draw trying to find something for this massive headache. Then I think Bryce, what is going on?

"*Oh, Rich, do you remember the pain I promised to bring? Well I'm bringing it to you now. You're such an idiot, you made our mate angry with you again.*" What did I do?"*You don't even know?*" Then the banging starts again. Please stop. Thank you, Bryce. What did I do to make you mad? "*You upset our mate again.*" She misunderstood what I said. "*It doesn't matter, Rich, you must apologize.*" I tried, but she's really stubborn. And the banging begins again. Bryce, I get it already, I'll apologize as soon as I see her, I'll beg on my knees for her forgiveness.

"*Good, Rich, now let me explain. You in your infinite stupidness said 'good', I know you were referring to our Beta not smelling our mate as his mate, but our mate thought you were referring to her beloved friend freezing when she ran outside. Then, in your continued infinite stupidness, you failed to correct that assumption in an appropriate time frame to prove that you are not callous and insincere. So, in one day you have been a callous ass to our mate twice in reference to two people she holds very dear.*"

I was just upset about the possibility of Pete smelling her I couldn't think straight. "*Well, you have to get better, Rich. At this point I don't think she's going to want to be our mate unless you fix things with her.*" I will next time I see her; I promise you, it's what I want as well Bryce.

Chapter 3

BETA JANE

I don't understand what that was. It was stupid to run out into the cold without a coat, but I couldn't think of another thing to do. This isn't the type of cold I'm used to, I would phase and run, but I'm not familiar with where I am, and that could put me in a worse situation. I walk around the side of the lodge, thinking there's probably another entrance I can find, and sure enough, I see a garage up ahead. I start jogging in that direction, and I swear I hear my name being called, but I'm not stopping in this cold.

Whoever is calling me will just have to follow me if they really want to talk. I'm sure I know who it is, who else would come out in this cold after me? Jay is relentless when she wants to be. *"You know it isn't Jay, you can smell him as well as I can."* I'm not going to acknowledge that I smell anything, Joy, and this can't be happening. We already found our mate. *"Maybe this is another mate for us, Jane."* We don't get second mates; we can choose a second mate and I'm not choosing a mate. *"You would have chosen Tim to be our mate."* Yes, Joy, I knew him, I liked him.

"You loved him, Jane." I could have loved him, Joy, given the chance, but he found his mate. We have no mate, as our mate died. *"I know that, Jane, then explain what we smell?"* I take a deep breath,

I smell minty spice, like my favorite tea, but this is not possible, I keep jogging. I reach the garage and to my consternation the doors aren't open. Why is this door not open? I kick it with my foot like that'll open it. The minty spice smell is close behind me now.

"We lock it at night to keep any unwanted wild animals from getting into the pack house."

I tense up, the smell of him is that much stronger with him standing soo close.

"You should have a coat on in this weather. I wasn't sure where yours was, I chose to bring you one of mine"

He placed it over my shoulder, and his smell explodes in my senses. I inhale deeply, and I feel at home, relaxed like I usually feel with a warm cup of tea after a long day of work. I was about to turn to face him when he reaches around me punching in the code to the door. I push it open and rush in even though the warmth from his coat as well as him behind me has lessened the cold in my bones. I was going to run to my room and put off whatever this was but I'm no chicken. I stopped myself and turned to face him.

He's tall, at least six feet seven, shoulder length black hair, brown eyes, large nose, large succulent looking lips and I would not be disappointed to have him as my mate. Based on his oversized coat I'm wearing, and what appears to be very large feet I can only imagine what that means for the parts of him I can't see. I look back up to his eyes, catching him watching me. I see curiosity about me and worry, I wonder why worry? Then resolve.

"My name's Pete James, I'm the Beta of this pack. Beta Scott told me your name's Beta Jane Jamison and that you're from the New York City regional pack. I'm not sure what it was I smelled. I'm sorry if I frightened you back in the foyer, it was not my intention."

"No, Beta James, you didn't frighten me, I don't frighten easily."

"You kinda ran out into the cold night without a coat."

"I was surprised to smell you."

"That is surprising."

"Yes it was. Have you found your mate, Beta James?"

"Yes, but she died five years ago in a snow fall accident."

"I'm sorry to hear that. I have no pups, and my mate died four years ago."

"I have no pups either, Beta Jamison. Have you ever heard of getting a second mate?"

"No, I haven't, which is why I was surprised and confused, but this is what I'm smelling. Is it what you're smelling, Beta James?"

"Yes, Beta Jamison."

"But I wasn't ready to have a chosen mate."

"But we're not chosen mates, Beta Jamison. We're Goddess-mates, if what we're smelling is true."

I decided to test this theory and step closer to him. I reach my hand out, he reaches out his hand, and before we even touch, I can feel the sparks tingling between us. I briefly run my finger along his finger, and the exhilarating feeling running through my finger into my arm brings back familiar feelings and I snatch my finger back. "How can this be?" I want to grab him and touch him more, but I'm not ready for this; am I? "I think I need time to consider what this will mean for my life, Beta James. This isn't something I was ever thinking was going to happen."

"I understand, Beta Jamison."

"Thank you for understanding, but do you mind if I ask, are you involved with someone in your pack?"

"I don't mind you asking, and yes, but I'll tell her now, considering what has happened. I respect the goddess' decisions over our lives."

"Was this person going to be your chosen-mate?"

"No, I wasn't even considering a chosen-mate at this point in my life."

"Will it break that person's heart?"

"I don't think so, but we're wolves, and she will respect it as I do. Beta Jamison, are you involved with someone back in your pack?"

"No, I've had no one in my life since my mate passed. I did have feelings for someone, but he found his mate and moved away, and we were only ever friends. I'm going to bed now, thank you for the coat."

"You're welcome. Will I see you at breakfast?"

"No, I'll be having breakfast in the clinic with Beta Scott and Beta Parker. We can meet after to decide what we should do about our situation."

"That's agreeable, Beta Jamison, but I would like to go on record with saying I would love to accept you as my mate, and I will hope you choose the same."

"Good night, Beta James."

"You can call me Pete."

"Very well. Goodnight, Pete, and you can call me Jane."

"Goodnight, Jane."

I move into the pack house, rushing forward to the stairs and hurrying to my room. I push in my code and rush to my bed. Joy, what do we do?"*We accept him as our mate! What's the worst that can happen? We are happy again and hopefully he will be good for us. We have been lonely, and we want pups, don't we?*" I thought we did. "*We do, Jane, why not take the gift from the goddess and accept Pete as our mate?*" I don't know, Joy.

I get up and go into the bathroom, look at myself in the mirror, pulling the ties from my dark auburn hair. I shake my head, realizing how long my hair has gotten. I've been so busy and have had no time to get it trimmed. I undress, jump in the shower, and for the first time, I start to wonder what my future looks like without work being my only companion. I quickly finish my nighttime routine and put on my pj's. I pull back the covers, getting into bed. I hit the light feeling more tired than I was before I got in the shower. I feel like tomorrow is going to be a long day.

B*eta Pete*

I listened to ensure Jane made it to her room safely. This is a surprise for sure. What could have made the goddess give me another mate? I've asked for one lately, wanting something like

I had with my Marley again. But after so many years, I thought it would have to be on me, and just last year I decided to date. I'm sure Anne won't care, she's looking for an Alpha. What she gets from me is sexual, keeps her warm on the cold nights, as she likes to say. I didn't mind, after four years of celibacy I wasn't picky at first, but after smelling Jane, I know I've been missing out on something more.

I walk up to the next level where my suite is and am happy to see Anne there waiting for me. She asks what took me so long and I tell her I had something happen, and honestly, I'm not sure how she's going to feel about it. She walks up to me, putting her arms around my neck. I grab them and place her back from me. I take a couple of deep breaths before saying, I have a mate. She laughs asking what I'm talking about so I explain to her how I just smelled someone amazing, and she is my goddess-mate.

She tells me that isn't possible and inquires if I've been drinking. I remind her that she knows I don't drink like that anymore. I met my mate, her name is Beta Jamison, she's here with Beta Scott, from New York City. We touched and we're true goddess-mates; maybe because we both lost our mates early, we've been given second mates, but it is true. "I told her about how I would tell you we're no longer in a relationship because you respect goddess mates just as I do." I could see the pain on Anne's face, and it surprises me, then I saw anger.

She says that she thought we would eventually be chosen-mates. "I thought in a couple of years maybe, I wasn't even sure you felt that way, but that won't happen now. I have a goddess-mate; you do understand that right?" She says yes, but then asks me, why I think she should be happy about it. I told her because I would be happy for her. Obviously I would be sad for myself, but happy for her because it's a goddess-mate.

I step closer to her, wanting to hug her and apologize for not knowing she felt this way, but then she pushes past me, snatching open the door and rushes out. I didn't think I would be hurting her this badly. I must make sure I let Jane know before she runs into Anne and thinks I lied to her.

I wake early the next morning, determined to catch Jane before she leaves her suite. I knock on her door, and when she opens it, I'm not prepared for the sight in front of me. Her hair is down around her shoulders, reaching past her butt. Wow, it's thick, dark auburn with highlights shining through it. She has on black jeans, a white camisole and nothing on her feet. She calls my name and I look up at her.

"Come in, Pete, I have to finish getting ready. I imagine if you're here, something important happened? Is Beta Scott alright, did your Alpha send you for me?"

"Oh, no, I came for my own personal reason." She closes the door and goes back into the bathroom, leaving me standing by the door.

"I can hear you from here if you speak."

"When we spoke last night, Jane, I told you I was involved with someone, her name is Anne. After we spoke, I returned to my room and she was there, but nothing happened, I want to assure you of that." She comes into the room, looking at me now, forgetting her hair that is now falling back down from its bun. I like it down; I wish she would leave it. "I told her immediately about the goddess giving me another mate, you, and she wasn't happy."

"But you said, Pete, she would be alright with this and happy for you."

"I was obviously wrong about that. I thought it would be nothing. Apparently, Anne was under the impression in a couple of years that we would be chosen-mates. I can't lie, I wouldn't have been apposed to that if our feelings developed to that point. But now I've been given a goddess mate and that's not an option for me."

"Are you sure, Pete?"

"Yes, absolutely, Jane."

"Then why are you here again?"

"When I told Anne, she got very upset."

"You said that part already, Pete."

"She pushed me away and rushed out of my room without saying anything to me."

"What were you expecting her to say?"

"That she at least understood and would be fine."

"If she wanted to be your chosen-mate, I can't imagine she is, maybe she just needs to heal her heart."

"I just wanted to let you know. That way, if she comes to talk to you, you know the facts. I wouldn't want you to be caught off guard."

"Thank you for letting me know. Is there something you're not telling me?"

"Nope, I've told you everything."

"Then we're good, and I have to get ready for my breakfast meeting now. Are we still on to meet afterwards?"

"Absolutely, Jane."

"Good, I'll see you then, Pete."

I turn to leave but turn back. "Your hair is beautiful, Jane, you should leave it down."

"Thank you, but it's a wild mess when I do and not very manage-able. This bun is the only way to control it, especially when I'm working."

I turn to leave.

"Pete, thank you for giving me the heads up about Anne, I'll keep an eye out for her."

I open the door and head out feeling good about what I've ac-complished in securing my mate. And she smells amazing like liquid honey. I love honey, it's my favorite thing to add to my tea. I wonder what her favorite drink is. I can't wait to learn all about her. I rush down to my office. I've quite a bit of things to finalize for next year's season. Alpha Richard is having all the lifts re-placed. I must get them all ordered and have the contractors selected and set up to get started on that work as soon as the snow melts and the roads clear.

Our lifts will be done last, of course, but still it's a lot of work to get done in nine months. It's doable if I get the planning done, supplies ordered and stored in our warehouse, and get the contractors set up. The plans have been approved already, so things should all move smoothly. This will keep me busy along with all the regular season things I have to do. I enter my office to find Gamma Marcus sitting at his desk looking all smug, commenting that there are words going around that I've been given a goddess mate. "How is that out in the rumor mill already?"

He tells me it got out that I broke it off with Anne. It spread like wildfire once she told one person, it's now a rumor. "Yes, it's true, but she hasn't officially accepted me, now please leave it alone." He says he hopes she does because I deserve it. "I hope so, too, but Anne is devastated. It's funny because I didn't even think she liked me that much." He informs me that was her plan, to get me hooked and now she can't even leave her room, and she knows my new goddess-mate is some kick-ass Beta. And she has no chance against her.

"Beta Jane wouldn't fight her anyway, that's not who she is." We agree that's a good thing because we both know Anne hates to even sweat. We laugh at that before he asks if I think she'll accept me. "I think so, she said I could call her Jane. She's beautiful. She has the longest hair I've ever seen, way past her ass, and it's looks thick and its' color is a dark auburn with highlights. She has the bluest eyes, intelligent eyes. I don't think I could lie to her if I wanted to. She's tall, making me feel less like a giant next to her. She's at least five eleven with legs that look like they go on forever.

Today she had on black jeans with a very plump round one from what I could tell and very fit. Plus, she had on a camisole, I can tell she's not overly busty but enough to keep me happy. I hope she accepts me." Marcus says he hopes so, too since I already sound like I'm in love and he asked if I kissed her yet. "Naw, but I smelled her, and she smells mouth watering." He laughed because we all think our mates smell that way. I tell him she has a working breakfast then she'll come to my office for us to talk.

Until then, we must get started on work, I turn on my laptop and take a sip of my tea. Now every time I take a sip I'll think of Jane.

B *eta Jane*

    I'm glad Pete came to let me know about Anne. But he delayed me for my breakfast meeting, and I hate being late. I rush to get my hair into this brain pulling bun, put on my boots, which are practical and comfortable. Why am I even thinking about my wardrobe? It has never been something I thought about before. *"Having a mate now, Jane, makes you care about your appearance."* See, Joy, another thing my brain will think about now that we must consider Pete.

I finish up and grab my laptop, rushing out the door. I press the lock code and walk as fast as I can to make my meeting. I hope I'm not holding things up, but see I have not when I get to Olivia's room. Both her and Jay are sitting around a small table that's full of various breakfast items. Not the normal hospital food, so it must've come from the pack lodge kitchen. I love the thought of bacon and scrambled eggs on toast, but mostly I want my morning tea with mint leaves, my favorite. I rush in, apologizing for my delay. "Beta James had something to inform me of this morning and threw me off my schedule."

"No worries, Jane, it's just breakfast. How was your conversation with Beta James?"

"Not a conversation we can have right now. Let's eat and then get on with what we need to do. Then we can talk about my Beta James issue." Olivia looks to Jay, then to me.

"There's a Beta James issue, Jane? Who is Beta James?"

"Can we stay focused? The sooner we get through our working breakfast, the sooner we can move on to discuss Beta James, ok." I take my seat, placing my laptop to the side so I can have breakfast while I go over things with Olivia. We agreed I would be the one to relay what we think is the issue to her. I look over the options for tea and to my enjoyment I see a small cup with mint leaves in it. "Thank you, Jay." I put some in another small cup with a tea bag, then add hot water. While that simmers, I begin to build my breakfast sandwich. "Now Olivia, we've figured out you're actually the intended target for all the attempts we thought were on Jays life."

"Really, why do you think that? I'm not as important as a Ruler's Regent."

"That's what we thought, but every time Jay has been attacked, you've been in the vicinity. This made us think that maybe the reason we can't figure out who this is, is because we're looking at it the wrong way. We think you know something that you're not aware you know."

"Well, that's helpful. How can I know something I don't know that I know, Jane?"

"We think it's something you don't think is important, but it'll reveal the person that's in charge of what's really going on. In California when the arrow was shot, you were in the path of the arrow, but Jay heard it and snatched it out the air."

"Yeah, she did because she's a bad ass."

"Whatever you say, Olivia, and then at the club, you were standing on the dance ledge next to Jay, and maybe the bottles got mixed up?"

"Possibly, but how could they control who took which bottle?"

"That, we can't know, but everyone was drinking a lot except Jay. She didn't really need a lot of water, but you and the rest of the girls did. Think about it, you drank almost your whole bottle, if you would have gotten the poisoned one you probably would not have survived it. Now this time with the arrow, you were shot directly. We figure the tree was put down after they knew your and Jay's schedule, and they knew Jay would always shift to the right to stay ahead of you.

But because the log was larger, you both chose to be safe going over it, staying on your side, and they chose then to shoot the arrow at you, not at Jay."

"This all makes sense when you put it like that, Jane, but what could I possibly know that would reveal who this horrible person is?"

"We know it has to do with Curtis, because he's a part of whatever it is. We need you to think about all the times you and Curtis were together, where you went, who you met, even the little things might let us know who this person is."

"I will do that, Jane. I still don't think I'm the target, but I will try."

We continue our breakfast while Olivia writes down all the times her and Curtis traveled off pack lands. When they went out on dates and who they met up with or ran into. I set up a program to do research on all those locations and individuals to see if and how they could be connected in any way. I set the program to run scenarios on possible outcomes that would be affected by the Ruler's come to power and any unknown outcomes my brain hasn't thought of.

After about two hours, I feel good that we have enough to start on and Olivia looks and feels good enough that the doctor is letting her leave the clinic. Jay has been quiet most of the morning, I look at her and ask, "What's up with you?"

"It's just, I still feel like this has more to do with the Ruler than Olivia."

"I agree with you, Jay. I think the end game is the Ruler, but I think Olivia might know something that can interfere with whatever the end game is. We need to figure that out so we can then stop them from killing Olivia."

"Yes, let's do that part please."

"We will, Olivia. Then we will also stop whatever they have planned for the Ruler. Now, can we move onto my problem, Jay?"

"I didn't know getting a goddess mate was a problem."

"WHAT?"

"Olivia I could have sworn I paid you a million dollars to stop doing that."

"Yes, Jay, you're right I'll remember that starting right now. But Jane, you got a new goddess -mate?"

"Yes, Olivia, last night I smelled, well you know something good, and it was attached to the most gorgeous man, Beta Pete James. It turns out we both lost our mates early after finding them and now we have both been given each other as goddess mates. He has already said he wants to accept me."

"Do you not want to accept him, Jane?"

"I wasn't expecting this, Jay, it surprised me."

"I'm sure it surprised him as well, Jane, but what do you want to happen?"

"I don't know. I haven't truly thought about even having a chosen-mate, let alone having the goddess give me another mate."

"I know if it was me, I would accept the goddess mate and not care about anything else."

"That's easy for you to say, Olivia, as you haven't found your mate. But I did and it was wonderful and amazing and then it was devastating. I can't go through that again."

"So, what you're saying, Jane, is that you would let your fear of the devastation you felt loosing your mate, keep you from the possibility of a wonderful and amazing lifetime with another chosen-mate and potentially have pups."

"You both agree I should accept him as my mate, but how do we handle that we're from different regions? I don't want to live on this mountain, I love NY. What if he doesn't want to live in New York, Olivia?"

"That's something you both will have to decide, Jane, once you decide you want to accept each other."

"Also, there's a female he was involved with that he thought would be alright with what happened, you know, respecting the goddess-mate. But this morning, he informed me she didn't take it well. If I wasn't a Beta she would challenge me for him."

"Was there a plan for them to be chosen-mates?"

"Not now, Jay, but he did say that in a couple of years, if they were still together, it was something he would have considered. But he immediately said he's choosing me as his goddess mate and then he saw my hair this morning and thought it was beautiful and I should wear it down."

"Why don't you wear your hair down, Jane? I saw it once it's gorgeous and very thick I wish I had hair like yours."

"Well, Olivia, if you knew what I went through to control this mess, you wouldn't feel that way."

"Jay what do you think?"

"I've never seen your hair down so I can't comment."

"I'm not talking about my hair, Jay."

"Oh, about Beta Pete. I think you should accept him as your goddess mate. You deserve it, and he probably deserves it as well, or the goddess wouldn't have made the match."

"I'm supposed to have a meeting with him right after our breakfast, and Jay, you need to go and talk with Alpha Peterson."

"I don't want to talk to him at all."

"You said your wolf said you needed to be at this pack, it's the reason you had us come here instead of going to Haven. That means you need to talk to him, you listen to your wolf, remember your promise."

"You're right, Jane, I'll go meet with him while you're meeting with Beta James. But first, let's get Olivia settled in her room."

"Sounds good to me guys, I'm tired of this clinic! I need a long bath and to put on my own clothes, then I will feel like myself again."

Chapter 4

BETA JANE

We get Olivia up and out of the clinic and settled in her room at the lodge. On the way up I ask the front desk for directions to Beta James office. As I head out to go to Beta James office, Jay, calls to me, wishing me good luck. I smile awkwardly back at her, It's not something I do often, and I can see the surprised confusion in Jay's eyes. I head out, admitting to myself that I'm very nervous about my upcoming talk. As I raise my hand to knock on the door, it opens before I can make contact, and standing there is Pete, looking as nervous as I feel.

"I'm glad you're here, Beta Jane."

Behind him I see another gentleman that he introduces as Gamma Marcus Solt, who was just leaving to go do something. "Nice to meet you, Gamma Solt." He steps past me and exits the office while saying it is nice to meet me. When I step into the office, I notice it's set up like how my office was with Tim. I turn when I hear the door closing.

"I hope your working breakfast went well, Beta Jane."

"Thank you, it did. You have a nice office, Beta Pete." I notice he has a tea station set up and I smile. "Do you drink tea?"

"Yes I do, I know most men like coffee, but I'm a tea person. I actually bought this station a couple of years ago. People don't realize how many tea selections there are in the world."

"That's correct, there really are, I'm also a tea person." He smiles at me.

"That's something we have in common, Beta Jane. Would you like a cup?"

"No thank you, I just had a cup with breakfast, my favorite is with mint and a little spice sometimes."

"Mine is anything with honey, I'm always trying different blends of honey. I actually have them shipped in from overseas."

"I do, as well." It's crazy how we both do that. He offers me a seat across from his desk. "I've decided, Beta Pete, to accept you as my mate."

"We're going to jump right into it."

"Yes, Beta Pete, I'm a 'don't waste my time' kind of person, will you be alright with that?"

"Of course, I will, Jane. There will be some things we have to determine, of course, but first I'm open to everything. You're my goddess-mate."

"I arrived here with Beta Scott, I had only planned on being here for a month, but with this development I'll stay longer. This'll give me an opportunity to get to know you, and your pack, and Minnesota. I love New York City but I recognize you're the Beta of a Regional Pack while I'm not, and to ask you to give that up doesn't seem reasonable. However, I'm Head of Security for my pack's security firm and that's a prosperous position as well. I also might become a partner in Beta Scott's firm so I might be able to give up my current position. With that option I can be located in any state."

"Jane, this all seems like something we can figure out over the three months that you're here. I look forward to getting to know you."

"I've been the only one speaking, Pete, do you have anything you would like to add?"

"No, you have covered all the important logistical things. I think the rest will come with us getting to know each other."

I rise to get ready to leave, as I have work to do for both the companies, Pete rises when I do.

"Are you leaving already?"

"Yes, I have work to do, and if there's nothing else, I'll get to it."

"I would like to have dinner with you, Jane, this evening if you are amenable to it."

"That would be nice, would you like to meet me in the dining room?"

"Actually, I would like to cook dinner for you at my house."

"You don't live in the pack house?"

"No, I have a house I built after my mate passed."

"You didn't build it for your mate?"

"No, she wanted to stay in the pack house until we had pups, but none came. I have a room in the pack house that's assigned to me, but I have a house I built to keep me busy and help to deal with her loss. The house I had planned to build when we had pups she never got to see. Would it bother you to come to that house?"

"Not at all, Pete, and I would love to have dinner with you. What time?"

"Six sound good? I'll send directions to my house to your room, and Jane, thank you."

"For what?"

"For accepting me as your mate."

"Thank you for accepting me as your mate, Pete." I turn and leave, thinking the meeting went well, and now I must decide what to wear for dinner. I head to my room because I do want to get some work done before my date. I haven't said that in years, but as I turn down the hall maybe a little excited, I see a female standing in front of my door. I brace my shoulders for the confrontation I'm sure is coming since Pete told me about his conversation with Anne. "How may I help you?" She asks if I'm Beta Jamison. I inform her I am, then ask who she is, even though I'm sure I know. She says she's Beta James' girlfriend. I take a deep breath, it's going to go like this. She stares at me, asking why I'm here ruining her life. I move forward to go into my room, telling her I'm here with Beta Scott, the Ruler's Regent.

And if I'm not mistaken, she's no longer Beta James girlfriend. According to my mate, he broke it off with her last night, so if I was her, I would stop making that statement. She says I'm obviously not her and I have no place to tell her what to say. "You're correct in one thing, I'm not you." I step close enough to not have to raise my voice. "But what I do have is the right to tell you in clear terms to stay away from my mate. I have accepted Beta James as my mate, and he has accepted me as his." I see the hurt lighten in her eyes hearing those words, "I'll give you this day, Anne, to get a hold of your emotions. I'm not unsympathetic to your feelings, but I will not allow you to come between what the goddess has chosen. You're not that special, I suggest you remove yourself from my door.

I have work to do and you're stopping me getting on with it." She screams how dare I, when I have interrupted the plans, she had for her life with the man she loves. "That's something you're going to have to take up with the goddess, now won't you? You make it sound like I came here and went after Beta James and seduced him from you by unscrupulous means. That is not the case. The goddess chose him for me and me for him, and you don't get to stand in the way of that. Now again, remove yourself from my door so I can get to work." Again, she refuses to move. I step forward to move past her intending to not touch her in any way. Then she raises her hand to strike me with anger simmering from her. I grab the offending hand, twist it around and turning her away from me, pushing it up behind her back.

I step close behind her, holding her arm and listening to her whine about me hurting her. "Be lucky you still have this arm, as you've attempted an assault against a guest of your Alpha, against the mate of your Beta, but worst of all, a guest of the Ruler's Regent of the next Ruler of all wolves." I hear her take a deep breath to that last statement. "I don't know what the punishment will be by your Alpha and Beta, but I'm sure the punishment against the Ruler is death." She starts saying she didn't try to assault me, but I say, "So the camera I have installed outside my door will show me walking past you to enter my room and you don't raise your hand against me? If that's the case, then I'll send the proof to your

Alpha, and he can judge for himself." She says I'm trying to get her killed preventing her from being competition for Pete's affection.

"I'm not worried about you being any competition what-so-ever." Her next tactic is to warn me that she's been warming Pete's bed for almost a year, and he loves it. "I'm sure he did, but he hasn't shared my bed yet, and I'm sure when he does, he'll forget all about you. Now, are we done here or am I breaking this arm and sending that footage?" After a few seconds of her struggling to get loose on her own she finally says we're done for now. I push her away while releasing her arm. "No, Anne, we're done for good, because if you involve yourself in my or Beta James's business again, I will send the footage to your Alpha. That's a promise, and trust me, I'll keep it." She threatens that Pete will not like it when he hears how I've treated her. "Well, when we have dinner tonight at his house, I'll tell him, then you don't have to."

She yells about how I'm lying, that he would never take me to that house, that he built it for his mate after she died. "Yes, I'm aware, but I'm the mate that will be living in it now, starting tonight." I turn and enter my room, slamming the door shut. I guess I'm not working today, I'm packing my bags and hoping my mate won't turn me away when I show up at his house, bags in tow. Besides, I don't want to have to keep showing up with this witch at my door.

B*eta Jay*

After getting Olivia settled in her room and ready for her bath, I square my shoulders and head down to Alpha Peterson's office.

A part of me hoping he isn't there, so I don't have to deal with him right now, but Jane is correct. I must listen to Jewel, and if she says we need to be here, then we need to be here. Unfortunately, he's there.

"Please come in, Beta Scott."

I turn the knob, peeking in the room, seeing him sitting behind his desk. I look around to see if any Alpha females are sitting comfy on the couches and I see no one, so I enter.

"Are you looking for someone in particular, Beta Scott?"

"No, I just want to make sure I'm not disturbing you."

"No, I was waiting for an opportunity to speak with you in private. Please have a seat."

I move forward and take the seat directly across from him. I feel nervous for some reason. Jewel, what is happening? "*I don't know, I don't feel nervous. Maybe you're feeling his feelings? That's strange, Jay, you are feeling his feelings.*" Wow, is this a new power? It's not one that I want, and this came on fast and sudden, maybe it's my imagination. "*No, I feel his nervousness, Jay, that's crazy. A big bad Alpha all nervous over little old you.*" I look over at him. "Alpha Peterson, you want to talk to me. I'm here, so talk."

"First, Beta Scott, I want to apologize for last night, I would not want anyone to freeze. I was responding to Beta James' response that he was not smelling you."

"Really, and why would you care if he smells me?"

"If he smells you, that would mean you might be his mate, and for some reason, I've had this strange feeling since I heard your name that you're important to me, to Bryce."

"Who's Bryce?"

"Oh yes, that's my wolf. I'm going to say something that might sound strange to you, Beta Scott. The best way to explain my response since I first set eyes on you yesterday, is to tell you my wolf is sure you're our mate."

I look at him intently, waiting.

"When I saw you, I felt an instant connection and you smelled sweet like the ripest strawberry. Then Bryce started moaning and screaming "claim, claim, claim," at the same time you were talking and trying to introduce yourself, and then you reached out your hand. I knew if I touched you and I felt it at that moment there would have been no way I could have controlled Bryce from trying to claim you right there. Then again, last night I was very happy when Beta James said he didn't smell you, but then you thought I was referring to your friend and was upset, which you had every right to be. I hope you accept my apology for the miscommunication on my part."

"Alpha Peterson,"

"Please call me Richard."

"I do understand, Alpha Richard, and please accept my apology. It was a very difficult day for me with my friend being injured and having to leave Tony so quickly. Then the reception here after Jewel said we needed to come here."

"Who's Jewel?"

"Oh yes, she's my wolf."

"She thought you should come here?"

"Yes, she said we needed to be here for some reason, and then last night, your callousness towards my friend's well being. Well I can understand now that I know this. How about we start over?" I stand and he stands, I reach my hand out, "Hello Alpha Peterson, I'm Beta Jay Scott, it's nice to meet you." He grabs my hand, and the electric sparks shoot into my hand, up my arm, into my chest. What the hell?! It took weeks for me to get this response from Tony and I got nothing anywhere near this with Jarrod. I release his hand and fall back into my seat. What the hell, Jewel? *You're closer to your twenty fifth born day and you have met all of your mates. I can say for sure now you have three mates, and this is our last one, which is why your response to him is stronger and your power is coming on faster.* What the hell is this power Jewel? *We'll see Jay, over the next few month's, won't we?*

I finally gather my thoughts and look at Richard, but I'm surprised by the look on his face.

"There is a good chance you're my mate?"

"I will tell you, Richard, there's a chance I'm also Jarrod and Tony's mate as well, so take that as you will. Until I turn twenty-five, we'll not know."

"Have you enjoyed your visits with the other packs? I apologize but there are not many pack members who reside at this lodge during the winter due to the freeze. About a third of them are here and the rest reside at the other lodges lower on the mountain. We're a good representation of our pack as a whole though."

"That's nice to know, and again I'm sorry about not being able to come when I was scheduled to. Will I be able to meet your parents?"

"Yes, they're actually in residence during the winter months and are looking forward to meeting you. We've closed the lodge a week early due to your arrival."

"Why would you do that? It must have cost you quite a bit to ask your guests to leave early."

"Not much, and according to Beta Jamison, they didn't have the security clearance to be in the presence of the Ruler's Regent, which is appropriate."

"I'll reimburse you for the funds you're out, of course."

"Don't worry. From my understanding, I have a lot of those funds because a certain person has been looking after our financial well-being. I think I probably owe you, actually."

I feel better about where we are now and relax back into my seat, and I think Alpha Richard does, as well. I'm not getting any nervous energy from him, he has a little smile on his face and I wonder what that's about. I begin to ask about it and he speaks.

"Beta Jay, my wolf would like to meet your wolf."

I'm surprised by the request, "Right now?"

"Yes."

"No. Why?"

"Because Bryce is trying to determine if they've met before. I told him he was dreaming, but months ago he said your wolf came to him. He couldn't see her clearly through the fog, but he could sense her. That's why he's confident you're our mate, and he feels if he meets her now, he will know for sure."

"Well my wolf says no, she doesn't want to put herself on display for a wolf she doesn't know. He'll have to wait until she's ready to reveal herself."

"I told him that would be your response. Bryce can be kind of like, well, an Alpha wolf. Would you be open to telling me why your wolf thought you needed to come to my pack?"

"I think she thought the isolation of your mountain would give us a chance to relax and reflect on what we've learned over the last six months. Plus, the Ruler wants to know about all the packs from an inside and personal perspective. That was the reason I was sent and none of the things going on should stand in the way of that. The Ruler will still need the information I'm going to provide to make the decision on who will be pack at Haven."

"Have you made any recommendations on that front?"

"No, I'll not make any until I've completed my visits to all packs. What I will tell you is I've been impressed with the progression of the packs overall. History has shown past Alphas have improved their individual packs and their individual families without regard to the wolf world. That's not the case now, I've seen growth by not only the regional packs but the smaller packs in each region. Growth within the regional packs has been impressive, and I honestly think it's because you, Jarrod, and Tony made the decision to become friends in Alpha training."

"I want to say you're right, Beta Jay, but I would say it was our fathers who initiated it. My father would say, 'Rich most of the problems I must deal with is making sure I keep the pack funded for the whole region.' Like those under me are too stupid to do it for themselves. I think if given the opportunity they would step up, but the other Alphas are all caught up in losing their power they wouldn't do it. I spend many of my days approving and denying what we spend and where, it's exhausting. I took this thought with me to Alpha training and strategically planned to bring it up with the Alphas from the regional pack. Believe it or not, they said their Alphas said the same thing. They all thought the other Alphas felt the same and our friendship began. It was not easy in the beginning, generations of false opposition and mistrust, but four years, a lot of beers, Tony getting us in trouble over human and wolf females, and this is the outcome."

I can see he smiles whenever he mentions Jarrod and Tony, and it's nice to know the friendship isn't just financially and strategically beneficial. It's built on real affection for each other. I'm looking forward to having them all in my life. "*Jay?* " Yes, Jewel? "*Do you realize you just admitted you want to have all three of them as your mates?*" Yes, Jewel, I think I do. "*That also means you now admit you want to be the Ruler?*" Yes, Jewel, it does. "*Now we're ready to start really training. We need to figure out who is trying to stand in our way. We will be the Ruler, we will fulfill this prophecy, and we will have our mates.*" I smile over at Richard. "Alpha Richard, this conversation has been an eye opener for me, and I'm looking forward to my time here with you more than I was yesterday."

"I'm glad to hear it, Beta Jay. I would love to have dinner with you."

"That would be lovely, I just need to check on Olivia and Jane. Jane is goddess-mates with your Beta, so that's something we'll have to figure out. She had a meeting with him, and I want to make sure she's good, as she wasn't expecting it."

"I know, but I think Pete is happy about it."

"I believe so. According to Jane, he wants to accept her as his mate already."

"I hope she accepts him, he's a great guy and deserves a chance to have a lifelong mate. Losing his mate was devastating for the whole pack, we all wish for him to be happy. Not all of us thought Anne was that person."

"It seems that all your wishes have come true, Alpha Richard. What's funny is that I wished this for Jane, as well when I was in New York. It's nice to know our Goddess is listening to us some-times." I rise to leave. "I'll meet you in the dining room for dinner, that way I can meet the pack members that are here."

"That's a good idea, and my parents will be there also. I look forward to seeing you again."

"Me too, Alpha Richard." I leave and head up to check on Olivia. When I enter her room, she's laying on the bed with a blanket over her, sleeping soundly. I kiss her on her forehead and leave the room, locking it back and ensuring she's not disturbed. I walk further down the hall to check on Jane. I knock on the door, and she opens it, looking very frazzled. "Jane what is happening? Are you leaving? Why are you packing?"

"I'm not leaving."

"Then why are you packing?"

"I'm not sure, Jay."

"How about you explain, then we can figure out what is happen-ing." I notice she's still wearing her jeans, but has removed her signature black button up top and is wearing a very pretty white camisole. Her hair isn't in its bun and now I can finally see she has long, thick, dark auburn hair, and it's as beautiful as Olivia said. Why has she been keeping that up? It's very long, reaching past her butt. I can't imagine how she hasn't had a splitting headache every day. She's still walking back and forth as I say, "Jane, can you sit down and explain what's going on? You have a month of clothing spread across your room, why?" She sits on the bed and spends the next thirty minutes explaining about her meeting with Beta Pete. Their dinner date at his house that's behind the pack lodge, her confrontation with Anne, and her decision to move in with Pete.

"Congratulations on the decision to accept Beta Pete as your mate. That's great news and I'm happy for you. But do you have to move all your things today? Can't you just take some of your items? How about enough for the next five days, that way you can spend that many days enjoying your new mate, and from what I hear, you probably won't be wearing much clothing anyway. Then you can come back with your mate for your clothing at a later date." Jane runs to me and hugs me tight.

"Thank you for coming to me. How foolish would I have looked showing up to his house with all this luggage. I would have looked like a crazy person."

"You're welcome, Jane. Now what do you say about me helping you go through what you should take tonight, and then we'll pack the rest, but leave them here in your room for now, sounds good?"

"Yes, very good, Jay."

"And Jane, I agree with Olivia; your hair is beautiful, why have you been hiding it in that awful bun?"

"It's extremely unruly when I leave it loose, but Pete says he likes it also."

"For dinner, maybe don't put it in a bun, then."

"I don't know any other style that won't end up with it in my face, around my neck, and in my mouth."

"Ever thought about cutting it, Jane?"

"Yes, but I promised my grandmother I never would, she said it was my strength. And then Ben, my first mate, he loved it as well. But I think I might need to."

"I think maybe you should leave that discussion up to you and your new mate, but I'll help you with some new styles."

"Thank you, Jay."

"How about we get started?" We spend the next two hours going through mostly her night wear. I was surprised to see she had a couple of nice pieces; I was also surprised to see she only wore thongs. She said why worry about your undies ending up in your butt if they start out there, and you eventually don't feel it anyway. I never thought about it like that but that's smart thinking, and those in themselves are sexy. I put a couple of comfy cotton bottoms with matching string tops she can wear around the house with a short robe just in case she wanted to cover up. We pack all her toiletries, and her small bag is ready. "This is all you need for now." The rest we pack away and set back into the closet to get later. I wait for Jane to get showered so I can do her hair before leaving to get myself ready for dinner.

When she comes out, she looks nervous. We decided on her favorite black jeans, but I convinced her to go with a baby blue cotton sweater she brought, which still had the tags on, and a pair of shoe boots. We're on a mountain in freezing weather, duhh. She wanted to be comfortable so I stuck with her bun but did a play on it, by pulling it to the top of her head instead of pushed back. I loosened it up so it's not as compact but secured it, making sure it wouldn't fall out without some effort. I put two braids from the top on each side and crossed them over the top to use up some of the length, allowing them to hang down on opposite sides of her face. I then pulled some tendrils to hang down her back, it looks nice, and she likes it.

"Now Jane, don't mess it up when you put on your sweater, and enjoy your first date with your future mate. I hope to not see you in the morning for breakfast." I hug her and head out to get myself ready for dinner, not doing as much as Jane, but I still want to look cute, as I have an Alpha I want to impress, as well.

Chapter 5

BETA JANE

I have nervous excitement running through my body as I head down to the lodge foyer. I received a message to my room with instructions that someone will escort me to Beta James' house at my convenience for our dinner date. When I get to the foyer, Gamma Solt, whom I met earlier, is there and proceeds to take my bag from me. I put on the coat that I was carrying over my arm as I ask if Beta Jame's house is far, and he responds saying it's about a ten minute walk behind the pack house. There's a path that is cleared that leads to a couple of homes in the same direction. it's an easy walk. Looking at him carrying my bag, it makes me realize how really foolish I would have looked showing up at Beta Pete's house with many like it, and how would I have even managed it?

I follow Gamma Solt, out the door, turning right, and I catch up, glad the path is ice free considering I'm wearing shoe boots instead of my trusty work boots. I notice he's correct, the walk was a quick one, and on the way, he regaled me with stories of the pack and how, when Beta James built his house, it inspired other mated pack members to do the same. I inquired why and he said I will see, it's very unique. He says him, and his mate love theirs, and being wolves who love the closeness to nature, it provides that along with the security of pack life. He wasn't wrong, there is nothing he could have said that would have prepared me for what seeing it for myself has done. Ahead of me, perched on three trees, is a cottage style house, but it looks more like a mansion in the trees.

It's made of all wood from what I could see, but it reminds me of my cottage at home, with a front wrap around porch and two large bay windows. I'm initially confused about how we're going to get up there but then I see there's an elevator underneath nestled, between the trees. When I approach, I can see behind it a set of stairs that circle around the furthest two trees that you could take up but the elevator is a convenient modern touch. Gamma Solt presses for it, and when the doors open, it looks like any elevator in a high rise building, not something you would find in the middle of a mountain lodge. When we enter, he presses a button and the doors close. A few seconds later they open and standing there is Beta Pete. Gamma Solt steps out into an open floor plan living room.

I can see a dining room to the right of me and the kitchen further back. He places my suitcase next to the elevator and I see the confusion on Pete's face looking at him. He hunches his shoulders and then turns to leave, saying it was nice seeing me again. I return the sentiment and thank him for escorting me and carrying my bag. I walk further in looking around while he speaks with Beta Pete. The elevator door closes, and Pete looks at me. It's strange how I didn't notice before how tall he really is, but in this closed in space his over six feet is really evident.

"I'm glad you're here, Beta Jane, let me give you the tour."

He walks further into the house, pointing out the living room, the dining room, and a very modern kitchen with a large island. I can see a hallway between where the kitchen begins and the dining room ends and he says this leads to a couple of bedroom en-suites. I see that the elevator opens up in the middle of the two bay windows with a door behind it so you can go onto the porch. It looks out to see the pack house. Adjacent to the living-room and kitchen is a row of floor to ceiling windows with a set of sliding glass doors. They lead to a back deck where there's mainly nothing but snow for as far as the eye can see. But, the best part of the house is the roof. It's made of glass, the entire roof, you can see the branches full of snow and the sky. "Is the roof in the whole house made of this glass?"

"Yes, but it's not glass, it's made of a thick polycarbonate plastic and it's cold formed for our climate. It was a bitch, excuse me, it was tough to get it delivered and installed up on this mountain, but worth it. And once we did it successfully the first time, the other houses were a no-brainer."

"How many houses do you have up here?"

"We have eight on this side of the pack house. At least a dozen more on the other side but further up. As well as some pack members are building them lower on the mountain, as well. Just not with the same roof. They don't get the privacy we get up here with nothing above us."

"This is beautiful."

"Thank you, the house is made from oak for its strength, but the floors are red maple for the beauty."

I look around more, noticing that the furnishings are sparse; a leather couch with a matching chair, a dining table with two chairs even though it could take four, and an island with no seats at all. "I can tell based on the furnishings that you don't stay here much."

"No I don't, mostly when I want to get away. I have had a couple of the guys here, but that's all. I think Alpha has been here a couple of times also."

"Whatever you're making for dinner smells good."

"You are in for a treat. I made the Minnesota staples, have a seat at the table and I will serve you."

"Do you mind if I hang up my coat?"

"Of course not. I'm sorry, over by the elevator there's a hook, and past that is a half bath you can use to freshen up. You look amazing, by the way. I noticed you still have your bun but different. I like it but I still think it would be beautiful down."

"I will keep that in mind for our next date." He smiles saying he likes the sound of that. I go over and hang up my coat and to take him up on the offer to freshen up. Once I get in the bathroom I starting to question the bag. It was impulsive, but can I change my mind? Of course I can, but do I want to? *Are you talking to me?* Who else would I be talking to, Joy? *I don't know, some people talk to themselves.* Well, I'm talking to you. *I think you have the bag here, might as well stick to your guns. Why not go for it? Plus you probably have cobwebs in your private parts it's been so long since you had anything in there. Not even your own fingers have made their way in there in the last four years.* Why do you have to be so crass? *Well you, asked* You're right, I'm sorry. I was talking to myself now that I know what your response is going to be.

I splash water on my face and grab a napkin off the counter to pat it dry. Alright, lets get it done. I go back out and see Pete standing there looking at the bag, then he looks at me.

"Want to talk about this?"

"Not yet," I notice he has set the table and it all looks good. "Maybe after I have some food in my belly we can talk about it."

"That's fine, would you like something to drink?"

"I don't usually drink, but some liquid courage would be nice. Do you happen to have some of that California sangria?"

"I do, but I have something better I thought you might like. It's a drink we usually have during the summer, but considering your love for all things mint."

"Wait, how do you know that?"

"Your brand of tea, and your standing order for mint to be delivered with breakfast."

"Checking up on me"

"Kinda, I wanted to know what you like, then I could impress you for dinner."

"Well if you have something good with mint in it, you will."

"Good, and if you don't like it I have the sangria you mentioned, just in case."

He hands me a glass, and after a sip, I smile. "I love it, what is it?"

"It's called The Bootleg. It's a mixture of limeade, lemonade, and mint, with whatever signature liquor you like. I added our famous Duluth Vodka for that added courage you wanted."

"It's very good. So what's for dinner? I'm famished as I missed lunch in preparation for tonight."

"I'm glad you have an appetite. We will start with a wild rice soup, and then we'll have pan seared chicken breast smothered in yellow morel mushroom gravy with green beans and homemade mashed potatoes. And for dessert, I got a Bundt cake from the pack house because, well, I suck at dessert, but its very good."

"That all sounds delicious, let's dig in," He passes me a bowl that he then fills with the wild rice soup and a saucer with bread rolls to start. During dinner, we talk about our lives at our packs, our families, the roles we play outside of pack life, our mates, their passings, my lack of a dating life since my Ben passed, and his dating life with Anne, which began last year. "I guess this would be the best time to discuss my luggage. Anne was at my room door when I returned after our meeting today."

"Really? I apologize for that."

"Why, did you send her there?"

"No."

"Then you have nothing to apologize for. We didn't plan this and didn't intend to cause her any harm. So she was, as you can imagine, not very happy I was here to, wait how did she put it ruin her plans for a happy future with you. I kindly informed her that she should take that up with the Goddess, since she was the one who made us mates. Needless to say, that didn't go over well, and no amount of patience on my part or understanding about her hurt feelings mattered. I think the only thing that would have been acceptable would have been for me to say I was leaving or that I would not accept you. When I told her that we both agreed to accept each other, she lost it and tried to hit me, but I didn't hurt her."

"I'm sure you didn't. That doesn't seem like something you would do."

"I did blackmail her though. I told her I had her on camera trying to assault me, and that I would send the footage to her Alpha, her Beta, and to the Ruler's Regent and what the repercussions would be."

"That is nice, she believed you?"

"Yes, but it wasn't a threat, I do have that footage."

"You installed a camera outside of your room?"

"Of course, I need to ensure my safety in a strange place."

"We have security."

"You do, and we should discuss that, but at another time. Well, then Anne proceeds to tell me that you have become attached to her love and you would miss her and kick me to the curb. Well, I informed her that I would ask you about that during our dinner at your house, which she didn't believe. She said you would never take just anyone to this house as you built it for your mate. I then informed her that I was that mate now and that after you were with me, you wouldn't remember her at all." He smiles at me.

"Then does that explain the luggage? Are you staying with me in my house?"

"Yes, if you will invite me to stay."

"Absolutely, I invite you to stay."

"Good, because it would be embarrassing to have to carry that bag back to the pack house." We both started laughing, and I finally felt better about the bag. "If you really want to laugh, you should have seen my room when Jay showed up. I was packing all my belongings, planning on bringing them all with me tonight with no thought on how I was going to get them here. Obviously at the time, I didn't even know where here was." He laughs even harder and it brightens his eyes and lightens the mood even more. I probably should have started with this story.

"Would you like some dessert?"

"Maybe later, but I would like a glass of that sangria now."

"As you wish my, lady."

He rises and I follow, wanting to look out at the view from the back. I continue turning and watching him moving around in the kitchen. He has no shoes on and his feet are huge, at least a size twelve with nice, very manicured toe nails. I decided to pull my shoe boots off to get more comfortable. I walk over and place them next to my bag along with my socks, and I can't believe how warm the floors feel against my feet. I am glad Jay drags me along for pedicures every time she gets them because I have a nice peach color on my toes, something I haven't cared about in years. He comes over, holding out the glass with my sangria. When I grab it, our hands touch, and the tingles run through me, igniting tingles in other parts of my body. I take a quick sip of my drink and I notice he isn't drinking. "Do you not drink?"

"Not really. After my mate died. I drank a lot and wasn't in a good place because of it. I almost lost my position as Beta of my pack. So I stay away from it, only small amounts once in a while."

"Is it a problem for me to drink?"

"No, I can drink. but I like to keep a clear head, and this sangria is said to knock some on their asses."

"Yeah I have heard that as well."

"You want to have a seat?"

"Sure." We move to sit on the couch, looking out at the snow and up at the night sky. I decide that I'm doing nothing that would prevent me letting my hair down. I start pulling out the strategical-ly placed pins, putting them on the coffee table then shaking my head to loosen my bun. I hear Pete take a breath beside me and glance over to see him watching me. He leans over closer, taking my glass from my hand and placing it on the table on the other side from where we are sitting. He helps my hair down the rest of the way, putting his hands in it. It feels good to have a mans fingers in my hair for the first time in years. I thought I would feel the pain of missing Ben, but I don't feel pain. I feel nervous, excited, anxious, and scared, but no pain.

He starts rubbing the back of my head with a hand full of my hair still in his. He's looking at me like I'm precious cargo that can't be broken, but there's nothing weak about me. I lean forward, grabbing his neck and placing my lips to his like my life depends on it, like the future I didn't know I wanted depends on it. I deepen the kiss and he follows, letting me set the pace, still rubbing the back of my head and the nape of my neck. I lean forward wanting to be closer, wanting to feel more of him. He's tall, I like it, like a tree I can climb. I raise myself up climbing onto his lap. He looks up at me surprised by this action, but he's about to find out that I'm not the precious package he thinks I am, and maybe he will change his mind about me. But he needs to meet me before he can accept me.

I straddle over him, pushing myself down over his package, wanting not just him but both of them to pay attention to me. I rub my hands over his shoulders, loving the width of them, reminding me of a mountain man, he is going to be my mountain man. I unbutton his shirt, wanting to feel his skin against the palm of my hands, exploring what there is, and he assists me, letting me know that he's just as anxious as I am to see where this is going. He pulls the shirt off, tossing it away and I reach out, rubbing all the huge muscles bulging from his chest, his shoulders, his massive neck, the pecks and his nipples that look like ripe berries. I lean down and bite the one closest to me, while rubbing the other so it doesn't feel left out. He hisses from the small pain and moans from the pleasure my tongue brings afterwards.

I do the same to its partner and then move up to kiss and bite on all the exposed muscles that he has on display for me to enjoy. I bite, kiss and blow every inch of his chest and neck, his chin, cheek, nose, and finally his lips. They are soft and juicy and taste like the minty goodness I love. I suck on his bottom lip liking the huge bulge poking into me from below, letting me know he's enjoying all that I'm doing. I'm losing myself in the kiss when I feel his hands running up under my sweater. He releases my bra and rubbing my back from top to bottom, releasing the tension I didn't even know I was holding. He starts pulling my sweater up and I moan in complaint because it requires I release his mouth. I did because it would free me of the encumbrance of my clothes that keep me from feeling my skin against his.

He tosses my sweater with my bra somewhere, I don't care where, and with his free hand, he grabs my breast, tweaking my nipples between his finger and thumb sending my juices flowing into my thong. He pushes me back, allowing him to get a better look, smirking at me from hooded eyes. It looks like he likes what he's seeing, I know I sure do. He leans forward, placing those beautiful luscious lips around my right nipple, making more of my juices flow, he moans loud around it sending tingles into my belly. I'm sad when he releases it, but happy when he treats its partner to the same wonderful treatment. He finally pulls me up after I thought I could take no more torture.

"You smell delightful, can I see if you look as good as you smell?"

"I would be disappointed if you didn't." He gets up with me still in his arms, saying we should take this to a place more comfortable as he heads toward the back of the house. We enter a room and he hits the switch to turn the light back off. He lays me gently in the middle of a huge bed, definitely larger than a California king. I unbutton my jeans and he pulls them off, one leg first then the next. I go to remove my thong but he says no, let me, I pull my hair from under me splaying it out, then I lay with my hands above my head, watching him massaging my feet, as he steps back and starts unbuttoning his jeans pushing them down. He's not wearing underwear, when his jeans pass his hips, his big ass beautifully engorged penis juts out making me catch my breath.

I don't think I have ever imagined a man having a dick this large. I know wolves are larger than most humans but this shit is huge, and I'm now nervous for a different reason. I look up at Pete to see he's smiling with a sadistic smirk on his face'

"Don't worry, you can handle him, and I will not hurt you."

I looked him in the eye, I only see and feel truth from him. I lay back, prepared to either have the best orgasms of my life or die. Either way, this is going to be a night to remember. I hear him kick his pants away before he pushes my legs open as he climbs up the massive bed. At some point I wish I had been further up the mattress, he had further to climb before he reaches me with that thing. "*Don't be a chicken, Jane. You're a bad-ass Beta, you can take it.*" That's fine for you to say, you're not the one he's about to try to put that big shit in! "*I'm hoping his wolf's is just as nicely hung, actually.*" I can't respond because at that moment I feel an open mouth kiss on the inside of my right knee, warm and wet, sending tingles into me, uumm that's nice. I close my mind deciding to trust my future mate and just enjoy it.

He continues his onslaught of kisses with soft lips and a masterful tongue all along my inner thigh. He passes over my thong, kissing me through the thin material, only heightening my imagination of how it will feel when the material is gone. He travels back down my inner thigh to the other knee and I love it. He finally puts my legs up, pulling my thong along and tosses it away. He places my legs open on the bed and I open my eyes to see him staring down at me.

"You're absolutely beautiful, Jane."

He leans down kissing my belly with those crazy open mouth kisses that soon make it to my clit. He kisses me there briefly but doesn't linger traveling to my center where he sticks a long delightful tongue inside of me igniting more tingles and more of my juices. His hands are roaming over my belly before they grab me around my inner groin area, spreading me open and giving him more access. His fingers play my clit like a guitar while his torturous tongue pushes far inside of me it feels like I can feel him in my belly. I can feel myself getting ready to come and it will be hard and strong, but then the tongue retreats and the fingers stop. I groan in frustrated pain. Pete starts kissing around my lady lips like he wants to soothe me for the release he denied.

We don't forgive him, as his lips keep traveling around until it encounters a very angry clit pulsing from four years of neglect on my part and long moments of teasing on his. I'm sure he can be forgiven if he tries hard enough, which he does, with gusto, as he flicks that tongue we love and hate. He sucks with the lips and he bites with teeth that we're not sure if we love or hate, but the combination of all this stimulation is again increasing the pleasure inside and I'm close again. To top it off, he puts a couple of those lovely fingers inside of me and starts stretching and rotating. I start rotating my hips with him, it feels good. I want more, I need more and at this point I don't care about the size of his member I just want it in me and I mean now, but now is not fast enough.

He keeps on stretching and rotating adding another finger, and I love it but I still want more. He keeps on stretching and rotating and sucking. Flicking, and biting on my clit as I keep rotating my hips, pushing for the release I can feel in every limb. I'm mumbling, saying I'm there, close, oh my, close, so close and right then faster than I can even think, he pulls his hands from me, grabs my right knee raising it while simultaneously shoving his huge ass monster in my pussy. He grabs my nipple with his mouth, sucking like his life depends on it, while rubbing the hell out of my clit and it feels good. I didn't even get a chance to acknowledge the burn from my lady parts being stretched so wide. The amazing fullness and the deep tingling heat surges into my belly and the over stimulation to my nipple and my clit sends me over the edge with the hardest, strongest, most painful release of my life.

I scream loud and hard it hurts my throat. The pounding I'm getting makes my release last even longer and I don't think it will ever stop. But the added lubricant eliminates the pain from the size of him. He feels good and moments later I feel his seed rush into me and I have no doubt it's in my belly. I thought he would collapse on me but I was wrong. Instead, he rolls to his back taking me with him and I'm now straddling him while he's still hard inside of me. I relax trying to catch my breath. I can feel him pulsating, is he going to go down? Not yet I guess, as he starts smoothing my hair out over us.

"I love this. It feels like I'm in a cocoon of honey."

"Why honey?"

"You smell like honey to me. I love your hair."

"I hate it."

"Really, why don't you cut it?"

"After I catch my breath I say. "I promised my grandma I wouldn't. She used to say it's my strength, but its very unruly."

"I think she would understand if you cut it to a manageable length for you. I can see how it would get to be a lot to handle every day."

"Yeah, hence the daily bun." He starts rubbing my back, by butt, my thighs.

"How do you feel, Jane?"

"Good, Pete, relaxed and comfortable."

"That's good, but I meant your insides."

"They're sore, you shoved a small tree in me."

"Yeah, but you handled him well."

"How do you feel, Pete?"

"I feel great, you make me feel like I'm wearing the softest, snuggest honey glove, I could live here all day and night."

"We know that's not happening, we have life to live outside of this bed. If you keep rubbing down my body, Pete, I'll fall asleep on you just like this."

"That's fine by me, honey"

"Really, I can stay like this?" And to his word he does and I do, only I'm not sure it lasts for long because I'm awakened by heat radiating down my thighs, up my back, into my stomach. My nipples are hard pebbles against Pete's chest and he's pumping up into me while I gyrate myself down on him. The sloshing sound from our activity is filling the quiet room. I raise my head to look at Pete and see his eyes are closed but he can't be sleeping so I lean forward, kissing him, and his hands grab my ass cheeks and start rotating me at a faster pace against his monster penis, causing me to loose the slow rotating rhythm I had going. I stop and let him take over. The fullness inside of me is mind blowing but no longer scary and I like it very much. I contract my muscles trying to get more of him inside even though there is nowhere for more of him to go.

I grab his hair, deepening the kiss and the faster he rotates my ass cheeks the deeper I kiss him and within minutes I feel his release and mine follows. I collapsed back down, catching my breath. "That was a wonderful way to wake up, thank you," I say. He immediately starts laughing.

"Why are you thanking me, Jane? I was laying here minding my business trying to convince my guy to take a nap so I can take a nap with you and you start gyrating on me. First I thought you were just adjusting to get comfortable, but then the gyrating got deeper and deeper and you started moaning and I realized you were sexing me in your sleep. And then I thought why not join in and enjoy it. You were gyrating in your sleep for over twenty minutes before you finally woke up. I think it was me finally losing my shit and started to pump into you that woke you up, honestly, but I couldn't keep still any longer."

"You're not telling the truth."

"Yes I am."

Joy, is he telling the truth? "*Yep, you have four years of pent up juice in there. Your body said let me get out while she's sleeping and this penis is available.*" "I'm embarrassed. In the court of law they would call this a form of sexual assault."

"Well I was a willing participant. I did leave myself inside of you, hard. Don't worry, its just between us mates."

I cover my face with my hair, this is the one and only time I'm glad to have it.

"Its fine, Jane, I loved it actually. You can climb up and gyrate on me anytime you want."

"I think I'm going to climb off now so it doesn't happen again." I get up and with him not inside me I actually feel empty. I go to climb off the bed and my legs are numb. I lay down and Pete spoons me from behind, pulls the throw from the foot of the bed and covers us. Its still early in the morning, I just snuggle back into him to sleep, glad that I brought my bag to dinner.

Chapter 6

BETA JANE

I wake with the warm sun shining down on me. I stretch, feeling better than I have in years, and I can honestly say I have not fallen asleep without my laptop in a very longtime. I'm sad Pete's not still in bed with me, but since I can smell bacon, I know where he is. I sit up and there's a t-shirt on the bed, so I grab it and run into the bathroom, needing to clean from the last nights activities. I turn on the water and set it to warm then use the toilet. I look around seeing a hand towel and new tooth brush on the counter, he's so thoughtful. I use them, then wrap my hair in a messy bun on my head to prevent it from getting wet. I jump in the shower and wash using the soap that smells like Pete and I like it. I get out and towel off quickly because the smell of breakfast is calling me. I pull the shirt over my head, and when I come out, I see my bag.

I was going to go through it and find my clothes but decided to keep on his shirt. I rub on some deodorant and go to feed my belly. I find Pete standing at the island with a cup in his hand that smells like tea. "Can I have a cup of that?"

"Of course, honey."

He reaches over and hands me a cup of tea with a mint leaf at the bottom. "Hhmm, my favorite," I say, then sip on my tea and grab a piece of bacon to munch on. "So what's for breakfast?"

"Besides tea? Bacon, eggs, toast; is there anything else you want?"

I look at him. "I can think of something but I think I need to get some food in my belly."

"Oh, I see, how about I feed your belly and then we can discuss the other thing you want for breakfast."

"Sounds like a plan. How can I help?"

"It's mostly done."

"Good because I can't cook a lick but I can boil water for tea."

"How about you butter the bread for the toast?"

"I can manage that, I can't manage the toasting part though."

"It's almost ready, just add butter."

When the buzzer goes off, I take the toast out to butter it and place it on a plate while Pete scrambles us eggs. I take the bacon to the table and bring the things we'll need for our tea along with a couple of bottles of water because I really need to stay hydrated. We have a mostly quiet meal, me not wanting to bring up the gyrating thing as I'm still a little embarrassed. I agreed to wash the dishes since he cooked and he said great, he could get a shower. While I clean up, my imagination runs wild with how good he probably looks with the water running down his body. I'm getting hot and bothered with the warm soapy water sloshing over my hands thinking about Pete in the shower. I'm about to say fuck it and join him when I hear the water shut off, opportunity missed.

I finish up the last couple of cups, putting them in the rack, and when I stand up, I feel Pete behind me. I mean really feel him behind me, which means he isn't wearing bottoms, or a top and my excitement kicks into overdrive. He turns me around and I look into his eyes.

"You said you wanted more than toast, eggs, and bacon for break-fast. I do have another meat you can have, if you can handle it"

He lifts me, placing me on the island.

"Did I tell you I love seeing you in my t-shirt, but what I love most is that it gives me access to all your parts."

"He lays me back on the island, reaching over and grabbing a small bottle of I don't know what.

"This, my dear, is something I created just for me, it's a type of lubricant I'm sure you're going to enjoy."

He pushes his shirt up, exposing me, spreading my legs wide open for him to view. I take the initiative to push them further apart, wrapping them around him, locking my ankles, and loving the feeling of his huge penis touching up against me while I try to create friction.

"Easy hon,"

"He turns the bottle upside down and the small suction cup tip is right over me. He uses his fingers to spread me open and places the cup right on top of my clit, the sensation is soothing. Then he squeezes the bottle and I feel a warm liquid touching me and it starts heating up, not burning, but warm like a tongue laying against me. He looks at me, asking if I like it. "Yes it's very nice." He removes the bottle, squeezing some of the liquid onto his finger, then looks at me and says get ready. He places his finger inside of me and starts rotating it while he uses the finger on his other hand to rotate my clit in the same way. After a few moments I can feel the tingles radiating from inside to out. The double stimulation is mind blowing and I'm heating up faster than I ever remember.

"Hon, are you ready?"

He removes his finger, drops some of his magic liquid on the head of his penis and slowly starts pushing into me. He then tells me here is the rest of the breakfast he promised me. And believe it or not, there's no pain, only fullness that burns on my insides. He continues pushing in and out of me as he pushes on my clit with his finger while I lay there biting my lip. I am trying to control my body that I seem to have no control over because of the pleasure this man is creating. The king of pleasure I've never had before. My whole body is vibrating and shaking and I know my release is coming. If he pulls out denying me this release, I will kill him, I swear. But he doesn't and I release so hard, screaming into the trees I know are above me. I must have passed out because I come to with Pete rubbing my face, rubbing my breast, rubbing my body.

"Jane, are you good?"

I look at him saying, "I'm great and I wholeheartedly accept you as my mate." He smiles down at me saying he accepts me as his mate, as well. He pulls me up, hugging me tight, and I feel his heart beating up against my chest. I know I'm happy I accepted him. I grab his hair, pull his head to the side licking and kissing his neck as I feel my canines tingle then extend before I bite down. I'm tasting his blood as it fills my mouth until I feel my bond snap in place. I hear Pete suck in, moaning while I take my fill of him. Then I release him and lick the wound, helping it to close and heal. I look at it, seeing my mark on his neck as I feel him wrapping my long hair in his hands and I turn my neck ready for his mark. He's still thick, long and hard inside of me and I know where this is leading to.

When he finally bites me after seconds of sucking on my skin. I'm ecstatic when I feel his bond lock in. The thought that I'm his and he's mine increases my juices, and my mate lifts me from the island carrying me to his bed. He crawls up the mattress kissing my lips, while I gyrate my hips, seeking that pleasurable release I know is coming and within minutes we come hard together. But this time, Pete removes himself from me despite my protest.

"I know, he is all yours now hon, no need to stay in there all day. We do need to let you heal; we have to take care of her as well."

"Alright if you say so." But I really do feel empty without him in me now.

"I think you have become addicted to my dick."

"I think I have, too," I say and we laugh. I crawl up to look at my mark, "It looks good on you."

"So does mine. Are you good?"

"I'm good. We have a lot to figure out."

"I know, but I'm sure we will figure it out. We have a couple of months to do that, but let's just enjoy ourselves for now. Plus, we're on a mountain and we have a lot to get done before we do anything about us. You want to contact Beta Scott to let her know how you're doing?"

"No, she said if I didn't show up for breakfast she would know what decision I made and would have my things delivered to your house, and that I should take the next five days to enjoy myself."

"That's great, I'll reach out to my Alpha this afternoon and update him on our progress, and let him know I will be out of commission for the next five days, satisfying my insatiable mate."

I cover my face but he tells me don't be embarrassed, he likes me just the way I am. I look at him between my fingers and he grabs my hands and pulls me close to kiss me. We plan on spending the next four days getting to know each other. Exploring more of each other's bodies inside and out, and I can say with confidence that by the time we come out of this house, that Anne will have gotten the message that Beta James is no longer her future.

B *eta Jay*

I chose a winter white dress that falls to just above my knee, and I think it's appropriate since I'll be meeting the former Alpha and Luna, my future mate's parents. The dress has quarter length sleeves and pleats below the waist with concealed pockets on each side to hold my phone without disrupting the flow of the dress. I pair it with black shoe boots, a pair of simple gold earrings, along with a matching bracelet. I put my hair in a Jane-like bun at the back of my head, minimal makeup, as usual, and deem myself ready for dinner. I'm the only musketeer going to the dining hall tonight, but Mark said he was going to be there, so I won't be totally on my own. I grab my phone, refresh my lip gloss, lock the room and head down to the dining hall.

I'm happy to see Alpha Richard is waiting for me in the foyer. He's freshened up with a clean shave, black slacks and a crisp beige shirt that looks great with his brown eyes.

"You look lovely, Beta Jay."

"Thank you, you look lovely as well, Alpha Richard."

"Most of the pack members are waiting for us in the dining hall."

"Really? I apologize for being late."

"No, you're not late. They're early, anxious to meet the Ruler's Regent."

"That's good to know, as I would hate to keep the former Alpha and Luna waiting."

"Oh, they're not here. They never arrive early, or on time. I think my parents don't know the meaning of time schedules, so who knows when they'll arrive."

I take his offered arm and we head towards the doors leading to the hall. I'm famished and the food smells good. As we enter, the talking quiets, and Richard takes this opportunity to introduce me to the group, letting them know I'm open to meeting with them and I'll have a desk set up in his office whenever they want to see me. I love that this affair is low key. Now let's eat. The pack hall is just a long table along the back of the room and about twenty rectangular tables in front of it full of pack members, most with plates of food and drinks already in front of them. Richard leads me to a table on the right about halfway down the room that already has a bunch of dishes on it. We have the option to choose from any or all, so I take a seat, grab a napkin with silverware and make a couple of food choices then begin eating.

It's all delicious, especially the wild rice soup, and the home-made mashed potatoes with some type of mushroom wine gravy, yummy. I ate more than one serving of each and downed a couple glasses of my favorite sangria while many of the pack members came to the table to introduce themselves. They extended invites for me to visit them, telling me about the businesses they own or work at, and I think the overall conversations were good. It was like a family-get together and Richard was treated like the head of the family. About halfway through the meal, the former Alpha Charles and Luna Loretta arrive and liven up the group even more, if that's possible. You can tell everyone loves their former Alpha and Luna. They join our table and begin to eat and drink and even more pack members come to the table.

Once the meal is done and the tables are cleared, the dessert options are brought out. I'm looking for the double chocolate option, but none appear. I'm disappointed but not every place has my favorite dessert, so I have a small piece of the Bundt cake with some chocolate ice cream. Not my favorite, but better than nothing. Overall, the welcome dinner went well and by the end I'm happy, full, and ready for bed. There is some fuss at the back of the room when I'm leaving and some female with blonde hair is not very happy. I wondered what it's about, but it must not be important because the Alpha isn't involved. I go over to tell Luna Loretta I'm going to turn in for the night and she hugs me, saying we will meet up tomorrow for lunch to go over the Luna responsibilities I'm probably lacking.

I smile and turn to leave when I notice the blonde lady from before staring at me like I offended her in some way even though I've never met her. Oh well. As I leave the hall, Alpha Richard catches up to me.

"I have something for you, Beta Jay."

I grab a bottle of water to take to my room, following him out. He leads me to his office, and I wait in the doorway. When he comes out, in his hand is a plate with double chocolate cake.

"How do you have this and why was it not in the dining hall?"

"Tony had it shipped for you, I had it cut up and put in the fridge. But I will admit I tasted a piece and if I would've put it out it would've been devoured before you arrived. The head chef is going to try to get the recipe to make it for you before this cake runs out."

I take my cake and look at him like he is the worst person in the world.

"Why are you looking at me like that, Jay? I got your cake and saved it for you?"

"Yes, Alpha Richard, but you ate a piece, knowing I have a limited supply. Wait until I tell Tony you ate a piece of my cake."

"Jay, you wouldn't! It was a very small piece."

"I don't care! Every piece of this cake was meant for me, and you violated it when you put a piece of it in your mouth."

"I apologize for eating the very tiny piece of your cake, I'll have to find a way to make it up to you."

"Yes, Alpha Richard, you will. I'm not sure you can though, as double chocolate cake is one of my most favorite things in the world. I don't have high hopes you'll be able to make it up to me, but you're welcome to try."

"We'll have to see what I can come up with, Beta Jay."

"You better hope your chef can figure out a good enough recipe or have Tony ship more cakes for the next three months if you want to be on my good side. I can forgive a lot when I have double chocolate cake." I take my cake and my water and turn towards the stairs. "I'll see you in your office in the morning, Alpha Richard. Can we have breakfast here? I would like to get some work done, go over your pack history and get it out of the way early."

"That sounds like a plan. I'll see you in the morning then, good-night."

"Goodnight Alpha Richard." I jog up the stairs and head to my room, enter the code, then sit in the chair and dig into my cake, yummy deliciousness. I finish the whole piece of cake, down my water. I change into my night shirt, crawl under the covers, hit the light switch and before long I'm off to sleepy land. Night, Jewel. *"Night, Jay."*

I wake up to knocking on my door and I crawl over to the end table, grabbing my phone to see it's barely five am. I know it's not Olivia or Jane because they know my code. I sniff, Samuel. I get up and open the door and he pushes past me. Rude much? I go and get back in bed. "What's the problem, and why are you in my room so early? Also why are you still here? I thought you left since I didn't see you at dinner last night." He's sitting in the chair in the corner, holding his head.

"I didn't leave with the rest, I have clearance to be around you.

Plus, I promised Alpha Richard I would stay and spend some time with Alpha Small."

This catches my attention; I sit up with my back against the headboard. "Alpha Small is still here as well?"

"Yes Jay, she's staying till the end of her trip."

"Samuel, explain why Alpha Richard wants you to spend time with Alpha Small." Not that I'm complaining, better him than Richard.

"Because he's been her twin's protector in the past and he would like me to take over that job, as he feels his mate is you, actually. And until her twins are old enough, she's protecting it for them."

"She's been doing a good job so far?"

"Yes, plus she's from my region and I would be closer, only she usually doesn't get involved with Alphas."

"Alpha Richard asked you to get involved with Alpha Small."

"Not really."

"Either he did, or he didn't, Samuel."

"Actually, he said it was not off the table since Alpha Small did inquire about my relationship with you and if I was available."

"Are you?"

"Am I what?"

"Available to get involved with Alpha Small?" I feel like this conversation is leading to a headache.

"I don't know, that's why I'm here."

"I can't tell you if you want to be in a relationship with Alpha Small, can I?"

"Can't you, Jay? You've occupied my mind in various ways for the last five years."

"Really? That's news to me, Samuel."

"I need to protect you, and I think my sexual attraction to you got twisted up with the need to protect you."

"Samuel, I'll have a mate, and I'm sure you're not him. But what I can say for sure is you should make the decision that will be best for you. I'm pretty sure I'll have more than one mate actually and I'm also sure you wouldn't share well if you were one of my mates. I think that's your problem, you would love to have me, but you also don't want to share me, so I'm not the one for you. The one for you will be the one that only needs you, and truthfully, you, more than anyone here, knows I don't need you."

"Really, Jay?"

"Yes, Samuel, really. We both know who I am and who I will be. Can you honestly say you'll be alright with that in your mate?"

"I don't think so, Jay."

"Your struggle with me, Samuel, is you know that. I would love to say it's different, but it's not and there's nothing wrong with that. The real question should be, what if you find your mate, what do you do about that?" He walks to the end of my bed sitting down.

"I found my mate years ago. She rejected me because I wasn't the Alpha of my pack and that's what she wanted, not a second son."

"I'm sorry, Samuel."

"Don't be. We never had a connection, the pain from the rejection was minimal."

"Were you alright with what she did?"

"I was alright I wasn't stuck with someone that felt that way, unfortunately she's still unmated, from what I know. Still waiting to find a chosen mate with the status that she finds suitable for her."

"So, from what I'm hearing, you're free to decide your future as you see fit You just have to face the fact of what type of union you want. Do you want to give it a go with Alpha Small, if she even wants to have a chosen mate, since from my conversation with her, the twins are her highest priority."

"We had dinner last night."

"You should have led with that, Samuel."

"And she made me a proposition and I'm here to ask you what you think."

"No."

"What do you mean no?"

"I don't want to have a say in what you choose to do with your life. What if you hate it and then in the end blame me?" He smiles.

"I'm sure I wouldn't be able to blame you even if it was your fault."

"Wait, you're right about that, I'm good like that. Can I at least use the toilet, brush my teeth and put on some clothes if we're going to have life changing conversations before the sun is barely up?"

"Sure thing, Jay."

I get up, trying my best not to reveal any of my lady parts, I know that's funny since he's seen said parts. After I finish up in the bathroom, I come out to find Samuel sitting in the chair looking off into space. I go into the closet and put on a pair of cotton lounge pants, then join him sitting in the other chair. "Now Samuel, how about you start from the beginning."

"I was getting ready to head down to dinner, figuring you might need some back up after your first meeting with Alpha Richard, when I received a knock on the door. I knew who it was before I even opened it. Alpha Small was standing there saying she wants to make me a proposition. I could tell she was nervous, but she just blurts out that she would like me to be her twins and her protector. I had an idea from Alpha Richard what it was going to be about, but I wasn't prepared for her to be a part of it. She says her and her twins come as a package deal, until they're old enough to take over the Alpha-hood in thirteen years. She went on to explain how she's a strong Alpha, which I can feel, but as a woman she's only been able to avoid challenges from other Alphas because they were aware she had the backing of Alpha Peterson."

"Really Samuel, only because of her personal relationship with Alpha Peterson." Samuel continues speaking like I didn't comment at all.

"But Richard getting a mate will change that dynamic, Jay, she knows that you're likely Alpha Richard's mate. She feels my brother won't remove his protection, not wanting to have conflict with another regional Alpha. My brother won't get into a relationship with her even if imaginary because he'll have a Luna of his own eventually. She doesn't know that'll be sooner than she thinks as well. She feels if she's in a relationship with me, his brother, no one would challenge me. Also, me having a connection to the Ruler along with his regent, is a plus. All these reasons are why she would be more than willing to have any kind of relationship I want in exchange for what I would provide for her and her twins. I will say, Jay, I was flattered to hear her say she couldn't do any better as an Alpha figure for her twins to emulate than the Alpha who trained the next Ruler, as well as she thinks I'm not bad to look at."

After Samuel finishes telling me what Alpha Small asks of him, I can understand a little bit why he's sitting in my room. "Wow, that's a lot to drop on an Alpha, taking away your decision about your life, how dare she."

"Jay, don't be an ass."

"Well, am I right, if you accept her offer, you're again in the situation where you have a female having control over your life? First it was my Nanna, then it was me and now it will be Alpha Small."

"You're going to continue to be an ass."

"Samuel, let me tell you what you should be focusing on, and that's where would your life have been if it wasn't on the path it's on, instead of second son to a regional Alpha. You were Alpha of our pack, not a large one, but one more important than your brothers. You were the Alpha in charge of training the next Ruler of all Alphas, thanks to my Nanna. And the next Ruler is going to be the best one in centuries and that's largely because of you. Because I was in your life, you'll have the patience and fortitude to not only deal with Alpha Small's twins but also her. We both know I was a handful, i.e. the twins, and the sexual frustration I caused in you and how you handled it will prepare you for what you have with her. I saw how you responded to her when we entered Alpha Richard's office. The inflection I hear in your voice when you speak of her even now. I suggest you think about the benefits you've gained from the she-wolves making decisions in your life before you let the fact it's a female turn you away from what might be the best decision for your future."

"I will take what you say into consideration, Jay, you do make a lot of sense."

"Of course I do, I'm me. Besides, I like you when you're not grouchy Alpha, and this whole conversation you haven't been grouchy Alpha once. That's a plus in my book. But Samuel, if I were you, I would ask for what you want from this arrangement from the beginning. Don't think 'let me wait and see where it goes, you always wait and then you lose out. Just imagine what you could have had if you would have taken what you wanted that day on the beach instead of walking away. It might not have ended up where you wanted, but you never know unless you try, so learn from that. Ask for what you want your future to be, you never know what can happen."

"What about you, Jay, how will I be there to protect you if I'm protecting Alpha Small?"

"Samuel, you know who I am, right?"

"Not like you let me forget it, Jay."

"Then will I really need you to protect me?"

"Until you're twenty-five and have found your true mate or mates, whatever, I think you will need strength around you."

"You might be right about that. Tell me do you plan on going to her pack before I go to Haven?"

"I don't know, Jay."

"Then now you have another decision to make in regard to what your future looks like."

"Thank you, Jay."

"You're welcome, Samuel."

A<u>lpha Samuel</u>

I rise to leave and once I open the door, I hear Jay in my head saying,

"Don't let what might be a great lady pass you by because you think you might have an opportunity with another great lady."

I don't turn, I continue out the door and close it behind me. I return to my room, get undressed and get into bed. I need the rest, my head is hurting from thinking about this whole situation. Sole, what do you think? "*I think what Jay says makes sense. I don't want to share our mate with Jake/Jarrod, or anyone else.*" We don't know that Alpha Lisa will want us to be her chosen mate. "*She might, Sam, if we love her good enough and only her. We are good enough, and Jay will belong to Jake/Jarrod.*" I think she will belong to more than just Jarrod and Jake, Sole. "*I think you might be right, Sam; I want our own mate that will not reject us.*" That wasn't our fault. "*It doesn't matter, we were rejected. It hurt me more than you and I don't want to feel that way again. You will have to find us our own mate, Sam, and even though we love Jay and Jewel, they'll never be our own mate.*"

You're right, buddy. Do you want to ask Alpha Lisa to be our chosen mate? *"Do you think she will say yes, Sam?"* I don't know, buddy. She's worried about us trying to replace her twins, and if we have pups with her, what happens then? *"What about if we don't become chosen mates until her pups are eighteen, then we can have our own pups."* Become chosen mates after her pup' become Alphas of their pack? Agreed. *"It's only thirteen years, Sam, we're wolves, we live long lives. Besides, I don't care about that, I just want our own mate."* You don't care now, Sole, but maybe in the future you will want your own pups. *"Maybe, but right now, Sam, I just want to know we will have our own mate. We will accept her offer, Sam, agreed?"* Yes, Sole, agreed. I take a deep breath; I feel better, night, Sole. *"Night ,Sam."*

Chapter 7

BETA JAY

S*urprise In Lutsen*

After Samuel left, I sat down thinking about the situation, and found that I have a good feeling he'll make the right decision. Even though Alpha Lisa attacked me, I know it came from a good place. I'm up, might as well get my day started, so I get in the shower. Today is a jeans, long t-shirt, and sneaker day. I grab my phone, my laptop suitcase and then head down to Alpha Richard's office. I didn't expect him to be there, so when I push open the door and see him sitting at his desk, I'm startled. "I apologize for just walking in, I thought I would beat you here with it being so early. I want to get started with work today."

"Good morning, Jay, I came down early to get your workstation set up as you can see."

He points to the space on the other side of the sitting area that has a desk and chair.

"You can work from there, and for future reference I don't keep this door open, you'll have to choose a code for the door."

"Good morning, Richard. I didn't think of that, meaning I would've been standing in the hallway."

"Yes, you would have."

I smile, moving over to my makeshift desk, "Richard, can I ask you if I can get another chair moved in? I'll be working with Olivia when she's better."

"Sure thing, what about Jane?"

"She usually works on her laptop from a chair, so she'll sit in one of those. Have you seen Beta James?"

"No, I did get a call from him this morning informing me he has accepted and marked his mate, among other things. I'm sure we'll not be seeing him or your Beta Jamison for the rest of the week."

I smile. "That's good to know. I'll have to set up her belongings to be moved to his house."

"It's been handled along with his belongings from his suite here. They're being packed up and moved this morning."

"Don't forget to have food delivered, Richard."

"No food, groceries will be delivered, Beta Pete can cook pretty well."

"That's a relief, because Jane can barely boil water for her tea." We laugh at that.

"What am I going to do if Tony's Beta Jamison takes my pack Beta away?"

"I don't think you have to worry about that. Jane can do her work from anywhere until they find a suitable replacement. If she comes to work for my security firm full time, again she doesn't have to be in any specific location, she just needs access to great internet service. She might be able to stay here, letting you keep your Beta."

"I'm happy to hear that. Beta Pete is one of the best and he would be hard to replace. I'll go and get you another chair and have breakfast delivered while you get settled."

"Sounds good, Richard, thank you."

While Alpha Richard goes on his errands, I get my laptop plugged in and get logged on. I go through my emails to see if anything needs urgent attention, and nothing is imminent. I forward some things to Olivia's email that she can handle and return some emails to clients I want to only hear from me. I review invoices that have been paid, check the accounts and bills we've paid, and once I confirm all is as it should be, I move on to reviewing the footage Jane usually would if she wasn't enjoying her new mate. I'm so into watching the screen I don't hear Richard enter and put the chair down, or the tray on the table with our breakfast. I'm trying to determine if there's anything that's different from what we should be seeing on the west fence, and so far, nothing.

I review the notes the pack member provided on what they saw, and again nothing. My gut tells me this is the right way forward, we just need to keep watching.

"Beta Jay, you want to have breakfast?"

I log out of Tony's pack system and move to the chair to enjoy my breakfast. I grab a plate and pile on an everything bagel with an egg omelet and bacon and dig in. I watch Alpha Richard as he fills his plate with more than double what I'm eating, shoving food into his mouth not even caring about the mess he's making on his shirt.

I smile, liking that he's comfortable enough to not care. I pass him a napkin, making him realize he needs it.

"My apologies, Jay, I love food."

I smile at him, "I can see that, and so do I." We spend the next thirty minutes enjoying our food and light conversation.

"I would like to show you something I hope will make up for how we first met, after breakfast, if you have the time."

"I do."

"Good, I'll have someone clean up our breakfast and we can head out."

"Why? Do we have to leave the lodge? Because I didn't bring my boots."

"It's fine, there are over boots in the garage you can wear, and your coat is there, you'll be fine. We're taking the snowmobile, you'll not be walking that much."

"Sounds like fun." I grab my phone and follow Richard out, turning towards the back of the lodge going to the garage, and he hands me the galoshes to put on over my Nikes. I put on my coat while he puts on his overcoat, and we head out. He obviously had this planned because parked there is a snowmobile waiting for us. He gets on and I get on behind him. It's a familiar position like riding behind Tony on the motorcycle only there are so many clothes between us I can barely feel him in front of me. We ride for about fifteen minutes when I begin to smell something familiar. I would know that smell anywhere, and if it's what I know it is, Alpha Richard is very much forgiven. There's another few minutes of riding and before he completely stops the snowmobile, I'm off and running towards the barn I see ahead of me.

I push the doors open and rush in, taking a deep breath, breathing in the smell of hay, horse, and yes, old manure, but that comes with the animals I love. I move forward and see two horses each in their own stall. The first one, I hear Richard say from behind me is a mare and she is beautiful, standing at least fifteen one hands, depending on the depths of the stall bedding. She has the look of a Friesian like my Galahad, but not full. Something else is there I'm not quite sure about but the elegance of the Frisian head and neck is evident. She has mostly smoke grey coloring throughout her body with zebra looking gray and black stripes on her hind legs. The most interesting part is the white star on her muzzle.

I move forward to see how willing she is to introduce herself. I remove my gloves, shoving them in my pocket, then open my palm to give her the opportunity to smell my essence. I'm letting her know I'm only trying to be her friend. She smells me and lets me rub her muzzle, but not much more. I'm not surprised, as she's a mare and they don't accept you easily; you must work harder to earn their trust. As I move further into the barn to check out the next stall, I notice her tail is mostly black with strands of white somewhere in there. I move on to the next stall, and here Richard says is a gelding. I can tell he's not Frisian at all, but like the mare in some way. Maybe whatever the mare is crossed with, I imagine, is what the gelding is. His coloring is Dunn and he's shorter, closer to fourteen hands.

He's friendly and I move forward for me to pet his neck and muzzle. Richard moves behind me but not coming further into the barn, this is curious behavior. "Why are you standing over there like that?"

"They don't really like me."

"Why do you have horses if they don't like you?"

"I don't have horses; you have a horse."

"I know I do, at Haven, mine were delivered there to await my arrival."

"No Jay, I mean the mare, whose name is Star by the way, is for you."

I jerked my head in his direction. "Are you serious? Why? How?"

"Mark told me how much you love to ride, and I know you had to send your horses to Haven. When you were at Jarrod's pack you were able to learn to surf, and while you were at Tony's pack you were able to learn to ride a motorcycle. At my pack you were supposed to learn to ski, but due to things being changed, you will miss the ski season. So I thought about what I could do so you could do something and enjoy your time at my pack. This is what I came up with, only I didn't realize you would arrive at the lodge a week earlier than expected. The day you arrived is the day Star arrived, she hasn't had a chance to settle in and to get to know me."

"Richard, is this where you were when I arrived?"

"Yes, I was getting them settled and didn't get the call from Tony. But that's not important at this point. This is Star, she's eight years old, part Friesian part Criollo, trained in." He then pulls a paper from his pocket and continues. "Dressage and endurance and can go thirty miles in eight hours."

"Richard? Richard? This is a great gift, but you didn't have to do this. There was no competition between the packs, I just wanted to know them."

"I know, Jay, but I want to make sure our pack leaves an impression on you that's a positive one."

"Just being who you are would be impressive enough for me, but I'll accept your pack's gift because I love horses. Now what about this guy?"

"This is Sam, he's not yours, he's just here to keep Star company. He's ten, endurance trained only and full Criollo, he's friendlier than Star."

"No, it's not about being friendly, Richard, it's about trust. Mares, like she-wolves, take longer to trust, but once you have earned their trust, they'll give you their everything. I have stallions at Haven and have wanted to introduce a mare into my herd to breed both my guys with and I think Star just might work. We will have to wait and see how it goes. I've a question for you, though. If you don't have horses, where did you get this horse barn from?"

"It was an old barn we kept old equipment in and used for storage, I had it converted to a horse barn over the ski season. It was barely ready in time. I had to have a pole shed helicoptered in to store hay and feed and a separate water tank because I don't have the plumbing out here. I'm happy with the outcome from what my research told me. I definitely needed the insulation to keep the water from freezing, and don't get me started on the cost of hay for them. Wow, I'll be glad when they move on."

I smile at him. "Yes it can get costly, I only hope I get the opportunity to ride."

"Oh yeah, Jay, look over in that room."

I walk over, opening the door and see all the tack I would need for an endurance saddle and accessories. "How did you know what to get?"

"I didn't. Mark provided his assistance, as well as Shirley Kilt, the lady I purchased Star from. She knew what you would need based on the information from Mark. Will it suffice?"

"Yes, Richard, it's more than enough, but what I was referring to is if Star will let me ride. It's more a matter of her accepting me. It's not something that can be forced especially on an unfamiliar ice mountain. For sure I look forward to getting to know them both." I walk over to him and give him a big hug. "You did good, and you'll probably be forgiven for a lot. Just say Star when I get upset and I'll remember this feeling and will probably forgive you. Maybe, depends... I don't know but you can try."

"I will keep that in mind. Knowing me, I'll definitely need this get out of jail free card in the future."

I'm reluctant to leave but knowing they haven't had a chance to really get settled into their new living quarters I'll give Star a couple of days before I come back and visit. I feel good about the opportunity to build a bond with a new horse, a mare at that. We head back to the pack lodge, and to my surprise, I see Olivia sitting at the desk working on her laptop. Richard goes to his desk and starts going over documents he left there. "How are you feeling, Olivia?"

"Better, mostly back to normal. Where's Jane?"

"She's with Beta James after deciding to accept him as her mate, so we probably won't see her for the rest of the week."

Olivia smiles. "Good for her. I went to her room and saw them moving out her things. She must have known she was going to accept him because things were already packed."

"Yeah, I helped her pack before her dinner date." Olivia looks over to Richard.

"Alpha Peterson."

"You can call me, Richard."

"Thank you, I will, but Alpha Richard, I think there is going to be hell in your pack soon."

"Really why do you say that?"

"Because when I was leaving Jane's room, I saw a blond girl standing in the hall and she was smiling, happy to see Jane's things were being removed. She said she knew he was going to send that bitch packing and then she walked off. When she realizes she was not only not packed off but moved into his house and they accepted each other as mates and are probably marked by now, there's going to be hell."

"That does sound like something I should address soon."

"Yes, I think you should, indeed, before it gets out about what is really going on."

Richard lifts the phone and orders lunch be brought to his office for two.

"If you both don't mind, I would like to have lunch with my pack member alone in my office today."

"Of course." As I wait for Olivia to log off her laptop and put it away, there's a knock on the door. Richard says enter, and in walks the aforementioned blonde who gave me the hateful looks the previous night in the dining room. She addresses Alpha Richard, saying he requested she join him

"Yes, Anne, please have a seat here."

As we leave the room, we see lunch being delivered and hear Richard saying they need to discuss some developments and that he thought they could have lunch together while doing so. The door closes and I look at Olivia. I feel bad for her, but not to the extent I don't want Jane to have her happiness. I'm impressed with how Richard is handling this situation. By taking note the attention and support his pack member is going to need at this moment. Very Alpha of him and something his Luna would assist him with if and when he has one. I wonder why he didn't contact his mother, and just as the thought leaves my head, I see Luna Loretta heading in our direction to go to Richard's office. We greet her on our way but don't delay her because she's going to be needed very soon.

We head to the dining hall to have lunch, glad we're not the ones having to deal with a hurt she-wolf. I notice Olivia is quiet and I imagine she's remembering the pain of her breakup with Curtis. "Are you thinking about Curtis?"

"Yes, but at least I didn't have to deal with losing him to another she-wolf."

"It's not just another she-wolf, Olivia, it's a goddess mate, and I would rather lose to a goddess mate than to any other situation. But let's not dwell on it, we're looking to the future, and I've thought of a great plan."

"Yes, what's that?"

"I'm going to bring your mother and brother to visit you here. You were supposed to go visit them when you were hurt, so how about we have them come visit you here? Talk to them and see if they're open to it. They'll get to meet Alpha Peterson, and your mom can brag about knowing not only the Ruler's Regent but two Regional Alphas."

"That's a great idea, Jay, but you don't have to pay for it, I have funds, remember?"

"Yes, you're right, and after you took an arrow for yourself, you earned it, that's for sure." We both start laughing.

"You're right, Jay, but thanks for suggesting it."

"I'll discuss it with Alpha Richard, but I'm sure he'll be fine with it. Besides, they're already cleared to be in my presence, so we just have to see when the best time will be based on the business."

"I'll talk to them later on tonight. It'll be nice, and I do miss my mom."

"Let's get some food I'm hungry."

"Did you miss breakfast?"

"No, but I did have it earlier than usual. I was up early helping Samuel with his life and then Alpha Richard took me to the barn to meet Star, a horse he bought for me."

"What, he bought you a horse?"

"Yes, it's a long story, I'll tell you about it over lunch. But she is beautiful, and I can't wait to bond with her."

"That's great, I guess. Not sure why you love doing it, seems dangerous to me. But you are an adrenaline junky."

"Yeah I am, I still want to learn how to ski, too. Mark said we can learn on the baby slopes. They're smaller so there is less chance of killing ourselves."

"I want to learn as well, Jay; can't go home and say I came to one of the most famous ski lodges and didn't at least try to ski."

"We'll have to come up with a plan on learning without dying." We laugh as we look for a table. While looking around, I see Mark sitting with a female, he notices us and waves us over. When we join, he introduces us to his Samantha. "Oohh, so this is the infamous Samantha! Nice to meet you. I've heard much about you." She said the same to me even though she's heard nothing about me. That's to be expected considering what happened on the island was confidential. But she said it was nice to finally meet me, and now that I'm no longer confidential, she looks forward to learning all about me. I see Mark smiling and I can see the affection he has for her. I continue to hope she'll be his mate; it'll be heartbreaking if she's not.

We enjoy breakfast, getting to know more about Samantha and learning more about who Mark was when he was younger and during his home visits. We mentioned wanting to learn to ski and Samantha agreed to teach us if we agreed to never leave the baby slopes, which we did. Then we set up a schedule to start tomorrow after lunch. That way it's warmer outside and we get a chance to get some work done. I thanked Mark for telling Alpha Richard about my love of horses, and he is glad I was happy with the choice he made. He also told me he had nothing to do with what he chose, just gave him ideas. Which made me even happier. We finished our meal and decided to hit the gym with Mark as our trainer. We're going to need to stay in shape if we want to survive the ski lessons.

We each go back to our rooms to get changed and agree to meet in the lodge foyer in twenty minutes. I like Samantha and look forward to getting to know her better. She makes Mark happy and that's a bonus. He's become like a brother to me and a big part of who I am, especially when it comes to my training. Mark likes to think out of the box when it comes to hand to hand fighting styles. The unexpected punch in the right place can result in a win or loss in our competitions and in life. I'm excited to see what new techniques he's come up with to challenge me.

I watch Anne as she takes a seat. I'm dreading this conversation, but know it must be had. I want to wait for my mother to join, as Luna she should be here to provide support to the female she-wolves. But as Alpha, I take responsibility for all my pack members, regardless male or female. She's watching me with nervous interest and my stalling is up. "I want you to know I'm here to provide you with whatever support you'll need." She says that's great to know but wants to know if there's something wrong with someone in her family, commenting that she hasn't felt a loss and if her parents are ok. She then goes to rise before I stop her. "No Anne, have a seat." I hear someone approaching and to my greatest relief it's my mother. She punches in her code, enters and calls to me. "Luna Mother, thank you for joining us. Anne, my mother, as well, is here to provide you with support."

She says again that is great, but that I have failed to tell her what she needs support for. My mother looks at me, asking why I haven't informed her as to why she's here. "I haven't, mother, because I was waiting for you to get here." She reminds me that she's here now and that I should proceed. She moves to the seat next to Anne taking her hand. Anne then comments that we are both making her very nervous.

"Anne there's no way to say this that will not cause you pain, so I'll just say it. Beta Pete James has taken a goddess mate." There's quiet in the room, she looks like she didn't hear me, but I know she has. She barely whispers that it cannot be true because she saw just this morning that Beta Jane was having her luggage moved out of her room. I didn't respond to Anne's statement; she isn't a stupid woman. I let her brain take her where it would eventually go. I could see her thinking, and when she eventually realized where the luggage was being moved to, the distress on her face was painful to see. She starts screaming, No No No, telling me that's not possible because Beta Jane just got here. She says that Pete wouldn't do that, that he can't have moved her into her house.

"Anne, look at me, that was never your house. It was Beta James house to move into it whoever he chose, and if he would have chosen you as his chosen mate, it would have been his right. But since he has been given a goddess mate who accepted him as her mate, they've moved into his house as mates." I can see my mother holding her hand very tight as she tries to rise from the seat. "Anne, please look at me," I see the pain in her eyes, "I can only imagine the difficulty you're going to go through. Your Luna and I are here to help you determine what you'll need to begin to be better." She sarcastically responds that what she needs is Pete back.

"Well, that's not going to happen." Again she sarcastically says 'Why, because some she-wolf came and stole him away?'

"Anne, you keep forgetting the part about the goddess-mate. She didn't steal him away, she was goddess mated to him. They both decided to accept the gift from the goddess. You will accept it because that's what we do. We respect what our goddess has put in place for our lives." Anne looks at me with defiance before saying that she think if she had a chance, Pete would have chosen her. "I think you did have a chance, Anne; you and Beta James have been dating for almost a year, or am I mistaken?" She goes on with, No but. before I interrupt her. "Anne, you both had a chance to choose each other as chosen mates, and neither you or Beta James made that choice. Our Goddess did make a choice, and Beta James, Beta Jamison, and you, Anne, will respect it." I can tell by the look in her eye she understood this to be a direct order from her Alpha. She responds, 'Yes Alpha Peterson.'

"Good, now how can your Luna and Alpha help you in what we understand to be a difficult time?" She asks if she can ask me a question, and I nod my head yes for her to continue. She wants to know why I keep calling Pete, Beta James. I take a deep breath before responding. "Because from the moment you leave this room that's how you will address him. He will no longer be Pete to you, he will be Beta James. If and until he gives you the right to call him Beta Pete. He's this pack's Beta. and you will show him that respect, regardless of how you feel about him personally. I know in public you've always respected him as such even though we all knew of your private relationship. However, since you've come into my office and spoke of him, you've referred to him as Pete.

In my presence, he should have always been Beta James. In front of your Luna, he should have always been Beta James. I'm trying to help you, Anne, to again realize that. for you from now on, he can only and will only be Beta James. Do you understand?" She nods her head in the affirmative, but something in me tells me she doesn't really agree. "How can we help you?" She wants to know if there be an opportunity for her to speak Pete, even though she corrects herself before she says his full name and calls him Beta James. I look at her, dreading what I'm about to say. "Beta James has requested five days off to get himself and his mate settled into their new home. He moved his things from the pack lodge. Yes Anne, he has." She shakes her head as she wipes away her tears.

"Anne, I think you need to start thinking about what you need to do to help yourself begin to move on. Again, how can we help you?" My mother finally decides to speak, requesting they have the office, and she will let me know what they come up with. "Sure thing mother." I rise, and mouth 'thank you' to her as I head to the door. I turn to Anne, "I'm sad for what this situation is causing you, and remember, anything in reason we can do, we'll do. Mother I'll be in your suites with father going over some of the ideas for the new lifts. Find me there with what you both decide, and we'll implement them immediately."

I leave my office, glad to have that behind me and run into Mark. "Do you know where Beta Scott is?"

"Yes, she went up to get changed. We're going to train in the gym, you're more than welcome to join, Alpha."

"No, I have to talk to my father about the new lifts. Can you tell her I would like to have dinner with her this evening if she's available? If so, can she please meet me in my suite at six."

"Will do, Alpha."

I head up, taking the steps two at a time. My dad was the last one to update the lifts. I would love his insight on how the project went, and what, if any, issues he ran into during the installation. My father and I were practically finished with reviewing my plans when my mother walked in. I wasn't expecting her to be done with Anne as quickly. "What did she decide?" She informs me that Anne is leaving. That she's going to move to one of the lower lodges where she doesn't have to see the Beta and his new mate."That is a good idea, right mother?" She thought so herself when she suggested it. "Thank you mother?" She quickly lets me know that she didn't do it for me. That Anne and her wolf are suffering and she thought out of sight out of mind. "But do you think not being able to keep an eye on her is a good idea?"

My mother already reached out to Anne's mother, and she'll be going with her to get her settled. She understands the gift of a goddess mating and will do her best to help her daughter. Also, she says that I should have let Beta James inform her that he accepted his mate.

Chapter 8

ALPHA RICHARD

I take a couple of deep calming breathes before responding. "From what I was told, he did tell her, mother." No, she says, he told her that he told his mate he would accept her, if she wanted him. The fact they have accepted, marked, mated, and moved into the house together so fast was shocking to Anne. It's like she meant nothing to him all these months. My father jumped in, asking her not to be hard on me since she knows how the mate bond works. She agreed with my dad, reminding us of both that Anne doesn't. She was going off of falling in love with her heart, not a bond connection. A choice of the heart, and Beta James should have explained it to her in that fashion. Now he has created an enemy of Anne. She'll never forgive them and he's this pack's Beta.

"Do you think we should have him go to Beta Jamison's pack instead?" My mother shakes her head at me, saying of course not because that would leave us without a great Beta because of a she-wolf who can't replace him. She would rather send her away. But she promised to figure something out and will keep in touch with her mother to ensure she's recovering. My mom explains that when I left Anne in her room, she watched by the stairs and saw her run from her room to Beta James suite and found the door open. She assumed the room was empty, but she heard Anne whisper, "How could you do this to me, Pete? I know you love me, at least you did until she came." She says she didn't hear what I said. "No, mother, she heard us, she has chosen to not listen. I gave her a direct command."

Again, she disagrees with me, saying what I did was really an Alpha request, and that I need to go and make it official, and now, before she leaves. I get up, thanking my dad for his help. He says he doesn't envy my next encounter but knows I'm a good Alpha. I leave, hurrying down the stairs hoping I haven't missed Anne. I see her heading in the direction of the garage with her mother following behind her with some bags. I rush forward, grabbing them from her. "Let me help you with those." She thanks me for my help. "I'll escort you to the chopper. Anne if you have anything you need delivered from your suite, I'll have it packed and delivered for you." She says thank you, Alpha Peterson, and that she left a list in her room of the items and her mother will only be with her for a couple of weeks. When she comes back she'll get them packed and sent to her.

"Don't bother, Anne, I'll do it this week and have them sent; you shouldn't have to go without your things for that long." As we approach the chopper, I assist her mother in and load up the luggage. "Anne, I need to have a word?" She turns looking at me saying she's not sure what more there's to say. I take a deep breath before I start. "I, Alpha Richard Peterson of the Larojey-Slopes Pack, hereby order you, Anne Carlson of the Larojey-Slopes Pack, from this moment on, to respect and refer to Beta Pete James as such. Any further disrespect of Beta Pete James and his mate in name and or person will be in violation of this direct order from your Alpha and this official Alpha Command. Do you understand this command?" She struggles with composing herself before responding with yes,

Alpha Peterson.

She continues saying, 'I Anne Carlson understand the Alpha Command.' I walk up to her and give her a hug. "I know you're hurt and angry, but this is what's best for all involved." She says she knows that's what I think, but she's the only one who's doing all the losing in this situation. There is nothing I can say to that because she's correct. There was nothing I could do to change it but what I'm doing now. She pulls away and climbs up into the chopper. As it takes off, I have a bad feeling I've also made an enemy of a pack member with the Alpha command I just issued. We as Alphas don't like to issue them, but when we do, they're binding and causes physical pain if violated. I feel like this had to be done, I think. I shake my head, turning to head back to the lodge.

I've work to do on the lifts since Beta Pete is off on what the humans would call the honeymoon, leaving me to do his work. I head to my office thinking I'll talk to Jay about this over dinner, maybe she'll have a better outlook on what transpired today. I have a feeling I did something wrong, even though I don't know right now what that is. I'm positive Jay's going to say I screwed up with Anne. I prepare myself for her scathing down.

I want it to be an informal comfortable dinner, so I go with cotton sweats with a matching t-shirt and no socks. I refreshed my face shaving this morning. My shadow isn't too bad, though my hair is a little longer than usual. But she saw me this morning with no complaints. When the knock came to the door at first, I thought it was Jay, before I realized it's dinner. I ordered burgers and fresh cut fries, and I had a large piece of her cake brought up, hoping she would share with me, but not holding my breath. I open the door to let them in, instructing them to set the table near my balcony. It has a great view of the mountain. It's not as nice as the one from

Pete's house, but nice enough. After they leave, I make myself a shot of vodka, just a little liquid courage.

This time when the knock comes, I know it's Jay. I open the door with a smile on my face, and notice she too went with comfy, only she has on cotton socks, no slippers and a robe over the outfit. She looks great in winter white with her sun-kissed mocha complexion, curly black hair and hazel eyes. I'm sure I would love whatever she was wearing though. "Please come in." She moves into my suite, and I notice she doesn't have her phone. I like that she didn't want to be interrupted. I walk over to where I left mine and silence it. "I thought we could have simple fair; I hope you like burgers and fries?"

"I sure do, Alpha, as long as you have sangria to pair it with."

"I sure do, I also had them bring a piece of your cake."

"That sounds even better."

I follow her to the table preparing to enjoy a nice evening before I bring up the topic of Anne. I'll wait for that.

B *eta Jay*

When Richard opens the door, I'm glad of my choice of outfit. After the grueling training Mark put us through, I couldn't bear to put on anything that wasn't loose and soft against my skin. I can't believe how sore you can be from missing a couple of days of training. I can only imagine how I'll feel tomorrow. *"You could have phased to let me heal you, Jay."* No, that's cheating, Jewel. Besides,

I need to be able to take the pain, I'm stronger than I look. *"If you say so, Jay."* I do say so.

I look over at Richard, he looks good, with his barely there shadow on his face. I love his eyes, they're light brown, but not quite as light as mine, and they twinkle when he laughs. Not as full as Tony's but it's there, like he's cautious with his laughter. He doesn't share it as often. Well, we'll have to work on that. I can see the fitness in his arms, huge muscles, more fit than just wolf physique. I also notice his nice butt when he passes by the table. Again, not as plump as Tony's, but still a nice handful.

I must be missing sexual attention. I've been thinking about nothing but his physical attributes since I sat down. Calm down or he'll know my mind is in the gutter. *"He might want to join you there, Jay. Have you considered your mind is there because you're getting these feelings from him? Remember our new power, you can sense other's feelings and emotions."* Oohh, so that's what this is, I look up at him and smile. You little devil, Richard, you're the one making me feel this way. I look at him smirking, and he looks at me.

"What, why are you looking at me like that?"

"Oh no reason, just wondering."

"Wondering what?"

"Penny for your thoughts, Alpha Richard." I see him visibly swallow.

"No need, Jay, I was just thinking we should get to eating before our food gets cold."

His eyebrows scrunch together like he's confused by my statement. "Sounds good to me, Richard." I uncover my plate, loving they didn't skimp on the loaded burger, and the fries are plentiful too, and I dig in. I love crunchy fries that are soft on the inside, with ketchup on the side, just a little to not overpower the potato. I open a bottle of water to have with my meal, not wanting to start drinking until I have some food in my stomach.

"Tell me, Jay, how did things go in training."

"It was tough. Mark is a ball buster, especially when you don't have any, but you would think I'd be used to it. Yes, he never fails to impress with the moves he comes up with."

"Really? What moves?"

"Oh, I can't tell you, they're our secret."

"But I thought you were training with Olivia and Samantha?"

"Yeah, sort of, they're for female wolves only. How was the rest of your day, Alpha? I don't even want to imagine how things went with the blond female after we left your office."

"Anne."

"What?"

"The blonde, her name is Anne."

"Oh, Anne. I do hope she'll be ok."

"I do as well, I actually want to talk to you about how it went."

"Really, why?"

"To get your take on things, you know, you being a she-wolf."

"Why? I saw your mother going to your office, I'm sure she provided you with great support. But I'll help if I can, even though I'll tell you I've lived on an island for most of my life and haven't had to deal with anything like what happened today."

"I'll keep that in mind, I wanted to wait until we finished our meal."

"Wow, Richard, is what happened that upsetting?"

"Not sure."

"Wait, hold on a second." I take another huge bite of my burger and shove some fries in my mouth then grab the sangria and pour half a glass full. I finish chewing in a very un-lady-like manner. While Richard is smiling at me. I take a big gulp of my favorite drink and say, "I'm ready, hit me with it." For the next thirty to forty minutes, he went over everything that happened from the moment we left the office until she got on the helicopter and took off. I have so many conflicting emotions running through me about what was said and done. While he was talking, I finished my first and second glass of sangria, poured myself a third and am halfway through that now. I take a quick sip, put the glass down and get up and start walking over to him. Richard leans back in his seat; I can tell he's not sure what I'm going to do.

I stop in front of him, turn him towards me and give him a tight hug, then walk back and take my seat. "You're the best Alpha a pack can have. You were understanding of her pain, but also understanding of Beta James' right to happiness. You were sympathetic to the fact she would need to make changes in her life and willing to support what those changes needed to be. But you were also strong in your support of your Beta and the respect he's earned in his pack. You were smart enough to recognize you needed a woman in the room when dealing with a woman, who might understand better how emotional we can be. But also, how willful and vindictive we can get when we feel wronged. Your mother was correct that you needed to make the command an official one.

The hug was because you included Jane in that command, I'm grateful to you for it. You don't know her," He begins to speak but I stop him saying. "No, Richard, let me finish. I also agree with you in that you do need to keep an eye on her."

"May I speak now?"

"Yes, Richard, you can speak now."

"Do you agree with me because, after I told her the situation, she still went back to Beta James room? That she said if Beta Jamison had not come here, Pete would be hers while still using the name I told her not to use?"

"Nope, Richard." While popping my **P** loudly, I'm really feeling my sangria now. "The fact that, even though she knows this is a goddess mate pairing, she still doesn't care is the reason why you have a problem. We as wolves respect that above all else, even those of us who haven't found our mate. But not Anne, even after she knew it, was told it by Beta James, by Beta Jamison, by her Alpha, and by her Luna. She still didn't care. That, Richard, is the reason you needed to make it a command. That, Richard, is the reason you must keep an eye on her. If she doesn't respect what we all respect, the thing we all hold dear, that means even your official command isn't respected. The pain of violating it is nothing compared to the pain she may think she's feeling over losing what she thought would be her future. But Richard, you have to keep an eye on her, and I'm not sure sending her to the next lodge is the best way to do that."

"But maybe, Jay, it will be easier for her to heal if she doesn't see them being together every day. Her mother went with her, so hopefully she can talk some sense into her."

"I'll let Jane know what has happened when she comes out from under Beta James." I begin laughing because that was funny. I pour myself another glass of sangria and hand the bottle to Richard. "Here, you have to take this from me, I'm a lightweight and you don't want to know the kind of trouble I can get myself into when I have too much of this stuff."

"I'm sure I do, Jay." But he takes the bottle away nonetheless.

I start to feel warm and tingly in my bones, like liquid fire is running through me. I'm not sure if this is me or him, I look over at him watching me, eyes low like he's trying to figure out what I'm thinking. If only he knew I can feel what he's feeling though. I wonder, Jewel, can I hear what he's thinking? "*I don't know, Jay, but it would be an invasion of privacy. And I'm not sure that would be a nice thing to do especially while you are in this condition.*" You're right, but let's think on this later. I look at him, trying to determine if the warmth seeping into my breast and down my abdomen is my arousal or his. I lean back letting myself slide a little further down, my head rests on the back of my chair. "Tell me something, Richard, what's going on in that handsome head of yours?" He looks into my eyes.

"If only you knew, Jay."

"I'm asking but are you brave enough to tell me, or would you like me to guess?" He slides a little lower in his seat.

"I've heard you have some magical powers, Jay, but if you can guess what's going on in my head, you're a magician."

"Wait, are you saying if I guess what you're thinking I get something? What do I get, Richard?"

"What do you want, Jay?"

"I don't know yet."

"Then I'll owe you."

"I don't know if that's a good idea, Richard. You never know with me, I might ask for something you might not want to part with."

"I'm confident you'll never guess what's going on in my head, Jay, trust me I'm not worried."

I lean forward and take a large sip of my sangria.

"Especially the way you're putting that stuff away. I've only had two glasses of my vodka and it's nowhere near as strong as three, or is that four glasses of your sangria. What I'm drinking is made for humans, I've more of my faculties than you do."

"If you think so, Richard." I lean back and let my body tell me what Alpha Richard is really thinking. "How do I know you'll admit to it, if I guess correctly."

"You have my word as an Alpha."

I lean up in my chair and stare him in the eyes. "You, Alpha Richard, were thinking how great it would be if you could suck on my nipples. But no, not just suck, you would start with my right one twirling your tongue around my bud until it is as pointy as a bullet. Then suck it hard causing my juices to leak from me so that you can smell me. Then you would move onto my left one treating it to the same manipulations. Increasing the juices between my legs enhancing my sweet strawberry scent you got a whiff of earlier but you weren't quite sure what made it occur." I continue to stare in his eyes. "Want me to tell you what made it occur earlier? I was thinking about how handsome you look with your barely-there shadow beard. How it would be nice to run my hands over your soft face.

How kissable your lips look and how I would love to suck on your bottom lip. I was marveling on how my hands wouldn't be able to fit around the bulging muscles on your arms. How I wish I could see what other muscles you had that bulge. Lastly, I was thinking about how juicy a handful of your bottom would be as you passed by to sit, but then I stopped myself before I released my arousal into the air but obviously, I failed in that attempt." Richard swallows and gets up from his seat and I'm able to witness an amazing bulge that is for sure a lot thicker than Tony and Jarrod. I lick my lips as he walks towards me with his penis bouncing in his sweats. It's obvious he's not wearing underwear to hold that weapon in place, he reaches me and leans down.

"That's exactly what I was thinking. You are either a magician or a mind reader."

He's so close enough to my mouth that I can feel his breath and he leans further down, kissing me softly on my lips, sending sparks tingling into my mouth. I reach up grabbing his face wanting to touch him since he passed by earlier. I lean up, deepening the kiss and getting my first real taste of Richard. My third mate. The heat in my body explodes making moans escape from me. I deepen the kiss before biting his bottom lip. He grabs me lifting me from my chair and I wrap my legs around his waist, feeling the head of his bulge hitting me in a spot just right to help this heat to its needed conclusion. He carries me to a chair in his living area where he sits giving me the leverage to push myself harder onto him sending more sparks into my belly. I break the kiss needing oxygen to breathe, giving him access to start kissing on my neck. Open mouth kisses that feel like hot lava inside of them.

I start pulling my cotton shirt above my head wanting to give him more of me. I'm on fire and this is new. It feels like my skin is burning up, but I know if I can feel his on mine, it'll be better. I was right, when his hands finally touch my bare skin the burning eases from unbearable to delightful. He massages my breast while kissing on my neck and chest. When those amazing lips finally suck my nipple into his mouth I lose all thought. I'm losing myself in the pleasure, my body wants more, needs more. He begins twirling his tongue around my nipple like he was dreaming of doing. He's squeezing my other nipple until it's pointy and painful and then starts sucking on the other one oh boy. The whole time I keep thinking I want him inside of me. Jewel keeps saying, but you promised.

I keep saying, but I want him inside of me. She keeps saying, but you promised, then he blows on the nipple, and I push and gyrate on his fat bulge that's barely fitting between my thighs. I can only imagine if it would fit in any hole on my body, but damn, I can't wait to let him try. He's treating my other breast to the same beautiful attention, and I continue my wishing. Wishing I could in some way just have a little of him inside of me. But I promised. While Richard is twirling on my nipple and I'm pushing down on him, trying to figure out how to break my promise, he does something that sends me releasing in my cotton pants. He bites the shit out of my nipple hard and won't let go. The pain hurts like hell and is kind of wonderful at the same time. Who knew I was starting to like some pain with my pleasure.

My release shakes throughout my body, and I collapse on his

chest. Once I can breathe, I lean up and look him in the face. "What the hell was that?"

"Well, Jay, you didn't seem to be paying attention to me. I didn't expect you would enjoy it that much, though."

"Well, I didn't either, but you're right, I was having a disagreement with Jewel."

"That's your wolf, I imagine."

"Yes."

"Would you like to tell me what about?"

"I was thinking I want you inside of me."

He smiles. "That can be arranged."

"Actually, no it can't because I made myself a promise I will save that part of me for my mate."

"We're wolves, Jay."

"I know, but I made that promise and I've kept it."

"Even with Jarrod and Tony?"

"Yes sir, I mean, we've done other things like what we've done and more, but neither of those penises have entered my vajajay."

"That's what you call it?"

"Yes, since I was young, but let's not discuss what I call it further, please? Anyway, Jewel was reminding me of the promise while I was trying to figure out a way out of it."

"There are other ways of bringing you satisfaction, like I just did, obviously."

"I'm aware, Richard, but for some reason the closer I get to my born day the stronger the want becomes. Don't get me wrong, I've had some very satisfying encounters, but I feel like that will be the ultimate one."

"I'm sure your mate will appreciate you waiting for him. What if you have more than one mate?"

"I'll have to figure that out when the time comes." I go to rise from his lap, but he holds me in place.

"You were right about my thoughts, and you let me enjoy them in real time, but you didn't tell me what you wanted in return."

"I'll have to think on that, but I will tell you one thing, you better not bite my damn breast that hard again."

"But Jay, you must have enjoyed it, you came when I did it."

"I don't care, that shit hurt, and if I wasn't a wolf, it would leave a mark. No marking my body."

"I apologize, but in the future, when we're hot and heavy like we were, can you stay with me and have conversations with your wolf at another time?"

"I'll try, but she literally has a mind of her own." I go to rise again, and he doesn't stop me. "I would love to help you with that, but I think it best I leave now. I have a promise to keep, and I came very close to breaking it tonight."

"That's alright, I have cold water in the shower."

"Good, I mean, well you know what I mean."

"Goodnight, Jay."

"Goodnight, Richard. Don't rise, I'll show myself out." I grab my shirt, pulling it on as I head out and rush to my room as quickly as I can. I don't bother with another shower. I just pull off my bottoms and jump in bed. I hit the switch to turn off the light. Jewel, that was close.*You know, Jay, that promise is stupid at this point?"* I know, Jewel, but it wouldn't be fair to Jarrod and Tony. It's the principal of it now. I can hold out until they join me at Haven. I'll tell them when they arrive that they are my mates, and then we can decide who gets the honors. I won't care which one of them it is by that point, I'll just want one of them to satisfy the ache I now feel. I wonder why it's so strong now. "*I think it's because Richard wants it and it's what he was thinking. That he wants to put himself inside of you, and since you can feel what he's feeling you're feeling it as well."*

Well, Jewel, we need to figure out how to control this feeling thing and stop him from thinking that for the rest of our stay.*Good luck with that, Jay."* Goodnight, Jewel. "*Night, Jay."*

Chapter 9

BETA JAY

During our daily ski outing, I'm convinced I won't get it. "I've been at it for almost two weeks, Olivia, and I still bust my ass every time."

"I think it's because you try too hard, Jay, you have to relax. You think it's supposed to be hard like everything else you do but it's actually very simple, like this."

I've been watching Olivia pick up the skiing from our first lesson with Samantha. She's a natural, me not so much. I broke my wrist the first day. It healed, I'm a wolf and I have faster healing, but so what, I still broke it. The next week I broke my ankle, again so what. Here I am still struggling with this, I'm not used to not mastering something quickly. But I do like how much Olivia is enjoying herself, more at my expense than at her skiing. "We're on the baby slopes, you know?"

"I do, Jay, but I'm doing well on the baby slopes."

We end our day and I'm actually happy, because after lunch, I get to go hang out with Star. She is still not my best friend yet, but she lets me hang out in her stall, grooming her, feeding her treats, and she listens to me complain about the skiing. I think we're becoming fast friends. I even figured out how to drive the snow mobile without much assistance, but the skis allude me. The training with Mark is going well, but I knew it would, so no more sore muscles. And I'm not surprised Olivia and Samantha quit on us. They said it was getting too hard and he was trying to kill them. They decided to work out together on their own. It's fine, I'm used to training with Mark. Jane finally came out of hibernation but all she does at work is smile most of the time and then heads home for lunch.

We never see her after we all leave for dinner. I'm happy for her, but miss hanging with her. I know she's working because I get emails about what's going on with the footage at the west fence line. There's been no complaints from the client accounts she's taken over. I told her what went down with Anne, and she was sad about it, but not much she could do. Might as well be grateful for the gift she was given and not waste it, which from what I could tell, she wasn't. I know Richard is happy Pete is back on the lift job. He has his Alpha duties to do, and the double workload was starting to get to him. I still haven't decided what I want for winning our bet, but we've had quite a few heated moments in both of our suites and the office when having dinner.

I'll admit, seeing his bulge live and in color makes me wonder if it was his wishful thinking or mine, because boy that thing is going to bring some painful pleasure. How did I see It, you ask? Well let me tell you. A couple of days ago, I had dinner plans with him in his office to go over pack history. The history conversations are boring at this point but must be done. As I approach the door, I notice it's not all the way closed, so I just push it open and walk in. What I see is his delicious bare butt. He was in the middle of removing both his jeans and underwear together, I imagine to put on his lounge pants. This has become our normal dinner attire.

But since he didn't close the door all the way, I just pushed it open and he was caught off guard and startled. When he turned around his mighty man was live and in color, and my response to seeing how big he was, even barely enlarged, was exciting. Him seeing my response to me seeing it made him get larger and grow wider.

It was like watching a balloon being inflated. It just kept getting wider and wider along with my eyes. It was like we were both caught in a trance. I moved into the office, closed the door and walked towards him. I stepped into his arms, putting mighty man into one hand while I grabbed his pup makers gently with my other. I started kissing him, he tastes delicious, and he felt so damn good in my hands. I massaged all I could manage to hold onto, rotating around his tip using both hands now, trying to feel every inch of him. The groans and moans that escape from him into my mouth were igniting more heat in my body, making me increase the speed of my exploration. Add the liquid moisture that seeped from his opening creating the smoothness and friction that ignited within seconds him coming in my hand. The excitement I felt knowing how I made him feel and respond just moments ago was immediately replaced with the embarrassment I felt seeping into me.

"Jay Jay."

"Don't Richard, we're both frustrated, and I caught you off guard. How about we re-schedule tonight's history review and dinner." I grab his t-shirt and clean my hands, turning to leave. He grabs me around my waist pulling me up against his front. I can feel mighty man pushing into my backside.

"Why are you running away from me, Jay?"

"I don't want to be an embarrassment for you, Richard."

"That's what you think? No Jay, the embarrassment is how fast I lost my jig in your hands like a schoolboy."

I relax. "Well you can owe that to my hand prowess." He laughs and it sounds like music in my ears.

"I promise you, Jay, I usually have more control over myself than that. It's just, you smell damn good all the time, and I wasn't expecting the skin on skin contact so fast. I didn't have a chance to fortify myself against the excitement you instantly illicit in me when you are around. That's what you do to me, Jay, to my body. Please don't make me eat dinner alone. I ordered you that seafood pasta you like, and the chef thinks he has mastered the double chocolate cake. He sure would be disappointed if you don't tell him how he did."

I take a moment to consider, "Well, you need another shirt because I used yours to clean my hands."

"It's fine, I can do without for one dinner, if you can control yourself, you know how irresistible I am."

"Oh, I think I've put my hands on you enough for tonight."

He laughs. "Touché, my lady."

I head to the powder room to wash my hands and get control of myself, and let him put on his pants. When I come back out, he said he's asked them to deliver the food.

"How did you get in without me hearing you enter the code?"

"You didn't close the door all the way. I just pushed in and the sight of you was, well you know."

"Yes, I'll be more careful next time."

"I did enjoy the view, and I enjoyed, well you know."

"Yes, I do."

While we waited for the meal to come, we went over what I knew about his pack's history. I knew more than he thought I would, and he was impressed as well as happy the Ruler will have a good knowledge of his pack. We went through the businesses his pack members have started or taken over, and I informed him how happy the Ruler will be about it. We discussed the status of the new lifts being installed and how Anne was doing. So far so good, so that's good news. He assigned one of the Gamma wolves to keep an eye on her. He's keeping an eye on her for her safety, and he reports back to Richard every week, so far nothing of importance to report. When the meal was finally delivered, we were ready to dig in, and the event from before was behind us but not forgotten. And that is how I finally met Mighty Man in full view.

I'm still thinking about what I want for my win, when Jane gets my attention.

"Jay, I'm reviewing the footage notes that were delivered to my inbox this morning and I think there is something we should review."

I get up and walk behind her to read over her shoulder. The email reveals a couple of the wolves that were on their security run yesterday and were horsing around in their wolf forms when they ran into the fence and a part of it opened. They originally thought they broke it, requiring them to phased into their human form to fix it. The quickly realized they could just push in back into place. They immediately reported it, but the report hasn't made it up to the security office yet.

"I'm reviewing the footage now, Jay, and now we know why the fence was ruined."

"Jane, we have to get someone out there to see how much of it is like that."

"Probably just enough for someone to fit through, Jay. They could get onto pack lands. We can't make any repairs until the report comes up to the security office or the culprits will know we're onto them. No one has used that fence line since you and Olivia were attacked, Jay. It was done just to be able to get on the pack lands to harm one of you and now that you're not there it's not needed. Whoever they are, they've left the pack weak to an attack if that fence is ever breached."

"Sure Jane, but that would mean someone not a part of the pack would have to know about the fence."

"Which means whoever did this is a part of the pack and hasn't involved anyone outside of it. They're also not strong enough to have climbed the cliff either, Jay."

"Would that have been an option to breach pack lands without being seen on camera?"

"We don't have footage in that area, remember."

"You're right, I forgot, Jane. We now know why the fence was tampered with, but we still don't know who did it, and we're still not completely sure about who the target was." At that exact moment, Olivia comes into the office looking like she saw a ghost.

"I can say for sure I was the target."

We look towards her, "Really? How do you know that?"

"Well, Jay, you know how I said I needed to borrow your extra charger for my phone until mine came?"

"Yeah, I told you it was on my nightstand, I think."

"Yes, but I didn't see it on your nightstand, I went looking and I opened the drawer."

"It wasn't in there, Olivia, I don't recall ever putting anything in there."

"You're right, Jay, it wasn't in there. What was in there was a book, and I picked it up thinking maybe the charger might be behind it or under it. When I didn't see it, I put the book back and then thought maybe it fell on the floor. I got down to look under the bed and that's when I saw a picture. It must have fallen out of the book that was in the drawer. I went to put it back and looked at it and thought the guy in the picture looked familiar, but I couldn't figure it out at that moment. I put the picture back in the drawer, and continued my search for the charger, which I was right it was under the bed. I grabbed it and started on my way back down here and on the way, I started thinking, how can a picture of some random man in a book in a drawer in a pack I've never been to have seemed kind of familiar?"

"Then it hit me. I saw that man in Miami, about a month before you came to our pack, Jay. Curtis was on a trip to Miami for some kind of computer training. He never takes me on his trips, always making excuses about having to work, but this trip to Miami was special because it's a neutral zone. I don't need to have permission from my pack to travel there. I bought a ticket and got one of the guys I know who works for the security firm to tell me what hotel he was staying in. I was going to surprise my man and have a great weekend in Miami. When I got to the hotel, they wouldn't tell me his room, but they did tell me he was having lunch in the hotel restaurant. I went there, and he was standing there talking to a man I had never seen before. They were shaking hands like whatever meeting they had was ending."

"I called Curtis's name and they both turned to me and had this look like I caught them committing a crime. I didn't pay much attention to it. I was happy to see Curtis and be in Miami. I ran to him, jumping into his arms. He caught me and kissed me and in the process the gentleman left. When I got control of myself, he was gone and Curtis said he was just one of the participants from another pack there for the training and he wasn't important. I initially thought he was mad at me but then I brushed it off because we went up to his room and spent the rest of the day and night catching up. Jay, Jane, that guy I saw, he's the guy in the photo I just saw. I mean he looks younger in the photo, but it was definitely him. That's why I think I was the target all this time, and that means Curtis has been trying to have me killed because I saw his partner in crime when I surprised him in Miami. I'm sorry, Jay, you could have died because of me, three times."

"It's not your fault, Olivia, you've helped us at least figure this part out."

"Jay, do you have any idea about this book, you said you haven't put anything in the drawer?"

"I don't, Jane," then I remember. "Mark, Mark said he accidentally took a book from the island that belongs to Edmond. He wants me to give it to him when I get to Haven so Edmond won't be mad at him for taking his things. Edmond is funny about his books. But Olivia has met Edmond if it was him, she would have said so."

"No, it wasn't Edmond in the photo. But now that I think about it, they could be related, a relative. I mean, he also could have been related to Alpha Tony as well."

"I forgot all about that book being there."

"I guess we're going to have to look through this book. Jay, why are you so quiet?"

"I'm having a hard time thinking Edmond could have anything to do with all of this."

"It might not be him, but maybe someone he knows. Olivia did say the person was older, and Edmond doesn't know Beta Shaw, from what we know. Whatever the truth is we have to find out for everyone's sake, Jay."

I start feeling sick to my stomach and a bad feeling is building in my gut. Could someone I love like a brother really be a part of trying to kill an innocent person? We're wolves and we all have it in us.

"Do you want me to go get the book, Jay?"

"No, I think we should head up to my suite and review this book right now. It could have the information in it we need to figure out what's really going on and hopefully why."

"I would love to go over this with you, Jay, but my mother will be arriving this evening."

"I forgot about that, Olivia. You've helped us already, and we can catch you up on what we find, and if we have any more questions, we'll ask you tomorrow. What about you, Jane, you've been incognito every evening, not that I don't understand."

"No, I'll be there, I just want to go to Pete's office and let him know I won't be there for dinner."

"Are you sure? I can review the book by myself and let you know what I find."

"No, I feel like you might need my support for this."

I'm secretly glad Jane's going to be there. We finish the rest of the work we had planned for the day and Olivia leaves to go meet the helicopter that will have her mother on it. Jane left to go to Beta Pete's office, and I wish I had something to occupy my mind, and then my phone rings. "Samuel, this is perfect timing, where have you been all this time?"

"Hello, Jay, I decided to escort Alpha Small back to her pack, my unspoken way of letting them know I will be there to protect her and her twins. I will be here until you leave to go to Haven."

"I guess that means she accepted your terms for your relationship?"

"You can say that, but I'll catch you up when I see you next."

"If that isn't why you called, then why?"

"Before I left, I wanted to tell you I was close to figuring out there was a connection with the three regional packs. I wasn't sure exactly if what I had been told was true. I wanted confirmation before I told anyone, well, I have confirmation."

"What is it Samuel?"

"I sent you pictures to your secure email; you need to be very careful with this information. It affects someone we both care about."

"I think I know who you're referring to." I don't want to think that it's possible we were wrong about this person all these years.

"Well, the connection might explain why, if it is who we think it is, but it doesn't have to be. There are others involved, keep this information close to you."

"How close Samuel?"

"You have a group you trust Jay; I mean, that are close."

"What about Richard?"

"No, he has a musketeer of his own and that's a deep relationship that might tug on his heart. That means not him. One more thing, Jay, Beta Shaw is no longer in the custody of our pack."

"WHAT?"

"Jay, I'm a wolf with wolf hearing."

"I know, I'm sorry, I say that to Olivia all the time, it's just so unbelievable. How did that happen?"

"His brother thought he could get him to talk to him. He used that relationship against him and walked right out as if he was him. No one realized it wasn't the pack's Beta Shaw until he was already off pack lands. There has been no sight of him."

"When did this happen?"

"Today which is why I'm calling you, Jay. I know he knows where you both are."

"Yes, but we should be safe here, not sure how he can get on this mountain unnoticed."

"Just let Alpha Richard know and be careful."

"I will, Samuel. He hasn't tried to move the money in his account because I would have been notified, and the funds would have been moved into other accounts, anyway."

"That could mean whoever he's working with could have provided him funds, protection, and whatever else he might need."

"Thank you for letting me know, and Samuel, I look forward to hearing how that conversation with Alpha Small went."

"Sure thing, Jay, later when things settle down."

"Alright, talk to you later, Samuel."

Chapter 10

BETA JAY

T<u>*he Plot Thickens*</u>

I hang up with Samuel and head up to Richard's suite, I know he went to change for the gym to work out, so hopefully I catch him before he leaves. I see him in the hall, "Richard, I need to tell you something." He stops, pushing the door back open. "I just got off the phone with Samuel and he informed me Beta Curtis Shaw is no longer in custody in California. Long story short, he tricked his brother and escaped, or his brother helped him, he wasn't put to death. Either way he's out and we have no idea where he is."

"It'll be hard for him to make it up this mountain without being seen. However, I'll let the lodges below know to keep an eye out for him. Are we still on for dinner?"

"Actually no, I have to meet with Jane tonight to go over some security issues we're having, sorry. I actually have to hurry, she's meeting me in my suite after she talks to Beta Pete."

"I'm going to miss you."

"Me too." I lean in, kissing him softly. "Have a good workout."

"I'll definitely need to now that I won't have you to help me burn off some frustrated energy."

I smile. "Tomorrow I got you, mighty Alpha man," and he laughs. We both know when I say that I'm referencing the mighty man in his pants. That's my name for him, and the little inside secret I get to say out loud. I kiss him again quickly and head out. As I pass by the stairs, I see Jane coming. "You ready?"

"Yes I am."

We get to my door, and I enter my code. As I step in, the lights come on automatically and I feel dread seeping into my gut.

"Stop it, Jay, you don't know anything, you haven't even looked in the book."

"We're about to find out, are we not?" I go to the end table and open it to see the book. It looks like a pack history journal, like the many ones I've read before. I grab the book and open it, and the picture Olivia mentioned is there. It's only half of a picture as it's torn, but you can tell there was a female in the picture based on the painted nails that can be see. She was torn away and just his half was kept. I can understand Edmond tearing her away if it's his father's mate, knowing how she felt about him. But since I didn't meet her, I have no way of knowing if that's her. I hand the picture to Jane. "Do you know if this is Alpha Edward's mate?"

"I'm not sure, all I see is a female's arm. I know Edmond didn't have a very good relationship with his father's mate. If that is her, it would explain the torn photo, but if it's not her, I don't know why it would be torn. But this is definitely Alpha Edward."

I start looking through the book and to my disappointment and relief I don't find anything incriminating about Edmond. All that's in the book is about what happened surrounding his birth, which he told me about. I spend the next hour or so reading through the book and relaying to Jane what Edmond relayed to me about his mother being an Omega. After we review the book, we know no more than we did before and were only a little further in our investigation. What we did know was Alpha Edward and Beta Shaw are involved. I take this time to inform Jane about Beta Shaw no longer being in Alpha Jacob's custody. I tell her what I know about the situation, as well as the email I was waiting on from Samuel. I'm hoping it would shed some light on things. I grab my laptop while Jane is still reviewing the book.

We're looking for anything that will help us find a motive, anything that would help us figure out who is behind these attacks. I log on to find the email, and when I open it, I'm sure we've found something because looking back at me is a picture of twin baby girls. "Jane?" She comes over and looks at my screen and we read the document attached. According to it, there were twin Omegas born on an island to an unknown female wolf, and then gifted to two regional Alphas as incentives to give the best of their pack's as representatives to train the next ruler. I couldn't believe what I was reading, *all I keep thinking is that my Nanna sent those babies to the Alphas of those two packs to raise*. Having Omegas was a good thing for a pack because they could birth pups to any male, regardless of mating or being in a heat.

And one of those Omegas was Edmond's mother who died giving birth to him. What happened to the other, we don't know. And there is nothing in the book or Samuel's notes, but at least now we know what it could be about and why. I could be the target of the culprit's hate; my Nanna Grace put in motion the decisions made by others by separating the babies. That decision unknowingly resulted in Edmond's mother dying while in the care of one regional pack's Alpha and who only knows what happened to the other. I now understand why they needed to keep themselves secret. I still don't understand what Alpha Edward has to do with this, considering he was the Alpha that might have impregnated Edmond's mother. It's not like she was raped, it was common knowledge by all parties that she was a willing participant, unless that wasn't true.

But I've met Tony's father and he didn't' seem like the type who would violate a female, but who knows when you're young and full of alcohol. He might not have thought he was forcing himself on her. I feel like we have more questions than answers at this point. I finally say to Jane, "We have to find out what happened to the other Omega and Alpha Andrew is the one who might know."

"Jay, I'll look through our medical records and see what I can find out. She would have needed to be seen by medical staff throughout her life, there should be a record."

Jane grabs her laptop while I hack into the medical records of Jarrod's pack to see if there was more than what Samuel provided. He said there was a connection to all three packs, but I only saw two. What's the other connection? I review the email again; at first I only saw the picture of the twin pup girls that are Omegas, but then I see it, another picture. "Jane, there were three born but the third was a male pup. And not an Omega, not valued as highly, and gifted to the Minnesota pack. Maybe we can find out who he was and get more information." Again, I think to myself, they hated my Nanna Grace for separating them from each other. I hack into Jarrod's medical records and find the information on Edmond's mother. She gave birth to a very large male pup with difficulty that was hard on her.

He was delivered but she didn't survive long afterward. They didn't list a name on his born papers, just listed his parents as Edward/Andrew Mathews. Not even the Omega's name were on the born papers and I wonder why that was. On her health checkups, they have her listed as Omega Linda Jacobs. Up until that time, she was relatively healthy growing up, and every checkup recorded once she was pregnant. Nothing stating what caused the difficulty during her pregnancy. Nothing in her notes will tell me. I would have to talk to someone that was in the room if I wanted to know. "Jane, you find out anything from your end?"

"No, nothing."

"That sucks."

"No, Jay, I found out nothing, it's as if she wasn't at our pack, no check-ups when she arrived, none while growing up nothing. And I sure don't remember there being an Omega as part of our pack. I know they're usually kept secret and protected and they're very well taken care of, so why the secret? And if she wasn't in our pack, where was she and where is she now?"

"That's the question of the day isn't it, Jane? You know another thing that's funny, there's no born date for when the Omega was born. She was closer to the age of the Alphas, obviously, but why no born date on the paperwork for her in the California paperwork? They didn't add her name to the born papers when she birthed Edmond either, just added Edward and Andrew Mathews, like she didn't exist." This shit is weird, and I'm pissed, and I want answers. I think I'm more pissed at my Nanna Grace for her hand in this. "Jane, I know who I can ask, Ma Glenda. I think if anyone would know, she might. I'll contact her tomorrow and hopefully she can shed some light on things. At least we know more now than we did yesterday, also we have to make sure we keep this to ourselves. We don't know who the male pup is, and if he's here or if his relatives are, not even Alpha Richard can be told."

"I agree, Jay, and this has worn me out,"

Jane rises to leave. "In a hurry to get back to your Beta mate, huh?" She stops, turns to me with the biggest smile on her face.

"He's good, Jay, and very good to me. I went a long time without touch, I think I'm addicted to him. Every moment I'm away I feel like I can't take a complete breath. My heart flutters and my lady parts start to twitch just thinking about him. I apologize, but I have to run, literally I have to run."

She kisses me on the head, and I notice on the way out she's pulling her staple bun loose. I smile; I'm jealous for myself and happy for her at the same time. I thought we would work later than we did, [I guess I can see if I can meet Richard for dinner.] I send him a text asking if he wants to join me for dinner. He replies absolutely but he needs to get showered, he's just finishing up his workout. I reply that it's a date, I'll order food to be delivered in an hour and would see him when he gets here. I decide I could use this time to get showered and ready for my dinner date as well. I head into the bathroom, turn on the shower to warm. Not wanting to deal with wet hair I take the time to put it up before I get in. I take the time to freshen up all the hairy parts that have started to grow.

I bathe and rinse myself squeaky clean, get out, dry and moisturize. Since I'm not leaving my suite, I forego underwear and just put on a black nightshirt and cotton bottoms, very comfy indeed. I need some of my favorite sangria just to relieve my brain from the stress of the information I took in today. I fill my glass, take a seat in one of the chairs and have a swallow while I wait. But before I can get comfortable, I hear the knock letting me know Richard is here. His delicious smell always precedes him. I open the door and step back letting him enter, and as usual, I'm ecstatic by how good he can make t-shirts and cotton bottoms look. I'm happy to see mighty man, I guess a few steps down the hall don't mean anything to him and hopefully will be a bonus for me.

"I was happy to get your text."

"I was happy to make it. I ordered us salad and pizza for dinner since it was last minute, as well as double chocolate cake. I also asked them to send up whatever dessert was made today because I'm not sharing mine." He laughs.

"Thank you, Jay, for at least thinking about me."

"You're welcome, Richard. Do you want a drink?"

"I would love one if you have more than sangria."

"Yup, you left your vodka here last time." I walk to the sitting area where the bottle is on the coffee table. I grab a tumbler and pour him a hefty one. "You have to catch up." Even though I've only had a couple of sips of mine, but he doesn't know that. He takes the glass, takes a gulp and sits in a chair. I sit on the corner of the two-seater close to him. "So how was your day, Alpha?"

"Long boring Alpha stuff. How was your day?"

"Long boring hacker stuff."

"Oh yeah, Jay, Jarrod called me to let me know about Beta Shaw, even though you informed me. I can keep an eye on you and Olivia."

"Do you really think he would come here?"

"I can't imagine why he would, but if he's motivated to, I imagine anyone could."

"That's the question, how motivated is he?" I told him about getting more info on our investigation into his accomplices but could not divulge any more than that and he understood.

"Very well, Jay, just assure me that you're being safe,"

I reply "I am, Alpha," and then a knock at the door announces our food. I'm hungry, and pizza will hit the spot. He opens the door, and I move to clear the table, making room for the dishes. While we ate, I regaled him with tales of my progress with Star, meaning she let me groom her and tack her up. I'm hopefully going to ride her tomorrow. He said he would join me, but I said no thanks, she didn't really care for him so I will ride on my own, but I'll stay close to the barn until I get a feel for her under saddle. I'm looking forward to finally being back in the saddle, even though it's an endurance saddle, different from what I'm used to but still, it's been months, and I've missed it. We went through the pizza and salad quickly, which meant we were both hungry, and after about three glasses of sangria and two goblets of vodka, we're both relaxed and enjoying each other's company. *"Jay."* Not now, Jewel. *"I just want to remind you about your promise."* I appreciate that, Jewel, but Richard promised to ensure I keep my promise.

"Jay, you talking to Jewel again?"

"Yes."

"You two are funny."

"If you only knew, Richard."

"I have an idea, if she's anything like my Bryce, it's like I have a split personality sometimes. Only I'm aware of the other personality and sometimes I wish I wasn't."

"Me too."

"Has Jewel ever caused you pain?"

"No, she can't do that, can she?"

"I don't know, but Bryce can. He makes this banging sound in his chest that vibrates in my head, I think it's what humans would call a migraine. I want to rip him out and beat him to a pulp when he does it."

We laugh over this, but Jewel isn't happy about us laughing about that. "*You know what, Jay, I'm going to leave you to your devices. Don't call me when you need me to save you from yourself.*" Oh Jewel, don't be that way. Jewel, Jewel, ok, whatever. I look over at Richard, I can feel he's tired. I can't tell if it's physical or mental. "Why so tired, Richard?"

"Just a lot of things happening in my head, in my life. A lot to consider, possibilities for the future of our pack with the Ruler among us now."

"I wouldn't worry about that. I have it on good authority the Ruler only wants what's good for the packs."

"That's good to know."

His exhaustion is making me exhausted as well,"Richard, would you like to sleep with me?" This perks him up,"I mean sleep, in the sense of eyes shut, bodies quiet, clothing on, type of sleep. We're both exhausted but we both need comfort, so how about we sleep.

I promise I won't take advantage of you, and this can be how you repay me."

"I can think of a better way to repay you, Jay."

"No, I would like you to spend the night holding me tight in your arms while I sleep, making me feel safe. I've never slept peacefully in a man's arms before and that's what I want, to sleep in your arms tonight."

"Yes, Jay, I can do that for you."

I rise and reach my hands out to him. He takes them and I lead him to my bed. I crawl up with him close behind me, pull the covers down, and get comfortable underneath with Richard spooning me from behind. He places his arm under my head, I feel his nose rubbing against my neck, it feels nice. I reach up and hit the light switch, flooding the room with the moonlight coming through the window. I settle in again, this is nice, I push a little more into him, and still when I feel Mighty Man, I close my eyes thinking I could get used to falling asleep every night like this if it brings this feeling. "Goodnight, Richard."

"Goodnight, Jay."

Chapter 11

BETA JAY

The warm sun is on my face and an equally warm Richard behind wakes me. I can feel him breathing deeply and hear him snoring quietly. I push my backside into him in the mood to tease him first thing in the morning. Richard might be sleeping but Mighty Man is waking up with a vengeance just from a little rub. Trying not to wake him fully, I carefully turn over and breathe him in. As he sleeps, he pulls me close with the arm I'm lying on. I place my arm around his waist, rubbing his side and back under his t-shirt while my other hand slides into his bottoms to say good morning to Mighty Man. Just holding and enjoying the feel of him pulsing and overfilling my palm while I slowly rub the twitching muscles in his back starts increasing my excitement.

I can tell Richard's still sleeping but enjoying whatever he's dreaming because his breathing becomes slightly elevated. My hand begins to warm as he grows larger and so much wider. I soon sense he's awake from his more controlled elevated breathing.

"Good morning, Jay, I thought you just wanted to sleep?"

"I did say that, Alpha, but now I'm awake and so is Mighty Man," and I massage him, hearing Richard moan softly.

"Well since you're awake Jay and I'm awake, and he's awake, how about we see if she's awake?"

He leans up and looks me in the eye. "Who is she, Alpha?"

"Oh, you'll see, Jay."

He moves down on my bed releasing my hand from his pants grabbing mine on his way pulling them from me tossing them to the floor."Oohh, Alpha, I'm not sure."

"Well let me talk to her and see."

He grabs my legs, pushing them up as he climbs towards me, looking at me with smiling eyes, kissing the inside of my leg on each side. This is torture for me but he doesn't linger this morning, and before I can even think about the path he's going to take, he's blowing on my clit, flicking it with his tongue then blowing again. He's on my thighs preventing me from moving and using his pointer and thumb from each hand to hold me open for this intense conversation. Between his tongue flicking me and the cool warm air from him blowing, the only respite I get is when he asks,

"Are you awake yet my little lady?"

I grab my pillow to scream my pleasure to avoid watching him. The sight of him is as exciting as feeling what he was doing to me.

"Look at me, Jay."

I toss the pillow to the side while breathing deeply as I feel myself getting close to my release. I look down at him.

"Look how enlarged she gets, Jay, just like Mighty Man."

Then his tongue starts flicking my clit. The pleasurable fire shooting through me borders on painful, but I need to come so bad. "Richard, please."

"Please what, Jay?"

"Oh my gosh, Richard, please."

"I know what you want, babe."

He starts flicking nonstop over and over until I think I'm going to split in two from the pressure of my release. When I don't think I can take anymore he grabs my engorged clit and sucks it hard between his lips. You would have thought he could suck my release up through my vajajay, into my clit and his mouth.

"Uuhhmm, that was delicious, Jay."

I look down and see him lapping me up.

"That's the sweetest breakfast I could have asked for, Jay, and I think it was a better payment for what you were owed."

He crawls up the bed kissing me on my belly, my breast through my shirt, my chin, my lips, softly. I turn my face. "Stop, Richard, I have morning breath."

He smiles down at me, "it's all good, Jay, I have vagina breath."

I looked up at him and burst out laughing. I push him off me,"I have to get a shower and get ready for breakfast. I'm meeting Olivia and her mother and I want you to meet her, it will make her day."

"Of course I will, but after, I have a full day with Beta Pete. We are picking the contractors for the new lifts."

"What about we meet in the dining hall, will that work for you, Alpha?"

"Sounds good to me, Jay."

He kisses me on my forehead and then turns to leave."Richard, thanks for sleeping with me."

"You're welcome and thanks for asking me, it was nice waking up with you in my arms."

As he leaves I get up smiling, it was a nice way to wake up and I could get used to it. I hit the toilet, and while brushing my teeth, I kept laughing about what he said about his breath. I turn on the shower and get a quick wash, not wanting to be late meeting Olivia and her mom. I throw on some blue jeans, a powder blue long sleeve sweater and a very stylish pair of dark powder blue tie up snow boots. We're hitting the baby slopes after breakfast while Ms. Parker is here. She's here for a week, meaning I won't be training with Mark, but Jane is still going to work and will let me know if I'm needed so I can spend time with them. I'm excited because Olivia's mother is like a sweet old grandma. We want to ask her some questions about the Omega and if she remembers her so we might find out some things. I also must contact Moon-Ma Glenda later on to ask her, as well.

I finish getting dressed, thinking I look very cute. I put my hair in a ponytail, letting my tight curls hang loose; it's growing like crazy, and I need a trim, but who has time for that. I grab my phone and head out, locking my door and rushing as to not be late. When I'm almost two levels down I see the Parkers, I rush to catch up to them, "I'm glad you made it here safely, I call her Momma Tilda, but her name is Matilda. She says it was nice of me to fly her out. I give her a big hug, and say, 'I'm glad you could come since Olivia wasn't able to go home.' It's all fine, she says, my baby is having an adventure, and with the Ruler's Regent no less. At least you got her away from that Beta Shaw. I knew he was no good for Olivia.

"I know how you feel, mom, let's go have breakfast and then we'll hit the slopes."

"Don't let her fool you Momma Tilda, she just wants to show off because she's really good at it and I suck."

"That's not true, Jay."

"Yes it is, Olivia."

"She's right, mom, but I want to teach you, and it's fun. Then we can have a girls' night and watch movies. I have the whole week planned of things we can do and you're going to love it, mom."

She agrees that Olivia can teach her because it sounds like fun, but warns if she gets hurt, she's going to spank her bottom. We're all laughing as we hurry into the dining hall and fill our plates with eggs, bacon, grits, sausages, and toast, and I grab a glass of orange juice. Momma Tilda also gets pancakes and I get double chocolate ones that the chef is now making because he knows how much I love them. I don't put syrup on them because they taste delicious just like that. We find a table and start eating while catching up on what's happening back in California. How things are going with the family business and her baking while Olivia tells her all about what she's learning about my business. After we're about an hour into our meal, Richard finally joins us and this lights up Momma Tilda. She gets to meet and spend time with the Regional Alpha from another pack and it's a big deal.

She whips out her phone and starts taking pics. I think Richard's face is going to fall off. Richard is a good sport but even so, Olivia keeps apologizing and thanking him for putting up with her mom. Momma Tilda wouldn't relent until we told her it was time to go learn to ski. We get up, clearing away our dishes before heading to the foyer to put on our coats, hats, and gloves, then head to the baby slopes. To my consternation and frustration, within an hour Momma Tilda is skiing like her daughter, saying she must be a natural like Olivia. I can't explain it, I'm still struggling. Olivia whispers that she thinks it's because I'm a virgin, since I've never had the real thing in there I can't get my balance. This makes her laugh louder, and I'm surprised it didn't cause an avalanche. "Whatever, Olivia, I don't think I want to ski with you anymore."

"Ooh come on, Jay, you have to keep trying until you get it, or get some."

They start laughing again, it's never ending. "How about I go sit over there and watch you and your mom enjoy yourselves."

"Alright, Jay, but once my mom goes home, we'll get back to teaching you because I'm determined you'll be a skier before you leave this mountain just like me, if my life depends on it."

"Whatever you say, Olivia." I head over to the rest area benches, taking a seat. I watch them laughing and enjoying being together. Watching them begins to make me miss my Nanna Grace and even Moon-ma Glenda. I take this opportunity to reach out to Glenda to see if she knows anything about the Omega babies. When she answers she sounds happy. She says she's glad to hear from me, and wants to know how my trip is going. "It's going, how are you doing Glenda? I hope you're settling well into your retirement quarters." She tells me she is, but that she's not ready to retire. "When I get there, I'm sure you'll be put back to work Glenda." She tells me she hopes I'm going to arrive with my mate and provide her with a pup or two to take care of. "Maybe, Glenda, maybe."

"I want to ask you about something I found out while on my travels. It's regarding three babies who were born on the island that Nanna Grace sent to the packs in exchange for the opportunity to select the people who would be sent to the island to train the Ruler." There is a moment of silence. "Glenda, did you know about this?"

"I know a little, not much. I don't know the parents of the babies. I know there were three born, two girls, both Omegas born seconds after each other, and then a boy born about three hours later. He was the one who caused the mother trouble. He was breach and difficult to turn, and with his mother being small, she struggled to birth him. I know the original plan was to raise them together on the island until they were of age. However, the Alphas of the packs wanted them to be raised with their packs, ensuring they would be like family. Grace told me she thought that would be a good idea for them to feel like they were a part of the packs they would be with and had them delivered to the packs."

"Do you know which packs received which babies, Glenda?"

"Only Grace knew and the Alphas of each pack, of course."

"Glenda, do you know why the babies were not given names?"

"I was told that, as well, was up to the pack Alphas. You have to remember they were only about two weeks old and going to families who wanted them to bond with their caretakers. There was no paperwork completed on Grace's part, all was done at the packs."

"What about the male pup, what of him?"

"I know that whichever pack he went to wasn't happy. I know the selection on which pack received an Omega was random and the pack Alphas only knew when the baby arrived."

"Was my Nanna Grace worried the pack Alpha who received the male pup that wasn't an Omega would be upset?"

"No Jay, because each of them knew that might happen, but they would then have the option to send their own representative to the island instead of Grace making the choice."

"Oh, that makes sense, Glenda, thank you for telling me what you know."

"Why are you asking about this, Jay?"

"I'm trying to find the babies; some things have happened, and I think it has to do with those babies being separated. Do you know anything about the family of the parents of the babies, Glenda?"

"No, I don't, Jay, Grace said I was safer not knowing."

"I found out about the Omega who went to California. She died in childbirth like her mother, Glenda, but the other two, there's nothing. I know one Omega went to New York, but there's no record of her ever being there, and the male pup is supposed to be here in Minnesota but I don't know who he is. Did Nanna Grace say if there were any identifying marks on them?"

"No nothing that she told me, but it's strange that the daughter died like her mother did, in childbirth. Was it because of a breached birth as well, Jay?"

"I don't know, there were no records that noted what caused her death. It just says. 'Complications from a difficult birth.'

Thank you, Glenda, this has been helpful."

"I'm sorry I don't know more, Jay, but if I think of something I'll call you."

"Thank you, Glenda. So, tell me how everything looks!" I listen intently as Glenda tells me how beautiful Haven is, and how much Pauley, is spoiling them with all the lush hay. And how fat they are both getting. Making me think how much work I will have to put in the get them fit when I get there. "It's will be fine, Glenda, and I'm bringing a mare with me, one I was gifted by the Alpha here in Minnesota. I'm hoping to get to ride her today, I'll keep you posted on my progress." She tells me she knows how great I am with horses, and she's sure I will win her over. "Thank you, Glenda. I have to go I'll call you again soon." I hang up as I see Olivia and her mom heading my way. "Are you done killing it on the slopes ladies?"

"Yes we are, Jay"

"Good, I'm going to get changed and ride Star. I'll meet you both for dinner and then we can have our girls' night. I'll meet you in the dining hall at, let's say six. Momma Tilda, did you enjoy it as much as you look like you did?" She quickly says, yes, but that she enjoyed the stories of how awful I was at it more. I smile before responding, "I'm sure you did." We enter the foyer, and they head towards the dining hall for drinks while I head upstairs to get changed.

After returning from the barn, I'm still excited about the progress I made during my ride on Star. I'm happy as can be, but that ends when I enter and see Jane waiting for me. I know my day's turning bad just by the fact she's here and not with Beta Pete. "Is this not something that can wait, Jane?"

"Sorry, Jay, I waited until you finished whatever it is you do with your horse."

"I'm supposed to have dinner with Olivia and her mother."

"I can talk while you get dressed, but I'm not sure you're going to want to after what I tell you."

We head up to my suite, I put in my code and we enter. I start pulling off my boots, setting them down by the side of the door. I walk over to a chair, taking a seat in what I've made as my little living area. "Hit me with it, Jane, what's the news?"

"I found out the reason there were no records on the Omega baby who was delivered to my pack. It's because it was deleted."

"How is that possible, Jane?"

"There was a worm created ten years ago to slowly delete the information from our system."

"But that means that whatever is going on started that long ago."

"No, Jay, it means whoever the Omega is didn't want anyone to know about her then. No way to know if she's connected to what's happening now. I found a trace of the deleted worm. Since it completed its job, the code was deleted. Now I have no way of connecting it to anyone."

"Send what you have to me, and I'll take a look at it and see what I can find."

"Alright, Jay. I also spoke to a friend of mine who relocated to DC, and he confirmed he doesn't recall knowing of an Omega being a part of our pack either. I think someone from the top agreed to let her disappear for whatever reasons and we should speak to Alpha Mathews about it."

"I agree, Jane, how about we get Tony on the phone now."

"No, I was actually talking about Alpha Andrew Mathews, he was the Alpha of the pack at that time. Let's call him now, Jay."

"Alright," I grab my phone and dial his number and he answers on the second ring, sounding happy to hear from me, but saying it's a surprise but a happy one for sure. He inquires about how I'm doing, and he knows I'm probably missing NY now that I'm in Minnesota with this special kind of cold. He heard why I had to leave and was sorry that happened to me and Olivia, but Tony told them she was better. "Yes, thank you Alpha Andrew, Olivia is well. I was calling because I want to ask you something, if you don't mind. Beta Jamison is here with me." He greets Jane, then asks what is this about and should he get Tony. "No that's not needed, we want to ask you about the Omega who was delivered to your pack in exchange for the last prophet's choice on who you sent to the island to train or educate the next Ruler." Silence was the answer, "Alpha Andrew, are you there?"

He finally speaks, saying he wasn't aware anyone knew of that. "I wasn't, but my mother lived on the island. She was aware of some things told to her by the prophet, but not much. However, we think some of the things happening now are connected to her, but we couldn't find any information on her. We found out all the information about her was deleted from your pack medical records. We thought something like that would have to be approved by the Alpha at the time so we're calling the Alpha of that time." He proceeds by telling us that this will be difficult for him to explain but he would give it a try.

"There was an Omega in our pack when I was growing up and into my late teens. My brother, Edward, and myself were young and rambunctious and were both attracted to her. For more than the obvious reasons we were forbidden from having a relationship with her. You know how Omegas are rare and valuable because they can produce

pups with any male without being mated or even in heat. Add with that her beauty and being labeled forbidden fruit probably made her more appealing to our wolves. As twins we tended to share all things, especially back then. It was bad, requiring my Alpha father to command us to not get involved with her, and believe me that sure worked. During the time that we were at Alpha training we met a fellow Alpha from the regional pack in California who surprisingly invited us back to his pack for a party weekend."

"Now we had no idea our Omega was a twin. We found out that the twin was in California, when we saw her there that weekend. She saw how attracted we were to her, she was flattered. She invited us to her suite, and we had a very nice time. Since our Alpha hadn't forbidden us from getting involved with that Omega and we had imbedded quite a bit of some new Sangria they just bottled, we overindulged for two nights with our lovely Omega. When we got back home, we thought it must have been a dream, because what were the chances there were two and our Omega was at home? But two months later our father called us into his office to inform us we might have impregnated an Omega in California. We realized it wasn't a dream and told our father the entire story, and he realized the Omegas must have been identical twins. It was decided that once the baby was born, whichever of us was the father would mate with the Omega. It's an honor to mate with an Omega, neither of us were upset.

More so, the opposite since we both wanted to mate with her, don't mention that to my mate ever. Before the baby was born, I found my mate, and since I was the older by 52 seconds, it was decided that Edward would be mated with the Omega and claim the baby. Then the Omega died giving birth to Edmond. Something about the baby being breached and the birth was very difficult, from what my father was told. However, our Omega found out about the whole situation and didn't want to be in our pack with her twin sister, who she never met, who would be mated to Edward who she wanted to be mated to. My father agreed to send her to another pack, very lucratively, of course. He made it as if she was never in our pack. He sent half those funds to the Alpha of the California pack and we took custody of the baby."

"Do you know what pack she was sent to, Alpha?"

"No, she requested neither of us know. She wanted to be with either of us, but with me finding my mate and my brother Edmond agreeing to mate to the California Omega, there was no room for her. Then the California Omega died and the baby survived, but by that time our Omega was gone."

"Thank you, Alpha Andrew. Can I ask you why you call her Omega instead of by her name?"

"After she left, we were not allowed to even talk about her and when she was here. She was only known to our immediate family, but her name was Gloria Mathews. She was given our name when she came by my parents. You know, we have a female who moved to New York about five years ago and her name is Gloria Matt. One day I saw her and could have sworn she was our old Omega, but she's way too young. I believe she moved here from Maryland with her Beta father. Supposedly her mother died and they wanted a new start."

"Thank you again, Alpha, you've been very helpful."

"I'm glad to provide any assistance I can, Jay, and I hope you find what you need."

When I hang up the phone, I look at Jane, "I know Beta Gloria Matt, she was a bitch during training."

"Yes, I know her too, Jay, she works for the security firm. She's alright at it and has her BS in computer science. I was considering taking her under my wing when my friend, Beta Tim moved, to DC. I can do some more research into her background, besides what we do for transferees."

"We need to find out, Jane, if her mother died giving birth. Also, what's with these Omegas dying in childbirth?"

"I'll see what I can find out. Sorry, Jay, but you've missed dinner."

"It's alright, I need to hit the showers and get ready for girls' night."

"I'll let you get to it then; you girls have fun."

"Will I see you in the office tomorrow, Jane?"

"Actually, you will. Pete's going to meet with some contractors, I'll be there most of the day."

"Good, see you then. Night, Jane."

"Night, Jay."

After Jane leaves, I text Olivia, apologizing for missing dinner. I let her know I'm still on for girls' night and asking if she'd order me a couple of turkey sandwiches with the works and a piece of my double chocolate cake. She responds saying that she would, along with a bunch of other snacks. I plug in my phone to charge and head in the bathroom to get showered. Afterwards, I get dressed in a comfy all-in-one sleeper and put on my thick cotton socks. I grab my phone and head to Olivia's room; Momma Tilda lets me in, letting me know my food just got there. I give her a hug and hurry past her straight to the table. I see two sandwiches, so I grab one, taking a huge bite as I'm starving, and the big bag of Lay's is calling my name. I rip it open and grab a bunch.

"Thanks for ordering for me, Momma Tilda." She says, you're welcome, and asks how my ride was and how she's freaked out that I ride horses. "It's not bad, most of the time they're more scared of us. At least you can ski, I'm still flummoxed by why it's hard for me." I continue taking large bites of my sandwich to signal my want to not talk about my sex life with Olivia's mom. Right then she comes out of the bathroom.

"Hey, Jay, what are we watching?" She asks as she grabs my chips.

"Hey! Those are mine, Olivia."

"You have a bunch on your plate already, Jay."

"But I'll need more for my other sandwich."

"I don't know where you have the room for all the food you consume, you have to share, Jay."

"Only lay's taste good with sandwiches, Olivia."

"You're right."

She passes them to me and I grab a bottle of water, opening it, I ask her what we are watching. She tells me whatever I want, "I don't care, Olivia, because you know I'll probably fall asleep within twenty minutes." We all start laughing because they know it's true. I can't stay awake long enough to watch myself once you turn on a tv.

Chapter 12

BETA JAY

The next morning, I run into Richard in the hall outside my door.

"Are you running late this morning, Jay?"

"I am, Alpha, I had a girls sleepover in Olivia's room and didn't take clothes with me. I had to come back here to get dressed." As we approach his office, he puts in his code, letting me enter before he leaves to go meet Beta James. Before the door can close, Olivia comes in behind me. "I thought you were going to hang out with your mom for the next week."

"That's the, plan Jay, but she's sleeping and I thought I'd come and check my emails or see if there's anything I could do for now. Mom wants to go skiing, again then we're going sledding and bowling. Want to join?"

"Nope. I've set today as a no skiing with you and your mom day, but you have fun for me." Jane comes and Olivia asks her what she's doing here.

"I thought I worked here, Olivia. What are you doing here? I thought you were taking this week with your mom."

"She's still sleeping, I'm just checking in. What about you?"

"Pete's out meeting with contractors, which is why I'm here to work."

She moves to the couch and sits down, crossing her legs. I can see the difference in her now that she's mated. No tight bun, now it's in a ponytail that's draped over her shoulder. Today she has on black jeans, a long sleeve blue pullover shirt, and her usual black work boots, with no jacket. Her hair down makes her look softer, but trust me, she's still a badass Beta.

"Jay, please stop staring at me. It's just hair, I know you've seen hair before."

"I smile. "Ok, Jane." I log onto my computer and begin running my system checks and updates for my clients.

"Jay?"

"I'm not staring, Jane."

"I know, I found something."

"Can you send it to me?" I get the file from Jane and it's a run down on Gloria Matt. Her father's Beta Joshua Matt and her mother was Belinda G Matt. Nothing shows if her middle name is Gloria, but it's a guess, and there's no record of her before the same time Gloria Mathews left the New York pack. It's a good bet she's the Omega that's the twin. She also died in childbirth. Nothing in the records say it was due to a breached birth but that's not something we wolves would care to make a record of. I remember the Omega from California was called Linda, close in names as well, that's doubly strange. "Jane, we need more info on Gloria, we need to see if we can connect her to all the accounts we're watching to see if she was the one helping Curtis, and if so, why."

I continue watching the footage on the west fence and then start reading the attached report. Nothing of note happens but it gets me thinking. "Jane, you know, the opening on the fence, it was small enough for a female to fit through. Beta Matt is trained well enough to have been our bow and arrow shooter, and she would have had access to the club to put wolfsbane in the water. She knew who we all were to have someone tell the waitress to give the bottled water to us, and since she's local, she wouldn't have been out of place. If she's proficient in computers, she could have hacked into the club cameras to find out where they were to tell her accomplice to avoid them. It all fits, now we just have to figure out if she's connected to the accounts."

She responds that there's no way to find out until the accounts are used, and there's nothing so far. Also, the pictures of me were from Gamma Stanley, who's still in holding and refusing to speak. Whoever our culprit is, she contacts him, and I see no contact on his or any of his family members' systems. I send Richard's pack login info to Jane, asking her to see if she can find anything on there that might help us. I continue working on my clients' things while Jane works on looking into this pack. After about two hours, I'm glad to see everything is running as it should for my clients. I add some additional checks on clients who have more secret software products and send them updated emails. I receive responses with approvals for the improvements within the hour and I'm happy about it.

"Jay, Beta Gloria Matt was in Miami the same time Beta Curtis Shaw was, and in the exact same hotel."

"That's more confirmation, Jane, but it's all circumstantial. Miami is a neutral zone, and Olivia was there, as well. She saw Gloria in New York and didn't recognize her, the other person in Miami wasn't her. She might have been there, but someone else that's more important than Beta Gloria Matt was there, as well. Until Beta Curtis tries to transfer funds, we just have to wait, Jane."

"Not exactly, Jay. Any transfer of funds attached to any of those accounts will trigger a trace but, I'll keep looking."

"Ladies, my mom is ready to go skiing. Jay, are you sure you don't want to join?"

"Absolutely not, Olivia, it's bad enough I have to listen to you laugh and tease, now add your mom to it? No thank you."

"Once Mom goes home, you're back on the slopes with me, deal?"

She heads out and Jane says,

"I can't imagine why you're struggling with it."

"It's not as easy as some would have you think."

"I can teach you, Jay if you like."

"Nope, Olivia laughing is enough for me. Besides, I have enough on my plate."

The rest of the week pretty much went the same with Olivia and Momma Tilda enjoying their vacation and Jane and I stressing over who we were trying to find, unsuccessfully. Olivia wants me to come skiing with them every day, and every day I say that's not happening. I'm determined to master at least the baby slopes before we leave, even if my time is running out with less than a month left here. I'll wait until Momma Tilda leaves, one Parker laughing at me is enough. I can also say my rides on Star have been the bright side of my trip, besides the time I spend with Richard. I've ventured out of the front pasture on my rides, up into some of the woods, but I worry about the slippery slopes, so I stay closer to the flatter areas. I can't wait to get her to Haven to really see what she can do and how she gets on with my stallions.

Today I'm working in the office on my laptop when I see a red start flashing in the top corner of my screen. "Jane, I think we have movement on the accounts!" I click on the blinking link and sure enough, one Beta Shaw is trying to transfer the funds to his offshore account. Everything works smoothly, the funds show up in his account as they should, only they're dummy funds. If he tries to use them or in twenty-four hours, whichever comes first, those funds will disappear, and I'll get another notification. I check the accounts I set up in the three Alpha accounts and the funds deposit show as they should. I immediately transfer those funds to the appropriate accounts based on the algorithm I created to determine which funds came into the other account and from where.

"Jay, what the hell was that?"

"Those, Richard, are the funds that were embezzled from your personal account from the hacker I told you about."

"It was that much?"

"Yes, and you obviously have too much money if you didn't realize you had that much missing from your account."

"Thank you for getting it back."

"You're welcome, Richard," I answer my phone when it immediately starts ringing, telling Tony he's welcome and yes, he needs to pay more attention to his personal accounts... "I know, I miss you, too... Alright I have to go, Jarrod is calling... Yes, probably about the same thing. I will call you later." I accept the call coming in from Jarrod. "Hello... yes Jarrod... I know right, I am that... Yes, you're welcome and yes you should... Yes you can, I usually get a percentage of what I get back for my clients... Yes, that would be nice of you, even though that isn't why I did it... No, I will not give you my banking info. You don't even keep up with your own info so I'm not giving you mine. I'll take my fee from your account, Jarrod... I have your info because I sent you your funds back... I'm hanging up with you. Yep, bye." I smile at how crazy my alpha man can be.

"Jane, Jarrod's paying us ten percent for recovering his stolen funds."

"That was nice of him, Jay."

"I'll pay that fee as well, Jay."

"Well thank you, Richard, and I'm sure Tony would do the same." I set up the invoice for each of the Alphas, then send them the authorization to transfer funds.

"Wow, Jay, that was fast."

"I'm good at what I do, Richard." I get a text from Tony wanting to know why he's paying me for giving him back his own money. I tell him because Jarrod and Richard paid me, and I figure he would want to do the same. His response was maybe, but sure.

"I wish I could see Beta Shaw's face, Jay, when he realizes all of his funds are gone. He's going to be pissed."

"It wasn't his money in the first place, Jane. I can see he's in Miami at an international bank and trust. Will you send the security firm in California his location, that way they can get on his trail? Unfortunately there's no way to find out what hotel he is in. Can you also check to see if Beta Matt is in Miami?"

"Not from what I can see, Jay. If she is, she didn't purchase tickets in her name. Beta Shaw must have credentials in another name, as well."

"That's not hard to do, Jane, so many forgers are out there. We need to try to hack into the FAA. Maybe we can run facial recognitions now that we know he's in Miami."

"That'll take a long time, Jay."

"But it'll be worth it. It's how Mark was able to make sure we were not on camera when we left the island. I'm sure it can find Curtis, we just need his picture."

"We have one from when we issued passes for them during the summit."

"Great, Jane."

"I'll set it up and let you know if we find anything. I also sent his last known location to his pack's security offices, and also sent it to my security office in New York City, as well. Since he's in Miami, any of our teams can pick him up, and since he technically committed fraud against all three regional packs. Alpha Richard, do you want me to send his information to your pack security?"

"Might as well, Jane, the more people looking for him the better."

I spend the rest of the week hanging out with Olivia and her mom. I enjoyed hanging out with her and wish I would have had my mother with me growing up. My Nanna and Moon-ma were the next best thing but not quite the same. Momma Tilda receives an open invitation from Richard to return during the regular season to try the other slopes since she mastered the baby slopes, unlike me who is still struggling. We're enjoying our last breakfast with Momma Tilda as she's headed back home, and it's bittersweet. I can tell Olivia has enjoyed having her mom here. We spend breakfast laughing over the adventures we've had during her visit and taking pictures on our phones to commemorate this vacation. As we help her load her bags on the helicopter, she gives me a huge hug, thanking me for being a friend to her daughter and bringing her along on this adventure, and that she's hoping she finally finds her mate when we go to Haven. I assure there's no need to thank me, Olivia's my best friend, like a sister to me. I would do anything for her and I'm hoping that for her, as well.

She moves on to hug Jane, who I can tell is very uncomfortable, but not as much as she used to be. After she hugs Olivia, she loads up and we move back, letting the helicopter get on it's way. "You'll see her again soon, Olivia."

"I know, Jay, but it wasn't until I left to go to New York that I was ever away from her for an extended time. It just seems like I've been away a lot lately."

"You can go home with her if you want, Olivia."

"No, I can't wait to go to Haven. Besides, if there are people out there trying to kill me, I don't want to bring that danger to my family. What do we do now, ladies?"

"I have work to do, I will see you both in the office."

We laugh as Jane turns and leave.

"She's a workaholic, Jay."

"That she is, but we actually have work to do, as well, since we've been mostly slacking off most of this week." We turn to follow behind Jane, and as we enter the office, Jane informs us that none of the security firms were able to catch up with Beta Shaw. "It's like he had a heads up that we were coming. We know whoever is helping him is at least a part of one of the packs, it's not surprising."

"It was a chance we had to try, Jay. I'm still searching through Beta Matt's online presence trying to find anything that'll give me a strain I can follow, but nothing. I also can't believe she's in my security company and I didn't know."

"Honestly, Jane, she isn't doing anything you would be looking for, and she didn't directly embezzle from the company. Let's just try to connect her to any other leads we have and not care about what we might have missed." There's some frustration when it comes to figuring out who and where the other Omega is. Did she really die in childbirth? Also, we still haven't found any real verifiable connections with Beta Shaw, even though the theory works. At this point it's just that, a working theory. By the end of the day, we're all tired from not having succeeded in finding anything.

"I'm glad it's Friday, Jay and I can relax; I'm going to sleep in tomorrow and get my room in order after my mom's visit."

"Will I see you for dinner, Olivia?"

"Nope, having it in my room. Night, Jay"

"Whatever, night, girl."

"But I'll see you bright and early Monday for breakfast and then skiing on the baby slopes."

"You're a tyrant, Olivia."

"Yes, but you promised to learn before we leave, and it's the only training we actually do."

"Ok already, Olivia. Next week we get you back to the baby slopes. Jane, you want to join us?"

"Absolutely not, I have other plans. Now, ladies, have a good weekend. I'm going to head out and find my Beta."

We smile as she leaves.

"I can't wait to find my mate if it makes you smile like that. See ya later, Jay."

I'm left to myself, thinking how I hope the weekend is a long one and dreading Monday's ski lesson. Richard walks in asking if my workday has ended. "Yes, Alpha, I've been left to my own devices for the weekend. Why? Do you want to do something?"

"How about I show you my mountain? I know you've ventured

some on Star, but it's beautiful when seen as your wolf."

"Sounds like fun Richard."

"Good, Jay, let's have a quiet dinner and then we'll go for a run early in the morning."

I wake early to head out for my run with Richard. Jewel's excited to run with Bryce, but we're both nervous about how he'll receive us considering, he thinks he knows us as his mate but oh well. I meet him in the garage, and I see he's standing there with just a pair of shorts on.

"You ready, pretty lady?"

"Yes, Alpha. "I kick my Nikes off. "You first." He phases into his large beautiful black wolf, but I can see his light brown eyes shining through his wolf looking at me, anticipating my phase. Here we go, Jewel, are you ready? *"Yes, Jay."* Jewel likes to jump into her phase, and we land several feet away from Bryce in our beautiful gray wolf with charcoal tips. He steps closer to me, rubbing up against me sniffing me. I use my muzzle to push into him, hinting I'm ready to get this run on. He turns and heads out of the garage and I follow. We travel in the same direction towards the pack's houses, and I can see why Jane loves her mate's house, the view is amazing. I can only imagine how it looks from inside where it's warm and cozy. We begin climbing and the Alpha in me wants to lead but I keep reminding Jewel we're Beta.

"Jay, Bryce senses I'm his mate, that came before, he knows." I don't

agree with her, but what can I do. I let her have her fun. I will admit it was a nice give and take of each of us leading and then following and I had a great time. I wasn't accustomed to running up snowy mountains. I fell back, catching my breath and letting Richard lead numerous times during our run. By mid-day, I was ready to head back, and he was happy to oblige. I will say the weekend was nice, seeing his mountain as Jewel was beautiful. I understand why Richard loves it here despite the splintering cold. The best part was cuddling up in his arms with warm food and a cozy fireplace to end the long days.

It was hard to get up knowing I'm about to let Olivia torture me on the baby slopes, but I'll keep my promise. I get up and dress, procrastinating for as long as I could. I try to get excited when I enter the dining hall and see the excitement on her face.

"You ready, Jay? I feel like you're going to get it today. This is the day you'll master the baby slopes."

"From your mouth to the Goddess' ears, Olivia." We laugh because neither one of us believe I'm going to come down those slopes without falling. Hopefully I'll continue to not break any more bones. We finish our breakfast and get all bundled up for the outside. Once we exit the lodge, we grab our skis and poles and begin heading towards the baby slopes.

"Thank you, Jay."

"For what, Olivia?"

"It was nice visiting with my mother, and she loved getting the chance to meet another one of the Regional Alphas. She'll get to brag about that for the rest of her life. Not only the Ruler's Regent but Alpha Peterson, as well. She is almost royalty."

"I was happy to do it, and sorry that your brother couldn't come."

"It's alright, I'll see him in two weeks. He couldn't leave the business right now. I'm surprised mom was willing to come, but the opportunity to meet a regional Alpha was more than she could pass up."

"Plus, she missed her daughter, you've been away for more than half the year at this point."

"I know, but we both know it wasn't me who made her come."

We laugh, knowing the truth. We notice Richard had some of the ice around the pack lodge raked so we can safely walk. We go down the slopes a couple of times with me falling and Olivia laughing. Even though I have yet to master the baby slopes still standing, it's a lot of fun. We keep at it for hours before I'm ready to call it quits. But Olivia is the one way more determined between the two of us and says, let's go one more time, you'll get this, I feel it in my bones. "No, Olivia, you just want another opportunity to laugh and take a photo of me on my ass."

"Not at all, Jay."

She smiles at me and up the baby slopes we go. Which brings us down closer to the front of the lodge. Where we can kick off the skis and run into the warmth. Once inside the pack lodge, we can end our day of fun and feed our bellies. I can say I've mostly enjoyed being here for the last couple of months, and according to Jewel, I have all my powers. They're just not at their full capacity.

When I finally turn twenty-five, they'll be stronger, and then when I mate, even stronger. I'm excited for the time I'll get to spend with all my mates. I'm nervous about how they will receive the possibility of having to share me. I don't know any Alpha that likes to share anything, let alone a mate. *"Jay, you don't know any Alph's period, so stop worrying about something you can't do anything about right now and try to get down the baby slopes without busting your ass,"* Whatever, Jewel, you're just as mean to me about these damn slopes as Olivia.

"Jay, stop procrastinating. I can feel it, you will do it this time."

That is what her mouth says but her eyes are laughing at me, saying something completely different. As we approach the top of the baby slopes, I hear a hissing sound, and Olivia falls and doesn't move. I drop my poles, ripping off my skis feeling dread seeping into me because I don't hear anything coming from her, and even though I don't want to admit it I know my friend is gone. I run over to her, whisper screaming, *"NO NO NO NO NO,"* not again! Thinking maybe I'm wrong, only this time when I turn her over, I see she's been shot in the head. I lift her in my arms, hugging her close, whispering *no, no, no, no,* with tears blurring my vision. Suddenly I hear a crunching sound. I carefully lay my friend down when I hear it again. I immediately jump up, phasing into Jewel as I take off in the direction of the sound, running as fast as I can go. I veer around a bend then a tree sniffing as I go.

I finally see someone running and more importantly I know that smell, and it's Curtis. I run faster, jumping and tackling him, quickly phasing back, staring at him with hatred and anger seething from my every pore. *"WHY WOULD YOU DO THIS TO HER?"* He smirks at me saying I ruined his life, ruined his future with her, he figures if he can't have her, neither can I. I couldn't believe what I was hearing. I was seething, furious I forget about being a Beta and scream for him to PHASE. He starts laughing, calling me a crazy bitch, saying I can't tell him what to do. I smirk at him. "I'm not talking to you." He looks around to see who else there might be, I see the confusion on his face. He snickers at me again. I say again in a whisper yell "PHASE, NOW." Seconds later, he realizes then what's happening and who's standing in front of him.

He says it can't be, hell no, it can't be. I can feel a lot of anger and see just as much fear flash in his eyes. I can see the panic set in him before he says never will we bend the neck to a woman, especially to me. "Really, Curtis?" I softly say. "PHASE," and even though he fights it, his gray wolf eventually appears, growling in anger. "HEEL," I say and after seconds of more growling and fighting with himself he goes down, practically to his belly. "BEND" I say and he quickly bends his neck. I walk over to him, looking down at his wolf, barely controlling Jewel who is fighting for it. "The rest of the wolf world might not, Curtis, but you have, and you won't be here to see it regardless." I extend the claws on my right hand and slice clean through his throat, practically decapitating him.

His blood splashes on my face as he falls, and I hear him gurgling while I look out, seeing it paint the snow red as I feel my anger and my grief fighting for supremacy in my mind. Anger and Jewel win and I phase, then begin slicing into him like I could kill him repeatedly for what he did to our Olivia. My sweet, sweet, innocent Olivia. I tear him to pieces, slicing and ripping away every part I can find. When his dead body phases back to Curtis, I phase back as well. I bend over him thinking about what he took from us, who he took from us, my very first friend. She was my chosen sister, the one I chose to be my family. My claws extend again, and I continue slicing at his body over and over, screaming for Olivia, over, and over and over.

A _lpha Richard_

I follow the sound of Jay's pained screams and when I find her, I'm terrified by what I see. She's covered in the blood of someone I can't even recognize with tears and blood streaming down her face and her naked body. "Jay... Jay, Jay." I calmly call out numerous times before she finally notices me. She looks up, misery shining through her eyes, she rises from the bloody mess and takes a step towards me, stops, looks into my eyes and sobs,

"She's gone, Richard."

I reach out, grabbing her in time before her body hits the ground. I lift her up, holding her close regardless of the mess. I can smell most of the blood isn't hers. I quickly run back to the lodge to take her to the pack doctor just to make sure. As I approach the lodge, I see that Olivia's body has been removed and Jane is standing in the doorway staring out, looking at nothing. She's probably still in shock, I imagine. I call her name, and when she sees Jay, the relief on her face is evident, as well as the tears. She follows me quietly, saying nothing as we head to the clinic. We'll have to wait for Jay to come around to know what really happened besides the bullet in Olivia's head. Along with the dead flesh Jay left in the snow. I put

Jay on one of the beds and the nurse begins cleaning her up. I let them know most of it was not her blood, but she does have some minor cuts.

I leave the room to let them work, knowing Jane will keep an eye on her, now that she's here. Now I'm going to figure out how someone got onto my mountain without me knowing. Were they trying to kill Jay again or Olivia this time, and what the hell is going on? Bryce, please stop howling, you're giving me a headache and you know she's fine. Go talk to Jewel or something. *"She won't talk to me, Rich, she's upset."* I can imagine, buddy, she just lost someone very dear to her. Lets give her some time. *"I know, Rich, but I'm worried for them."* Me too, but I can't think with you howling in my head. *"Fine, Rich, but you don't have to be mean about it."* You're right, I apologize. Now can you settle down; I swear you're like an old lady sometimes. *"I'm an Alpha, Rich."* I know, Bryce, then act like one.

Now, please, for Jay and Jewel. *"I will but I'll hurt you if you call me an old lady ever again, Rich."* Really, Bryce, and pray tell how are you going to do that? *"I have my ways, Rich. Remember before? I have my ways."*

Chapter 13

ALPHA RICARD

A <u>*Painful Discovery*</u>

I hurry to my office while texting Beta Pete and Gamma Marcus to meet me there. As I enter, I'm not surprised to see them standing there. "What have you found out, if anything?" 'Alpha, it's strange, we got no reports from anyone on shifts from any lodge below us or on ours,' Says Gamma Marcus. "How did he get this far up the mountain without being seen?" It's not possible, he continues, it means someone in our pack assisted him. "Exactly, so tell me who was working the shift that coincided with him passing through from both lodges. Work back to the time Beta Olivia was shot." The first name Beta Pete mentions sends warning signs through my body.

"Beta Michael Carlson was on shift."

"Was that his shift?" Beta Pete, Say,

"Yes, Alpha," it has been his shift since his daughter relocated to the lower lodge."

I now have a bad feeling about this. "Who was on shift on the other end?" Gamma Polson says Pete. I feel more dread hearing that name. "Not possible, Pete, I moved him from rotation and put him on a personal detail watching Anne Carlson."

"Yes, I was aware, Alpha. She was doing well, started dating and he requested to go back to his regular rotation. It was granted two days ago."

"Did you contact him to ask if he had anything unusual happen on his watch?" He responds that they have, but couldn't get through to him since he was relieved.

"I sent his brother to look for him with orders to bring him to your office, Alpha."

"Can you also have Beta Carlson brought to my office when Gamma Polson arrives?" They agreed but wanted to know if I thought they were involved with what happened. "I hate to think it, but it's the only way it could have happened." At that exact moment, I hear a code being entered on my office door, and in walks Jay with Jane following closely behind her. She's obviously not happy that she's here, saying she tried to get her to rest but she wouldn't listen to her.

"Jay, you've been through a traumatic event, maybe you should."

"Stop, Richard. Please don't try to manage me or my emotions. I know better than you what I've just been through. One of my best friends, someone very dear to me, was just murdered in front of me and I was unable to save her. So please don't talk to me like I'm not aware of what's going on. I'm here to find out from you how Beta Shaw was able to walk up your mountain unchallenged and kill my friend."

"That was Beta Shaw?"

"Yes it was."

"That's what I'm trying to figure out, trust me, Jay." I can see the frustration, and controlled anger on her face. I can't blame her.

B *eta Jay*

I look around the room. "So what have you found out?"

"I'm waiting to meet with the individuals who were on rotation during the time frame that would have allowed him to get through. This is a large mountain, Jay."

"Yes, but according to you, well protected. Remember you said that, Richard." I look around and see Beta Pete standing near Jane, close but not touching her. I can see the pain in her eyes but there's nothing I can do to help her as I'm dealing with my own pain at the moment. The emotions I'm feeling are flooding me, overwhelming me, I need to try and concentrate. "Can you all please leave the room so I can speak with Alpha Richard in private?" Beta Pete tries to grab Jane, but she pushes his hands away, saying, I'm not leaving, Jay. "Jane you are, I can't deal with your pain and my own, go let your mate help you."

"I don't want to leave you, Jay."

"Really, why, Jane? What can you do? Can you bring her back? No you can't, do what you can do and go." "*Jay?* "I know, Jewel, that was harsh but it's what I need right now. "Beta Pete, please take your mate and help her." I see Richard hanging up the phone; I didn't even recall hearing it ring. Beta Pete pulls Jane with difficulty out of the room and Gamma Marcus follows. I look at Richard and I can tell he's not very happy with me.

"That was harsh, Jay."

"I know and I'll apologize at another time. Right now I need to concentrate, and it was hard with her here."

"What are you concentrating on, Jay?"

I can't tell him, but I feel his frustration and I also feel his worry. "What are you worried about, Richard?"

"Why do you think I'm worried?"

"I sense it seeping from you."

"Really? Well, I may as well tell you, one of the people on rotation is Beta Michael Carlson."

"And that's important, why?"

"He's Anne's father."

"Why does that matter?"

"Do you not remember, she's the female that was dating Beta Pete."

"Why didn't they shoot Jane then? Olivia didn't become his mate."

"JAY."

"I know, I know, what else, Richard."

"The other person on rotation was Gamma Polson. He was the person I put on detail to watch Anne. He requested to be off the detail two days ago. Supposedly she was better and dating a new guy, no need to keep watching her. He went back on his rotation; we're trying to locate him now."

"So, what you're saying, Richard, is the two people on rotation in the area that Curtis could have passed through your mountain based on where he was located are the two people connected with the female who was hurt because Jane stole her boyfriend."

"Yes, Jay."

"That shit is crazy, Alpha."

"Yes, you're right it is, but that's the situation."

"I want to be here when you speak to them."

"You're not a part of the pack, Jay."

"I'm the Ruler's Regent and it was my assistant who was murdered under their watch. Technically their punishment falls to the Ruler, and since the Ruler isn't here and his Regent is, I will be here for the conversation."

"Only if you will let me talk and you will listen, understood?"

"Jay, you need to relax. You can listen and feel but you need to be relaxed." Ok, you're right Jewel. "How soon will this meeting be, Alpha?"

"Soon, Jay, they're actually on their way here now. That's what the phone call was about."

Jay, you need to relax, take a seat in the sitting area and try to calm your emotions. You need to be able to know who you're feeling things from to know who's telling the truth." Jewel, I'll try. *"And Jay, try not to be overly responsive."* I'll try, Jewel. *"I know, but you need to be careful and keep your head about you."* Alright already, Jewel. The knock comes and Richard gets up and opens the door. Entering is a young guy probably in his mid to late twenties. Richard greets the younger guy whose name is Gamma Polson. He directs him where to take a seat. Then he refers to the other as Beta Carlson, who looks to be in his late fifties, but well fit since wolves age well. Richard begins talking, while I try to settle my nerves to be most effective.

"Beta Carlson, can you also please have a seat."

I immediately feel two things, nervousness and curiosity, but I'm not sure what's coming from who.

"I wanted to speak to you both about something that happened on the mountain today. Someone was able to get through from locations where you both were patrolling."

I take this opportunity to stand. I walk towards the window closer to Richard's desk so I can see them both clearly. They look in my direction and I get a clear feeling of curiosity, nervousness, and hatred, that's new. I look harder trying to figure out which one's feeling that emotion. Gamma Polson speaks first, explaining that he didn't encounter anyone, and nothing unusual happened on his rotation, asking Richard if he was sure it was from his area. It could have been from another area. Whoever they were could have traveled, who knows how long they could have been on the mountain, Alpha. Richard smiles, like he knows he's not telling the truth, but nothing from Beta Carlson.

"Gamma Polson, you do know I can tell when you're lying, so tell me the truth. This is a command from your Alpha."

After a few minutes of struggling, he finally speaks, saying how

Anne joined his rotation. That they've been hooking up and they just snuck off for about thirty minutes to, you know. But he didn't see anyone or smell anything, and he swears nothing was out of the ordinary when they were done. Richard is breathing heavy, pinching the bridge of his nose.

"Let me get this straight. You left your area unattended for thirty or so minutes, but you're claiming no one got through, yet you can't be sure of that."

He stammers on about how there were no footprints in the snow besides his and Anne's and there were no smells besides theirs, all the things they would look for.

"Really, then how do you explain someone coming to the pack lodge and killing the Ruler's Regent's assistant this morning?"

He stammers that it's not possible again.

"Oh, believe me, it's possible Gamma, but I do think you were just used. Why would you get involved with the person I told you to monitor?"

He didn't know, saying that she's hot and she likes him.

"You're in a lot of trouble for your lack of judgment."

Richard picks up his phone and instructs someone to take Anne Carlson and her mother into custody, and to lock them away until further notice. Instructing them to accept no changes to his order from anyone. The whole time, I'm listening and watching Beta Carlson, looking for a response, but nothing. Waiting for a feeling, but nothing. I know now the hate must have come from him. A few seconds later, another knock at the door and Gamma Marcus enters. Richard instructs him to please take Gamma Polson into custody until further notice. He says no one is to see him, no one can talk to him, and that includes Marcus himself, no questions asked. Once Gamma Marcus closes the door, Richard looks to Beta Carlson.

"Do you want to now tell us why you would do this? Your daughter would have healed from her breakup."

He starts laughing.

"You think this is about some silly breakup? You're holding my mate and my daughter and they're innocent in all of this."

With those words I know this is all my fault. Dread seeps into me and it all falls into place. I whisper, "You're the male pup." He looks over to me with a surprise smirk on his face.

"How do you know?"

"I have my ways, Beta Carlson."

"You don't know that much about who I am, that's for sure, Beta Scott."

"Really, Beta, why don't you tell me what you think I don't know." He snicker laughs again before he starts talking.

"You grew up, Beta Scott, with some self-proclaimed prophet. I bet she didn't see this in your future."

"Really, and how do you know what she did or didn't see about me?"

"Because you didn't know about me until recently, I'm sure of that. I've been searching for my records for years, I know that much."

"But why kill Olivia?"

"Oohh, she needed to die, she saw someone who couldn't be seen yet, and now she's taking that to her grave. Besides, Curtis was like a dog with a bone because you stole her from him. He had dreams of running off with her to some island with a lot of money for them to live happily ever after, like that shit ever happens."

"So, what's the plan now, Carlson? Olivia's dead so she can't reveal some unknown person?"

"You'll find out soon enough, the worst thing that prophet ever did was to separate me from my family. My Omega sisters should have been treasured, instead they were basically sold off to separate packs without a care in the world. And what of me, shipped off to some stupid mountain, put into an orphanage for unwanted pups. Well, the Ruler will regret the day the prophet ever made that decision."

"Your plan is to what? Kill the Ruler? Then what? What's to keep us from telling others of your plan now that you've revealed it?"

"Things have been set in place, Beta, that can't be undone. Trust me, and I've spent most of my adult life putting things in order, and in the end my family will be the ones remembered in history."

By this time, I'm fuming, I feel nothing but satisfaction seeping from him. "Where's your sister, Carlson?" He looks at me with that satisfied smirk.

"I figured you knew about her if you knew about me. I'll never tell."

"I can command you to tell me as your Alpha," Richard says.

"You could try, but since I was an orphan, I wasn't born into your pack, like I said, you could try. Besides, I don't actually know where she is or who she is. We thought it would be better to not have a connection between us, ensuring there's less chance we would be found out. I can't tell you what I don't know. She's smart like that."

I look hard at him. "You know I'll find her, right, Carlson? I found you."

"Look how long it took you to do that, and you couldn't even save your friend."

"You're right. I didn't save my friend and that will haunt me for the rest of my life. But Olivia didn't take anything to her grave, she told me what she knew." He jerks in his chair

"Impossible, you're lying."

"Why would I lie?"

"You're trying to trick me up."

"Again, why would I need to do that?"

"You're trying to get me to tell you."

"No need for that, Olivia told us weeks ago, she saw Alpha Edward Mathews in Miami meeting with Curtis Shaw." There was that surprised look again, but there was also that smirk. There was something else that happened that weekend that was just as important that Olivia didn't know. But they weren't sure if she knew. "Yes Carlson, that was all she knew, the other person who was there that weekend, Olivia wasn't sure about."This caught his attention. "You see, you all thought she could bring you all down, but she barely paid attention to Alpha Mathews. If you wouldn't have tried to kill her in California when I was around, we wouldn't have thought you were trying to kill me and wouldn't have been looking for you at all. You all put this in motion, Carlson, and you would have gotten away with it if you would have just left Olivia alone."

"You talk like we still won't get away with it, Beta. As you say, you didn't mention the other person that was in Miami. That means you don't know."

"No actually, me not mentioning it means I'm sure that you don't know, and why would I tell you who your sister is?"

I could see the anger now, the emotion I was waiting for. I start walking towards Richard's chair and turn to continue facing Beta Carlson. Richard gets up and walks towards the door to his office. "Let me tell you a little bit about what I do know. I know your Omega sister who was sent to California and died giving birth to a son, fathered by either Edward or Andrew Mathews, and they cared little enough for her that they didn't even put her name on his born papers." More anger, I like that. "I know your other Omega sister who was sent to New York was never even acknowledged or recorded on their books and you weren't able to find her. She found you and brought you into her scheme of revenge. She didn't even bother to tell you her name or where she was." More anger from him. "I know you were sent to this pack and the Alpha couldn't find a family to take you, so they put you in an orphanage."

Anger is boiling in him now, and it felt good in my nose. I could also feel the annoyance coming from Richard not liking what I was saying about his pack. "I can tell you're angry, about to rip the arms off the chair you're sitting in. But I'm about to tell you something that is going to really piss you off, that I'm sure neither you or your sadistic sibling knows. It's that while you were planning to get revenge on the prophet for separating you as babies, using you as pawns with the regional packs to get their best to train and educate the next ruler. While you were running around trying to kill Olivia, making sure she wouldn't reveal who you were to me so I couldn't tell the Ruler and spoil your plans, Olivia was standing right next to *ME*." I whisper-scream. I see the confusion on his face and feel the confusion coming from Richard. "*Jay.*" No, Jewel, I got this. I sense more confusion from Carlson. "I see you're confused." I walk around standing to the left of him while he follows me with his eyes, his brain trying to figure out what I was saying.

"What are you saying, bitch?"

"Just what I said, Carlson, think harder about it. Think, Carlson, think. Beta Olivia Parker, every time you shot an arrow at her, I was there. You poisoned her water, I was there. You shot her in the fucking head and I was right there. "I could feel the realization seeping from Richard when he inhaled his breath. But still confusion from Carlson, "I can still see you're confused or just stupid, let me help you. Did you ever consider why the prophet would care enough to separate Omega babies? Send them to the most powerful packs in exchange for their smartest and strongest representatives to come to the island to teach and train the next Ruler?" He screams at the top of his lungs.

"*BECAUSE SHE WAS A SELFISH BITCH AND DIDN'T CARE ABOUT RUIN-ING MY FAMILY.*"

"But why, Carlson? Think, no prophet in the past ever had a hand in choosing the representatives so why this time, why this prophet?"

"*I DON'T KNOW AND I DON'T CARE WHY. THEY ALL WILL PAY FOR WHAT THEY HAVE DONE.*"

"Oh, Carlson," I lean towards him snapping my fingers in front of his face. "Look at me, every time you tried to kill my dear innocent friend," I see the smirk return to his eyes, "If you would have just moved a little to the left or right you would have accomplished your goal by killing ME." There it is, I see it, recognition, realization, comprehension, and anger. Anger over them all, the missed opportunities, anger over being played by my Nanna Grace, again. "I see you realize now who and what I am, Carlson, yes the prophet, my Nanna. Me, the next Ruler." I turn and step away from him to look out the window relieved to know this is one less piece to figure out in this craziness that has become my life these past months. I sense him move and before he can even yell or really contemplate what he wants to do. I turn with claws extended on my right hand and slice his throat open, and before his mind or body can react, I reach into his chest gripping his heart, feeling it *pump, pump, pump* slower after each *pump,* before ripping it out as his body falls to the floor, *pump,* in my hand.

I drop my arm, dropping it from my hand, while staring at Richard standing right behind where his body was. I'm staring into eyes that are reflecting, disbelief, anger, frustration, betrayal, all bundled into one, pushing into me through those lovely brown eyes. "*Jay.*" Yes, Jewel. "*I don't think you should have done that.*" You may be right again, Jewel, but he made it possible for them to kill Olivia. "*I wasn't talking about that, I was talking about revealing to Alpha Richard, we may be in danger now.*" You might be right, Jewel, but I'm tired of all of this, tired of not being me, just so damn tired of it all. Time to move on from this. "*I think you are in shock, Jay.*" You might be right about that too, Jewel, but let's deal with Richard. "Richard?"

"Jay, I don't know what to say to you right now."

"That's good as I don't feel like answering your questions right now."

"We will have to talk eventually about what happened and what I just heard."

"Yes, we will and now that you mention it." I take a deep breath before I say with as much authority that I can muster. "I, Alpha Jaidan Emerald Scott, Ruling Alpha Queen of all Wolves, command you, Alpha Richard Peterson, Regional Alpha of the Larojey-Slopes Pack, to not reveal to anyone what was revealed about who I am." I sense him shiver then shake, more anger, more confusion, and now hurt.

"You didn't have to do that, Jay."

"I didn't want to do that, Richard, but I need to not only keep myself safe, but I also need to keep you safe from yourself." I turn and walk into his office bathroom, cleaning my hands as hard as I can. When I come out and pass by Richard to leave, he grabs my arm. I turn and look at him but instead of speaking because I'm not sure how strong my voice will be at this moment. I whisper into his mind. "We will talk, my Alpha." His eyes get big, and he lets my arm go, I walk on, open the door and leave, head up to my room desperately needing a shower and my bed. I'm so exhausted, Jewel. "*You've dealt with a lot today, Jay. Lost a loved one, revenged that loved one, revealed.*" Ok already, Jewel, I know it. "*Oh, just thought I would give you the run down.*" Well, let's just give it a rest for the rest of today. "Fine *Jay. Jay?*" Hmm, Jewel. "*Thank you for killing those that took our Olivia from us.*" You're welcome, Jewel.

I sit in my office, staring at the blood spot that was Beta Carlson, wishing it had already been cleaned from my office floor. Beta Pete's sitting across from me, watching, waiting for me to speak, and honestly, I have no idea what, if anything, I want to say. I think I'm in shock myself. He says he is very sorry about what happened to Beta Parker. That the bullet she was shot with was coated in wolfsbane and there was no way she was surviving it. He informs me that Jane has contacted her mother who was blowing up Beta Scott's phone. She requests that we transport her remains to her in California. "Yes, Beta Pete, but not until Jay is ready," I can't in good form call her Beta when I know the truth. So many things make sense now and many things are more confusing than they were before. I understand the ruse. I think it'll be hard for the wolf world to accept a female as our Ruler, but with her power, she can force it. I've many questions about everything else. I would love to talk to my musketeers. Jay was right, I would be talking to them now if I could.

Anger seeps into my chest at her command but I'm reminded by it every time I want to call them, which reminds me, she was right, and it was needed. Bryce is purring with pride over our mate being the Ruler. He's been really quiet, I started wondering if he left me, but no, he is off consoling Jewel over losing Olivia. He says she's very upset over the loss. I'm upset about the loss, but I feel helpless today and I'm the Alpha. The quickness in which Jay killed Beta Carlson was surprising and impressive. Not something I thought was in my sweet innocent, Beta. I wonder Beta Pete says, interrupting my thoughts. "I'm sorry Beta Pete, I'm lost in all the events of today, please continue." He says he wonders what I want them to do with the daughter and wife of Beta Carlson. They're aware of Beta Carlson dying, of course, and have been trying to contact me to find out what happened. "Have them brought to my office in the morning. I'll explain what transpired and then we can determine what role, if any, that they played and what to do with them."

"They'll not be able to stay in Lutsen. Also, how did things go with transporting Gamma Stanley?" He tells me it went as well as can be expected, saying his brother is ashamed and wants it kept as quiet as can be. "I'm fine with that, night, Pete." I need to go to bed, I can't think clearly until I speak to Jay, and that won't happen tonight. I'm sure she has a lot on her mind. I head out of my office locking the door. As I start to go up the stairs my phone rings, it's Jarrod, I contemplate not answering, but answer it anyway. "What's up, Jarrod?"

"Is Jay ok, Rich?"

"Olivia was murdered by Beta Shaw today, and he and the person who helped him are dead. I'm actually not in a position to reveal anything to you at this time, however I will tell you now that Jay is safe. Mentally exhausted, but safe. You should call her, I imagine she would love to hear from you, Jarrod." I push in the code to enter my suite... "What I sound like, Jarrod, is tired. I'll give you a call when I can brief you... Yes, absolutely." I hang up the phone, walk into my bedroom, and drop it on my bedside table. I will shower and sleep, and maybe wake up tomorrow and this will have been a dream.

B *eta Jane*

I can barely feel my limbs, sitting here staring at the moon in the sky. The phones in my hand keep buzzing. One belongs to Olivia, I know her family is freaking out because they have felt her loss. The other is Jay's, probably Olivia's mother trying to find out what has happened to her daughter. I shiver as I remember the shock I felt walking out the door of the lodge after hearing a lone painful moan that sounded like it came from Jay. I didn't see her, but after walking towards the slopes, my legs stopped moving, heart beating fast, because I knew my perfectly good eyes were seeing a body laying in the snow. First I thought it was Jay, and I quickly ran up the hill, even though I knew whoever was laying there was gone. But as I got closer I realized who it really was. I approach her slowly like I would disturb her if I moved to quickly. I lean down, seeing the blood still seeping from the bullet wound in her head. I looked around not seeing Jay anywhere, wondering if she was taken or if she went after whoever did this to her friend, to our friend.

Over the last couple of months, even though I tried to fight it, these two she-wolves had become like my family and I don't know how Jay is going to survive losing Olivia. How will we be the three musketeers with just the two of us? I finally shook myself, needing to find Jay, thinking she may have needed help. I rose to try to get an idea in which direction she went I when noticed her phone laying on the ground. I moved to pick it up when I heard someone coming up behind me. I heard Alpha Richard breathing heavily moving up the slopes. I put my hand up, telling him that it's not Jay, that it's Olivia and she has been shot in the head with a bullet that smells like it was coated with wolfsbane.

He relaxes slightly, looking around asking about Jay. I told him that I thought she went after whoever did this to Olivia, and I was getting ready to go look for her when he came. I feel anger building up in me at what has happened here, and with only Alpha Richard here to take it out on, I say. "I thought you said your mountain was a safe place for Jay to be. Considering what has happened, I don't think you were right about that, Alpha." He looked at me, eyes lighting with anger before it quickly fades with his realization of what has happened.

"You are right, Beta Jamison, but I promise to figure out what happened, and those responsible will pay for what they have done. I am going to find Jay, would you please stay with Olivia? Beta Pete will be here shortly to help get her body moved to the pack clinic."

"Of course I will, Alpha Richard." He turned and moved further up on the run we're on, and a few seconds later I heard a phone buzzing, but not the one I'm holding in my hand. I realize shortly that it is coming from Olivia. I searched through her coat, finding her phone and silencing it because I knew I was not the one who should relay the information to her family.

Chapter 14

BETA JANE

M*usketeers of Two*

A few minutes later, my mate walks up to me, wrapping me in his arms, telling me how sorry he is about what has happened to my friend. He moves carefully, picking Olivia up from the bloody snow and turning, heading to the clinic. I follow behind him slowly before I hear someone quickly moving our way. I turn to see Alpha Richard holding a naked Beta Jay and relief floods through my body.

I shake the memory from my head grabbing the phones to bring them to Alpha Richard's office. Once I get there, I see him sitting there barely listening to my mate. I give him the phones and inform him that they have been ringing non-stop. Most likely it's Olivia's family trying to figure out what has happened to her and that I think the news should come from Jay, or at least him. He takes the phones and I turn to leave with my mate following behind me. I really need a moment to wrap my mind around what initiated this attack so that I can, at the very least, have some answers for my friend when she wakes up. I walk out the back door through the garage and head back to my mate's cabin, with him quickly on my heels. I can feel that he just wants to be here to support me, but I have never needed someone to console me, and I don't know how to accept that from him now.

I am angry and I don't think it will be fair to take it out on him. I just want to be by myself. I decide to take the stairs to get to the level to enter the cabin, and even though I am not answering any of Pete's questions, he continues to doggedly follow me. I finally stop on the first level on the stairs and turn to look at him.

"Please Pete, give me a minute to settle my nerves and then we can talk, I just need a second." He looks at me like he wants to argue but then decides to give me what I ask for and turns walking back down the stairs. I continue up, stopping briefly as I try to catch my breath, not from the stairs, but from the emotions overcoming me. I start struggling to breathe, trying to get air into my lungs and let the anguish over losing Olivia and possibly Jay out. I'm not sure why what happens next happens, but I didn't hear anyone coming up behind me until they were almost on me. Thinking maybe whoever shot Olivia was now here, my instincts take over and I turn punching whoever it is in the throat then the midsection before I hear the painful grunts of my mate and realize my mistake.

I immediately started apologizing and helping him up the rest of the stairs into our cabin. I hearing him trying to breathe through the pain and telling me to remind him not to get on my bad side in the future and to stay clear of my hands. I get settled on the couch joining him, now calm enough to let him provide the comfort that we both need at this moment. The next morning, I wake early and go to Jay's room to find her still sleeping deeply. I call her name to try to wake her without response. I quickly contact Alpha Richard and he has the pack doctor come to Jay's room to examine her.

The doctor informs us that he doesn't see anything wrong, and that she is probably just trying to recover from her ordeal. He tells us to keep an eye on her and just let her sleep, it's probably the best thing for her considering the events of yesterday.

Alpha Richard informs me that he spoke to Olivia's mother and she is on her way to the lodge to pick up her daughter and to see Jay. Within the hour, Olivia's mother arrives and immediately starts watching over Jay with me. After two days, she informs us that she must get her daughter back home to her family and requests that Alpha Richard and I keep her informed on how Jay is doing. They both leave to go down to his office where she can leave a note for him to give to Jay when she finally wakes. I find myself standing outside of Jay's room wondering if she will ever wake from this loss.

B *eta Jay*

I wake, feeling strong and feel energy pulsing through my limbs. I stretch out, feeling my power stronger than I ever have. I can hear movement outside like it's right in the room with me. Jewel, what's going on? *"The closer you get to your born day the stronger you'll be, you know this, Jay."* I feel rested, I must have slept very hard. I wonder what time it is. Olivia is going to be mad if I'm late for skiing. I'm determined to make it down the slopes without falling today, I'm positive, Jewel. Jewel? Jewel? *"Jay."* I open my eyes and stretch. Yes, Jewel? Why are you so quiet? *"Jay, do you not remember what happened?"* What happened? *"Olivia. To Olivia, Jay."* Then it all comes flooding back along with the pain washing over me. I feel the tears falling into my ears as I lay there staring at the ceiling.

I turn and grab my pillow to cover my face, to catch my tears and the noise of the screams coming from deep in my chest. Why, Jewel, why couldn't I save her like before, why didn't I try? "*She was dead the moment the bullet entered her head, Jay. There was nothing you could do.*" But what's the point of being the Ruler if I can't save those I love? "*Jay, you're not the Goddess.*" Why did the Goddess let this happen? "*The Goddess didn't do this, Jay, Curtis did, and you killed him. Carlson also did, and you killed him.*" Yes, but that doesn't give me Olivia. I must call Momma Tilda. "*You have to get a hold of yourself before you call her, Jay. You're in no condition to provide support to her right now.*" I turn looking for my phone. I must let her know how sorry I am that couldn't save her, but I can't find my phone.

Where's my phone? I push myself up, looking around my room, I don't see the bloody clothes where I peeled them off. I rise and make my way to the bathroom, use the toilet and brush my teeth, clearing the cotton from my mouth. "*Jay, Jay.*" Yes, Jewel. "*I need to tell you something.*" I don't think I can take any more. I have to talk to Momma Tilda. I throw water on my face to clear my senses. I rush into the closet and put on a pair of blue jeans, a blue long sleeve shirt, and my Nikes. I open my door, and standing there is Jane. I look at her, wondering if she's been waiting for me. "How long have you been standing there?"

"Today, for about two hours."

"What do you mean today? Why didn't you come in or knock on the door?" "*Jay.*" Jewel. "*Jay, you've been sleeping for three days.*" WHAT? "*That's what I have been trying to tell you.*" Why, Jewel, what's wrong with me? "*Nothing physically, but your mind needed to heal. You were not dealing with Olivia's death well, so you slept, and I let you.*" But Momma Tilda. I push past Jane, running to get to Richard's office. I hear Jane running behind me, when I get to his office the door is open and I rush in. He looks at me and I see relief on his face. I also see Momma Tilda sitting across from him. I stop, and she jumps up, running to hug me. At first I don't respond, I don't deserve her comfort, but then I realize she deserves mine. I hug her back and we cry together for our loss, for Olivia.

"I'm sorry I was not able to save her." We move to sit on the couch, and she wipes the tears from my face saying that she knew if I could, I would have. She continues, saying just like I did the last time, she's sure of that. Momma Tilda tells me that she knows how much I loved her daughter, and that I gave her more life in the past year than Olivia had her whole life, and she's grateful for that. She explains that she knows we will miss her, but that I'm her daughter, too, and I will always be. I hug her again, and just enjoy the comfort only she can provide. "I'm sorry I didn't call you, I've no idea where my phone is."

"It's here, Jay, I contacted Ms. Parker and brought her here, especially when you didn't wake up."

I look at Richard. "Thank you." Momma Tilda tells me that she's glad I woke before she left. The doctor assured them that I was fine; just trying to heal from the loss. But she must take her girl home to their family so they can say their final goodbyes. "I wish I could be there, Momma Tilda." She understands and says all that matters is that I was with her when it counted, and she was where she wanted to be. She gets up. "You're leaving now?" She nods her head, saying yes. That she's been watching me sleep. But, that Olivia is loaded and ready to go, and she was just talking to Alpha

Richard about what she wanted him to tell me when I woke up. I help her with her coat, and we walk to the helicopter. We hug again and I promise to keep in touch because she's officially my adoptive mother through my sisterhood with Olivia.

As she loads onto the helicopter waving, I feel the tears flowing again. I need the tears to stop. I feel Jane grab my hand and I hold hers tight. I must hold onto those I love even tighter now. We turn and head back to the lodge.

"Jay, I'm sorry about Olivia."

"Jane, why do you say it like you haven't lost someone, as well? I know you cared for her as much as I did. We are sad together, now tell me how you are?"

"Now that you're awake and talking, I'm better."

"I'm sorry Jane. I didn't mean to desert you in your time of need."

"It's fine, I know you needed to heal. That's what Alpha Richard, Pete and the doctors kept telling me. I have your phone here."

"I took it from her. We need to talk, Jane."

"I know, Jay, do you want to go into the office?"

"No, I want to go to my suite." We head into the lodge and up to my room. After I put in my code, we enter, and I head to the sitting area. I look at Jane and she is looking at me waiting for me to begin. "I killed Beta Shaw."

"I know, Jay, I saw the body when they brought it back."

"I killed Beta Carlson."

"I know that as well, in Alpha Richards' office."

"They were working together."

"I figured that much since they were both dead."

"Beta Carlson was the male pup."

"I guessed that, but good to have it confirmed."

"The other Omega sister used him; he didn't know who she was or where she was. They needed to kill Olivia because they thought she saw whoever she is, in Miami, but if she did, she didn't remember it or recognize them. The plan is to kill the Ruler, and they didn't want Olivia to spoil their plans, she was the target all this time. The crazy thing is Jane, she didn't even know she saw anything, this was all for nothing. We will not know that for sure until we figure out who or where the NY Omega is. Any news on your end, Jane?"

"No, and I have been looking at anything to keep myself busy. Pete's worried about me. I'm fine now that you're awake, though."

"We have to figure this out, Jane, and before we leave to go to Haven. I can't, no, we can't bring this danger to the Ruler. You are going with me, right?"

"Yes I am, I told Pete I'll not leave you until this is figured out. He'll be coming with us, as well, not letting his mate out of his sight."

At that exact moment we hear a knock on the door and I get up and open it for Mark. He immediately grabs me and hugs me tight, saying he's glad I'm safe and that he's sorry about Olivia. He knows she meant a lot to me but that I mean a lot to him and to please stop scaring him by almost getting killed. "I will do my best, Mark." He moves to sit in a chair, while I close the door. He starts immediately, wanting to know if it's all over with now. He asks if it's all over now? Since Olivia was the target all along. "Yes, she was but it's because she potentially saw the person behind the plan to kill the Ruler." He looks at me, eyes wide, saying, then it's not over?

"Nope, Mark, we have to figure this out before we all arrive in Haven." So, what's the plan, he asks. "Jane thinks we have to find a connection to the Omega who was sent to New York. She'll be the key and we're trying." Well Jay, Jane, you have a couple of weeks before we travel, he explains. So, we have that amount of time to figure out who and what the plan is to get rid of the Ruler. Samantha and him are traveling with me and it would be safer if we knew what we're facing, let them know how they can help.

"There's nothing you can do now, Mark. Everything we need to know will be online. We will know everything we need from your pack, but I need you to just be ready to go and I'll let you know if I need any other assistance. And Mark, thank you for always being there for me." You're welcome, he says, and there's no need to thank me. I turn to Jane. "I need to speak to Richard."

"I'll go to Pete's office to work."

We get ready to leave and my phone rings, I look at it and see Samuel's number. "I'll talk to you later Jane." As she leaves and closes the door, I answer my phone.

"*How are you Jay?*"

"As well as can be expected, Samuel."

"*I know what I heard from Jarrod isn't the whole story.*"

"Yes, but I don't have time to go through it right now. Why are you calling? Have you found anything else out?"

"I found out the Omega from our pack stayed with the Shaw family for the first twenty-something years she was in our pack. That's the connection to Beta Shaw, and we have to rethink who is actually behind everything, Jay."

"You're right, Samuel. Is it possible the Omega from NY would have moved to California?"

"That would have required Regional Alpha approval, Jay, and after speaking to my father, that didn't happen. Also, Beta Shaw's mother is a nurse at the clinic. I think maybe the Omega that's behind all of this is the California Omega, not the New York Omega."

"Thank you Samuel."

"You're welcome, I'll do anything to make sure you're safe."

"How are things with you and Alpha Lisa?"

"Things are as expected, Jay."

"Well, you have about two weeks to make sure things are in place because we will head to Haven at that time. I want you with me when I get there."

"I would be in no other place, Jay. May I ask who else are you taking with you to Haven?"

"At this time, you, Mark, his girlfriend Samantha, Jane and her mate Pete, why?"

"I was just wondering if you were taking any of your mates with you."

"I don't think it's a good idea at this point. The Regional Alphas are supposed to attend the new Ruler at a scheduled date. I think we should stick to that date. I need to prepare myself for who's coming for me, and I need people I know with me when I get to Haven."

"*That means you're going to reveal yourself to the others?*"

"Not until we arrive at Haven, I'm also having Edmond join me. His father is a part of this in some way, and he may be able to shed some light on what that might be. I will see you in two weeks and thank you again, Samuel. What you have provided has really helped clarify some things. Talk to you soon." I leave my room heading to Beta Pete's office instead of Richard's. When I enter, I don't see Beta Pete, but Jane is sitting at Gamma Marcus desk.

"Jay, what's up, are you ok?"

"Yes, I just got off the phone with Samuel and he informs me the Omega from his pack was placed with the Shaw family and was the one who probably has the connection with Beta Shaw. This means we're looking for the wrong Omega. It's probably the New York Omega that might have died in childbirth and the California Omega who survived and faked her death. She's the one behind all of this, Jane. Let's imagine the Shaw's helped their Omega fake her death, we need to figure out her motive for killing the Ruler."

"Why would the motive be any different, Jay?"

"I don't think it is, Jane, but we must investigate all possibilities to know for sure."

"I'll work on it, Jay."

"I have to go talk to Alpha Richard."

"You've said that, are you going to tell him what we've been working on?"

"I'm going to tell him what I can."

"Jay, I have this feeling you're avoiding Alpha Richard, is there more going on?"

"Yes there is, but nothing I can talk to you about right now. And don't worry, it's nothing that affects what we're trying to figure out."

"Well good luck with the conversation that you're clearly avoiding."

"Thanks, Jane." I leave Beta Pete's office and head down the hall in the opposite direction. Jewel, I have no idea where to begin."*How about you let him ask what he wants, and you go from there.*"That sounds like a good plan. I put the code in, and push open the door to see Richard sitting at his desk. I try to sense what he's feeling, but all I feel is nervousness, and I'm sure that's coming from mostly me. I walk in and take the seat across from him, putting my hands in my lap. I look into his eyes, waiting for him to at least acknowledge I'm here for the dreaded conversation.

"Jay, how are you?"

"Richard, I'm as can be expected, I just lost someone very special to me."

"I'm sorry about Olivia."

"Thank you, but I'm sure you have other things you would like to be discussing."

"Honestly, Jay, I have no idea where to start."

"How about you ask the question upper most in your mind?"

"Fine then, how will it work with you being my, Jarrod's, and Tony's mate, while being the Ruler?"

I look at him stunned. This is what he's most concerned about? Jewel, can you believe this? *Actually, Jay, I'm as stunned as you, but now that I think about it, it's a very good question. One that neither of us even considered.* Wait you're right, damn. I smile at him, "Richard, you've asked me the one question I've no answer for. I hadn't considered that with everything going on. Well damn, thank you for adding more to my plate. I guess this is something we mates will have to figure out together, don't you think? If that is something we all want. But if that's our situation it will be a challenge. I guess, Richard, that's my response to your question, do you have any other questions?"

"Why did you feel the need to command me to not tell anyone? I would not have anyway."

"If you think about it, you would have wanted to tell Jarrod and Tony."

"Don't you think they should know, Jay?"

"Not yet. I didn't want you to know, the more people who know, the more danger to me. Actually, until I have my full powers and my mates, I'm weaker, and we both know there are many in our world who will not want a female Ruler."

"Yes, but I think the Regional Alphas would have protected you."

"Really, Richard, you all would have protected me before you got to know me?"

"Yes, Jay, we don't kill for no reason or kill women."

"Really, so when you three met up in Miami, was that a meeting to discuss how to protect the next Ruler?" I could tell I hit on a sore subject, he looks into my eyes.

"How are you aware of that?"

"I know you traveled there; I wasn't aware of why, but you didn't do any business there, I figured it was personal. I thought to myself, why would the three most powerful Alpha's meet up after the notice went out the next Ruler was going to travel to the packs? Maybe planning, I knew what you all had accomplished, and I could understand you not wanting that to change. That was a large part of the reason I decided to travel as my regent. To give you all a chance to know me, to know what I thought about how you were running the packs now. To know how happy I was for what you all had done for your packs. I had no plans to change things as long as the growth was for all in your packs not just at the top. But tell me, Richard, was I wrong in why you all met?"

"Actually Jay, no you're not wrong. And thinking about it, I understand why you did it, which is why I didn't question it. I even agree with some of how you did it. You were right, and I'm sure I speak for both Jarrod and Tony when I say we would lay down our life for our mate and our Ruler. But after some of the things I've pieced together about you, Jay. I'm not sure you'll need our help."

"Oh, I will, Richard. I might be able to protect myself against a few, but there will be many who arrive in Haven who will not want to bend the neck." I see him contemplating what I say.

"Can you now tell me what was going on that resulted in Beta Parker being murdered?"

"Now this is a question I can answer." I spend the next couple of hours explaining everything that's happened, from the first arrow I caught while at Jarrod's pack, to what happened in his office the other day. I went over what we know and what we don't know about the plan to kill the Ruler and who we think is behind it. I catch him up on the development with Samuel and Alpha Lisa and those who will be traveling to Haven. He caught me up on the fact that Gamma Stanley was behind the blackmail, but it seems he was just one of the pawns. Apparently, it was a side job he came up with on his own to make some extra money in case he was found out. He finally revealed he was the one who shot the arrow in California, and he was given access by Beta Shaw. But when he saw me there, he remembered me from the competition with Gamma Mark who he knew from when they were young and figured it out.

Richard tells me, that the investigation revealed, that Gamma Stanley, thought it was safe to attend the summit. Even after he found out I was attending, that he was surprised I recognized him in New York, since I hadn't seen him in California. I informed Richard it was based off his smell from the arrow. He was transferred to the federal prison for our kind along with those who assisted him in his blackmail. He was understandably upset to know Mark would be leaving with me and taking Samantha without even informing him. "Technically, Richard, Mark is assigned to me until my twenty fifth born day, and would you deny him being with Samantha after all the time they've been separated?"

"No, of course not, Jay, since I'll be traveling as well."

"No, you have to stick to the plan, Richard. Whoever these people are, they need to think things are going as planned, making it easier for us to catch them. You must arrive when you were scheduled to with Jarrod and Tony. Another reason why I can't tell them, Richard. They would have arrived here and wanted to protect me. The other Alphas won't arrive until after you, Richard, and that's when they'll try whatever they have planned, so I'll be safe until then. So we stick to the plan. I'll have Samuel and Lisa, Mark and Samantha, and Jane and Pete."

"I knew my Beta was leaving me, he said he wasn't letting his mate out of his sight."

"Edmond will meet me there, as well. I'll have my pack with me, I'll work on fine tuning my powers and training, so I'll be prepared, Richard."

"Nice to know, Jay, you seem to have it all figured out."

"No, Richard, I don't, but I have all these people around me that will help me get it figured out."

"You will keep me informed with how things are going?"

"Of course I will." I rise from my seat, walk around, and then turn his seat to sit on his lap. "I know the Alpha in you wants to protect me, just as the Alpha in me wants to protect you, as well."

"You've been protecting me, Jay, for years it would seem. When will it be my turn?"

"Soon, my Mighty Man." I hug him tight, "I'm glad this conversation didn't turn into you hating me more."

"I could never hate you, Jay. But I'm disappointed you felt you needed to take on this without us."

"Maybe if I would have brought you all to me and divulged things it would have gone differently, we will never know." I look into his brown eyes, then lean forward and kiss him softly "I'm excited about the future we'll have together. I will admit I'm nervous about how we'll make it work with us."

"You know, Jay, that promise you made to yourself seems foolish considering I'm one of your mates."

I laugh. "You would think that, but until my born day, we don't really know for sure, now do we? So, we'll just have to wait. Besides, what will my other two potential mates think about it."

"I'm sure I don't care at all, Jay."

"All I know it that you three will have to figure that out between you if or when the time comes." I get up, giving him a quick kiss and then I head to the door. I must start getting my things together, as well as getting Star ready for travel. "Will I see you in your suite for dinner?"

"Absolutely, Jay."

Chapter 15

BETA JAY

F_inally, Haven_

I head to my suite, glad things went well and he was more reasonable than I probably would have been if the situations were reversed. Jewel, we'll have to determine how things will go for the packs if all three Regional Alphas are my mates. I'll not be separated from them. _"I'm sure it will figure itself out when the time comes, Jay. For now we have to make sure we actually become the Ruler, because someone out there doesn't want that outcome."_ You're right. I begin going through the things I can pack now that can be shipped to Haven. Then I get dressed and head down to ride Star.

She will begin her travel to Haven in the next couple of days so she can get settled in. I begin with getting her things packed for tranport. I already let Pauley know about her arrival so he could set up a stall and pasture for her separate from our stallions. He's excited to finally have a mare in our herd and I'm surprised to finally be starting the next leg of my journey. I'm standing in the foyer, surprised by how fast the last couple of weeks have flown by. We're headed to Haven and I'm excited to see the place I'll call home. Richard still isn't happy about me going without him but is trusting my judgment.

What luggage we have with us now is manageable, and the rest of my traveling crew begins to arrive, ready to load onto the helicopter while I've decided to have my plane ready to transport us. Richard approaches, hugging me from behind.

"I'm going to miss you this long month, Jay."

"I will miss you as well, my Mighty Man, but you have a lot to prepare for. Like making sure your region Alphas are cleared to meet the Ruler, as well as preparing your pack for not only your absence but your Betas as well."

"Please Jay, don't remind me."

I turn into his arms, kissing him softly. "Just think, Alpha, the reunion will be sweet for the separation."

"Please be careful with yourself, Jay. I would hate to lose you before we can even confirm you're my mate."

"Will do, Alpha, now let's go." We head out to the helicopter, with all our luggage loaded. I'm the last to board, wanting to get every second with Richard that I can. But eventually I must go. I lost a dear friend here and gained a mate, but I'm not at all sad to have this place behind me. I get on the helicopter, with Richard securing the door and stepping back. I wave again with a sad smile, even though I'm sure I'll see him again in a month. I take a deep breath, turning to Jane. "Are you ready for the last leg of our journey?" She was quiet for a moment.

"As ready as I'll every, Jay."

I know she's thinking about Olivia, we thought it would be the three of us, the three musketeers, but like myself, Jane found her mate in the same place she lost a friend. Mark grabs my hand; I know what you're thinking he says, and it'll be alright. Once the helicopter lands we walk through the security for personal plane owners, and Mark and Pete make sure our luggage is cleared and loaded on the plane. Mark comments on how much he likes the plane, that it came out well. "Thanks, it did, the boys will be comfortable when we travel in the future."

"What are you talking about?"

I look at Jane. "I had this plane commissioned so I can transport my horses for shows. There's accommodations in the back for them."

"Wow, that's nice. Every time I turn around, I find out there's a lot I don't know about you."

I look at Mark and shake my head. I'm waiting until I'm safely at Haven before I tell the current group who I am. In a couple of hours, they'll know all they need to know. We hurry to get on board, and soon, the pilot announces that we're ready to take off. Everyone is settled in their seats ready for the flight. Jane and I go over what we have on the potential California Omega surviving the birth of Edmond with no leads on where she went after that. We did get confirmation that Beta Gloria Matt was behind the hack into the Regional Alpha accounts and transfer of funds. Jarrod found a USB chip in Beta Shaw's belongings at his parents' home, which had the worm program he loaded on the pack computer, making it possible for her to move the funds. The program was very similar to the one that was attached to original invoices moving the money I found in California. It was on all the Alphas incoming invoices and put there by Beta Matt in New York and Beta Carlson in Minnesota.

This made us look for proof Beta Shaw traveled to Miami prior to when Olivia went there. We found the security footage of her in Miami with Beta Shaw. The footage showed them going into a hotel together, the room was booked under her name and they met there twice where Beta Matt must have given him the chip to load during the first visit. It turns out it correlated to when the funds started being embezzled from the Alpha accounts. Which meant that Beta Carlson must have met her there. But we couldn't find any footage or any documents to support his travel, or the name of the California Omega sister they met up with, but we're still searching.

Before I realize it, the pilot is announcing that we're landing. Beta Edmond, Alpha Samuel, and Alpha Small will be at the airport when we land in Haven. It's a private landing strip, so we won't have to deal with anyone from the public. I spent two hours last week going over the characteristics that verifies me as the Ruler. When loading them in the system, I updated what would be required to validate who I am once I arrive. I also uploaded my digital DNA signature.

When the plane lands, the flight attendant opens the door, and we begin disembarking. I grab my laptop bag, ensuring I have my phone. Once I exit, I see the rest of my crew standing inside the terminal waiting. Mark, Samantha, Pete, Jane, and we all grab our luggage and head in. Edmond immediately jogs to me, grabbing my bag and giving me a tight hug while whispering,

"I've missed you ,Alpha, glad we're finally heading to the end of our journey."

"Me too, Edmond, glad to see you." I move on to say hello to Alpha Small, she's standing with two very handsome little boys. I step close, "Alpha Small, it's nice to see you again, and who do we have here?" She puts a hand on each little boy's head saying, this is Alpha Jonah and Alpha Joshua, boys this is Beta Scott. I reach my hand out to shake their little ones. "Nice to meet you, and I'm happy to have you visit with me at Haven." I look up to see Samuel standing closely behind her. "Hello, Samuel." He smiles at me.

"Hello, Jay, how have you been?"

"I've been well, and you?"

"I have been well."

"I'm glad to see you took my advice, Samuel."

"Yes, thank you again for that."

Alpha Small grabs the hand of each little Alpha and turns, instructing their caretakers to follow us as I head towards the front of the terminal. I stop at the door and turn to look at the group. "Everyone, I have a couple of SUVs to take us to the main house. I need you all to meet in the conference room on the main floor immediately upon our arrival. I'll meet you there shortly. I have something to take care of first." Then I hear Samantha clear her throat, wanting to know if they will we meet the Ruler. "Absolutely, Samantha,"

I turn and they follow me, loading into the waiting vehicles. The ride to the main house doesn't take more than twenty minutes, and I'm glad everyone's quiet, giving me the time to reflect on what happens next. When we finally pull up in front of the house, I'm happy to see the renovations were completed as I requested. The previous Ruler house looked like an old southern antebellum plantation, home and being in the middle of Georgia, I wasn't surprised.

I had it modernized, painted all black with white trim and I had all the extra buildings on the property converted to individual casita suites. All the rooms inside were completely updated, giving it a more rustic modern feel decorated to resemble our house on the island. There's warm hard woods throughout and large windows. I removed some of the upper-level floors, the suites were all complete with entertaining quarters down and living quarters up. I'll not have a large pack here, so this will be my personal home, and most others will stay in one of the numerous casitas.

As we unload from the vehicles, I head to the front door, opening it to see Moon-Ma Glenda. I quickly walk in and give her a tight hug. "I've missed you Glenda. How are you getting on at our new home?" She hugs me tight. I've missed you as well she says and she loves her casita.

"I've decorated it nicely but I'm glad you're finally here, where are the rest of my boys?"

She asks and just then in walks Mark, who gives her a hug, with Edmond next, who she squeezes so tight. I've always felt like he was her favorite of the boys. Probably because he was on the island with her the most. He was responsible for my studies, which we did mostly on the island and rarely left. Then Samuel who has always been kind of to himself, even with Glenda. She finally sees Alpha Lisa and her twins, and this sets her off to do what she can't wait to have the chance to do. Taking care of little ones. She takes them off to the kitchen, their caretakers in tow, and the rest of the group head towards where she informs us the conference room is. She set up drinks and snacks for us to have after our flight.

I go towards the back of the house, finding the door I was looking for that leads to the security room I had built in what was the former cellars. I enter the code for the first door and once it opens, I step in. It immediately closes behind me and in front of me is a long hallway, followed by an even longer set of stairs that descend. As I walk, I prepare myself for the verifying tests that's are about to begin. Jewel, we need to get ourselves established in the system as the Ruling Alpha and get security in place now. *"Let's do this, Jay."*

I step up to the next door and look at the screen as I place my face on the chin panel, allowing my eyes to be scanned. Once I get the green light of approval, I place my palm on the pad, pressing my middle finger down and feeling a small prick, taking a sample of my blood to be taken and tested. This took a few seconds before it turns green then the door opens. I push my Alpha aura into the room, ensuring those insides would recognize it before they see me.

I enter, and in front of me are twenty-four computer stations manned by the members who have historically provided personal security for the Ruler's family. To the right and behind me is a huge monitor, which has the set-up of a hackers dream; Jane is going to love working out of this place. I step forward, ensuring they all can see me, and the responses that I hear and feel are as expected. Never, impossible, fake, I hear and feel it all. Jewel, here we go, "SILENCE." They quiet themselves, and I think to myself these Alphas and yes, they're all Alphas, knew I was coming for months, and now I'm here. They must prove they deserve to serve me, not the other way around and I don't have time to deal with this.

"SIT DOWN," and while some struggle they all take their seats. "Now, Alphas, I understand you're shocked, and some are even repulsed, by the idea of being ruled by a female. I'll give you a choice, you can get the fuck over it or leave. You've been trained your whole life for this job. All you have is because of this job, but you can retain what you have and leave. I personally only want those who are open minded enough to want to face the future and change. Those who don't want to be a part of that can exit this room from the way you entered. Those who want to be a part of the new and exciting future I envision, you can stay." I release the command to sit, a couple of the Alphas stand but I can feel their uncertainty. "How about this, I can sense you're not sure. so I'll give you a week to decide what you think about me, and then you can make your decision."

"This choice comes with some stipulations though." One of the guys who stood asks if they get to keep the payments they have received. "Yes, I would not pauper you, that's not who I am." After a few moments, they sit. Jewel, I'm ready. "As you're aware, since I left the island, I've been pretending to be the Ruler's Regent, Beta Jay Scott. I'm in fact, Alpha Jaidan Emerald Scott. You know the Ruler is born with certain characteristics that prove who they are. One of those are the eyes, as Beta Jay Scott, I have hazel brown eyes," I look up at them eyes wide, "as you can see." Then I reveal my right eye. "In reality, I have one hazel brown eye and one emerald green."

"Another of the characteristics is that the Ruler will have a mark between their shoulder blades. Rulers in the past have had a K to mark them as the King. I was born with a Q, as Beta Scott I wore this." I remove my long sleeve t-shirt, turn and lift my ponytail revealing my tattoo that reads Jay. "It looks like a tattoo," and then I reveal my Q birthmark. "The last characteristic is the Ruler will have a golden wolf. Beta Scott, as you know, would have had to be a gray wolf." I begin removing the remainder of my clothing. "However, my wolf, her name is Jewel by the way, likes to add a little flare." I phase into my gray wolf with the charcoal tips. I then change into my golden wolf and at this point I let Jewel speak to their wolves.

"Hello my protectors, I look forward to working with you to protect my girl and I know you're going to love her as much as I do." I phase back and begin putting my clothes back on. I can feel the amazement, some acceptance, a couple still skeptic, some dislike, but no hate now. I look up at everyone.

"As you can see, I was able to enter this facility because I also have the DNA markers of a Ruler. I know this is a lot to take in. As I've said, you have a week to make your decision. I've brought with me a team of my most trusted trainers, advisors, friends, and family and we'll be getting settled in. We have things of our own we're working on. Those who are on board and ready to accept me as their Ruler will have that opportunity in the morning during break-fast. Those who are still not sure, maybe you shouldn't attend."

"One last thing, I own my own security firm, I've known who you were, what pack you originated from, who you're mated to, or not, the balance of your bank accounts in the states and offshore. I have background reports on all of you and if you decide you don't want to be here, that's your right. However, you know that in the past Rulers, didn't allow security to just walk away, my first show of who I am is to let you do just that. I will let you live your life as you see fit with what you have, as long as you leave and agree to let me do the same."

"The moment you decide you want to involve yourself in what my future looks like, well, that won't be tolerated, and I'll kill you. Yes, absolutely dead your ass, and based on my research of past Rulers, I have more powers than any before me. Put that with the skills I've acquired, and you won't have a chance. But don't think

I'll stop there, absolutely not. I will eliminate your whole family, because they should have taught you if nothing else, loyalty, respect, honesty, and ultimately, to keep your word. If they didn't, they failed, as well, and I'll not risk my future family having to deal with your family wanting revenge, are we understood?" Yes Alpha, they say unanimously.

"Very good, now, I've a meeting to attend. I need you to get the lands fully secured because the Queen is in residence." I turn and head out the way I came, returning to the conference room, only this time I'm me, no more Beta Jay Scott. As I enter, everyone sitting in the room is quietly talking amongst themselves. I step forward, keeping my face lowered. I step to the front, clearing my throat. "May I please have your attention." I begin to feel the confusion coming from the people in the room and smugness from Alpha Lisa.

I look up at the people I've spent the last months with. "Jane, as my business partner you're the one person here I must first offer an explanation. I was hoping to make this to you and Olivia but, well you know, for both your safety and mine I've not told you the whole truth of who I am. Now that you're here, if you haven't already guessed, I'm the next Ruler of the wolves." She's looking at me saying nothing. I wait as she continues to look. "Jane, are you going to say something?"

"I figured as much, Jay."

"Really, how is that, how did I give it away?"

"You didn't actually give it away, your wolf did. She isn't very good at not being who she is. There have been times when I've wanted to bend the neck and it confused me. It had me thinking a lot, and honestly, the only person I've ever done that for is an Alpha, making you a Beta wasn't sitting well."

"Why didn't you say anything?"

"I felt you would tell me when you were ready, besides, I'm happy to be a musketeer with the Ruler."

"I told you that wolf of yours was telling on you."

This from Alpha Lisa, Jewel, do you hear that? *"Yes, but it's only because I felt very close to Jane."* And what about Alpha Lisa? *"Well, she pissed me off, I slipped."* Whatever Jewel. "Jane, I've another secret for you, you know the hacker you've been hunting who you think will be our competition?"

"Yeah, what about her? NOOOOO."

"Yes Ma'am."

"How can that be?"

"Nadiajlewej, it's my signature, which is my wolf and my name in reverse, Jaidan Jewel."

"Jay, but you were sitting right next to me when it disappeared."

"Yes, I was changing it while sitting there."

"Damn, do you know how many hours I've been chasing you? I could've been working on other things."

"I apologize for not telling you, Jane."

"I'm not sure I'm going to forgive you for this, Jay, I don't believe you."

"Well Jane, I've come clean about everything now. Are there any questions from the rest of you? Samantha what about you?" She says she doesn't have a question, but is wondering if I think I might have a problem with a lot of the older Alphas, as they'll not want a female Alpha as their Ruler."They're going to have to get over it, but that's for another day. Right now we have to figure out who's trying to kill me and why."

"I want to kill you right now, Jay, and I know why."

"Ok, Jane, but can you kill me later? Maybe?" Jane and I spend the next couple of hours running down what has happened and what we know. I can see Edmond is upset about his family's involvement, but I could feel from him he is as clueless about why as we are and is determined to help figure it out. Glenda has dinner delivered as we talk over varying scenarios, and finally Alpha Lisa leaves to make sure her boys are settled for the night. I placed them in suites in the main house since they have the twins and their caretakers and would need more space. As she heads out, I see Samuel following her every move. I smile happy for him, I look at him. "Go with her, make sure things are good, you won't be of any use if you're worried about her and the boys." He says thanks and gets up, leaving to go after her.

I see Edmond doesn't look happy to see Mark and Samantha talking and laughing, I forgot he had a minor crush on both from the island, poor Edmond. "I think we should call it a night, everyone, we've all had a long day." As we file out, I go with them to the front door. I grab Jane and give her a tight hug. "You can look on the bright side, our company has no competition at this point, the market is ours. So am I forgiven, partner?" She hugs me back saying she guesses. "Great to hear, Jane." I let everyone know the casitas run along the rear of the house, as per my instructions there are keys on the front hook to each. "Pick which one you want and then keep the keys. I hope you like your accommodations. Have a good night's sleep and I'll see you all for breakfast."

I turn and head to the hall at the far end of the house. This hallway leads directly to my suite, and I'm ready for a shower and a good night's rest. I enter my code in the door and I'm happy with what I see. I've periodically been looking at the progress online, but seeing it in person makes it feel real. Knowing this is going to be my home for the rest of my life. Once you enter, there's an open floor plan with a living area. At the far right, there are stairs that take you up to the sleeping areas. Ahead to the left is the dining area, and straight behind is the kitchen with a large island. In the living area on the same wall as the entry door is a floor to ceiling fireplace.

I can't wait to hang out in my space, but for now I need to rest, as tomorrow will be longer than today. I pull my phone from my pocket and send a text to my Alphas. I set up a group text for all of us, I let them know everything is going well and I'm heading to bed and will call them in the morning to give them the rundown of things. Now that I'm in residence, I can finally be me, no more hiding behind Beta Scott. I kick off my shoes, placing them on the shoe stand by the front door. There's a closet I set up specifically for coats and shoes, but I don't have time for that right now. I slowly drag myself upstairs, turning left towards my bedroom suite. I push open the doors and barely look around as I head to the bathroom. No time for admiration I turn on the shower to warm as I peel off my clothes tossing them on the hamper.

I jump in, happy that my favorite wash is here. I do my thing, jump out, and towel off. As I look at myself in the mirror, even I'm surprised to be looking at both my eyes again. It has been so long since I have seen them and it feels good to be me. I also feel the power I don't have to use to change myself flowing through me and it feels good. I can't wait to begin training. I've not really trained like a full blown Alpha in months. It's going to feel good to see what I can do after months of holding us back. I look through my luggage for a night shirt, pull it on and climb under the covers. Night, Jewel. "*Night, Jay.*"

Chapter 16

ALPHA JAIDAN

I wake early the next morning, wondering who among the group will bend the neck. This is the first time I'm asking this and I'm nervous about it. I stretch my limbs, procrastination will get you nowhere, Jay. I push my body up and head into my walk-in closet. It's massive because I love clothes, most of what I own has been delivered and put away. Glenda knows what I like and how I like it. I must thank her for the effort she put into getting my things put away.

I'm thinking I should wear something queenly, then start laughing. There's nothing queenly about me besides the Q on my body. I opt for a pair of black slacks with a beige long sleeve button up blouse and I pull my hair into a tight bun at the back of my head. I realize now that no one in the conference room required me to prove I was the Ruler besides seeing my eyes and taking my word for it. I wonder about that now; they should be more careful of people. I mean, my guys know, but the rest of them should have been more skeptical. I will mention that to Samantha, Pete and Jane, this morning. I feel like I'm ready, I grab my phone and head down, once again, not really paying attention to my room.

It's what I wanted but I have much to do and little time to do it.

When I get to the bottom of the stairs, I begin contemplating what shoes I'll wear. I hate anything that's a dress shoe, so I pick shoe boots, ones that aren't very high, are cute and comfy, my favorite kind. I put them on, pull up the zippers on the insides, and head out the door, pressing the lock code on the way out. The dining room is in the opposite direction of the conference room and as I approach, I can hear numerous loud voices. I enter and the voices quiet. "Good morning, everyone." They all respond good morning, Alpha. Really, well this is going to take some getting used to, even on the island I wasn't called Alpha.

I head to the front of the room where I see Jane, Pete, Samuel, Lisa, Mark, Samantha, and Edmond all standing waiting for me to join them. I approach and get the feeling something isn't quite right. I sense unhappiness. I slow my steps, not sure who it's coming from. With so many in the room I can't pinpoint it. I must work on this power the most. It can be my most effective tool if I can control it to the point where I can look at a person and narrow the feeling to that person specifically. That's what I'll work on the most while here, I approach my group, "I hope you all slept well."

"We did, Jay, but we have a problem."

"And that is, Jane?"

"Your security team thinks they have priority over who has access to you. We have to establish a pack order before we can move forward."

"But that's ridiculous, I can't choose a pack until I have my mates."

"We know, and Rulers in the past didn't have this problem because they were only needing a Luna. The Alpha usually arrived with his Beta and Gamma picked from the Regional Packs he visited along the way or the ones who were with him on the island."

"I know what I'll do Jane," because of course I can do this. "Let's begin. Everyone, the first order of the day will be to choose my ruling pack. I know my Gamma will be Gamma Mark. He was the Gamma with me on the island and like a brother to me. Mark please join me here." He comes to the head of the room, offers his hand palm up as I extend my claw. I slice his palm then I slice mine and I grab his hand, combining my blood with his. He takes a knee and bends his neck speaking loudly for all to hear.

"I, Gamma Mark Long, accept you, Alpha Jaidan Emerald Scott, as my Ruling Alpha Queen. I promise to Loyally Defend, Protect and Serve you with my life."

"Thank you, Mark and I, Alpha Jaidan Emerald Scott, Ruling Alpha Queen, accept you as my Ruling Gamma. I promise to Defend, Protect and Serve you with my life."

He rises and goes to kiss my hand, but I pull him up to give him a hug and kiss his cheek. He goes back to his seat a little less steady on his feet, I say into his head so that only he can hear. "You'll be stronger because of me sharing my blood, and all your strengths will be enhanced." He smiles at me, saying that's cool. I look out again. "I choose Beta Jane Jamison to be my Beta, please join me," she rises slowly and moves towards me.

"Are you sure about this, Jay?"

"Of course I am." She offers her palm and I extend my claw and slice her palm then I slice mine. I grab her hand, combining my blood with hers. She takes a knee and bends her neck.

"I, Beta Jane Jamison, accept you, Alpha Jaidan Emerald Scott, as my Ruling Alpha Queen. I promise to Loyally Defend, Protect and

Serve you with my life."

"I, Alpha Jaidan Emerald Scott, Ruling Alpha Queen accept you as my Ruling Beta. I promise to Defend, Protect, and Serve you with my life." When she rises, I hug and kiss her on the cheek as well, noticing she's way more stable on her feet than Mark was. "That's my strong girl," I whisper to her. "You're going to love the enhanced power you receive from joining my pack." I look out to the rest of the room. "My Beta and my Gamma will be the first line of contact to me. They will inform you on who you go to below them. Beta Jamison will be head of the Security team effective immediately. You'll soon see she's the best at that job, besides me of course.

Gamma Mark will be head of pack training. When I kick your asses during training, which begins on Monday, know you owe it to him for the years of training he's put me through. This morning begins with you now choosing to accept me as your Alpha, bending the neck or not. If not, you leave this room, those on the security team know your options and what your time frame on this is, but you'll not stay in this room today if you choose not to accept me now. I would like to add that a part of the original ritual does not include the word learn. However, I've learned a lot from many on my path to where I stand, and I'm open to learning more in the future.

I believe in an open-door policy and will accept all teachings that move us forward as a people. Shall we begin?" Samuel and Lisa are the first to step forward and the rest of the morning goes as it went with Jane and Mark, minus the palm slicing. That's a power I only share with my personal pack. Never the less, I have a personal greeting for each to let them know I can communicate with them because they all belong to my pack. When Edmond comes forward, he asks, how I knew he didn't want to be my

Ruling Beta? "You told me you wanted to teach, and being stuck on another compound wasn't for you. Just the same, I can find a position here if you want it."

"No, Jay, absolutely not. I was praying you didn't call me the whole time."

"I knew it, Edmond, and you have to catch me up on which university you chose."

"Later, you have a line behind you."

When the line is complete I notice there were only two of the security team who left, deciding they wanted to take some time to consider. When they leave the room, I see Glenda standing in the doorway, I walk towards her and feel sadness in her. "Glenda, why are you sad?" I thought you would choose Edmond to be your Ruling Beta, she says. "Oh Glenda, he didn't want that position, he wants to teach at university." She just looks at me and I hug her. "It's going to be just fine." She pulls away and rushes off. Samuel comes up to my side, asking what's wrong with Glenda. "She's sad Edmond won't be staying. She was sad I didn't choose him as my Beta, but he didn't want the position. He's going to teach at university."

"I'm sure he'll come back and visit with her, Jay."

"Of course he will," I turn to the room, closing the door. "Those of you who are here, I thank you for the commitment you've made to the future of our kind. Let's enjoy our breakfast and then we will move to the security offices to get to work." I head to my table, ready to dig in, but I have this feeling I just missed something, something very important, but I can't put my finger on it. Jane walks up next, distracting me from my thoughts.

"What's up boss?"

"You're not going to start calling me that."

"Fine I won't call you that, Jay."

"Thank you, Jane."

"I received the list of the Alphas who are attending the week after the Regional Alphas arrive. You're not going to believe who's on the list as security for my pack."

"Let me guess, Beta Matt."

"Exactly, also you need to contact Tony, he called thinking something happened to me when I dropped from my pack."

"That explains why my phone is blowing up. What did you tell him?"

"I said the Ruler will notify him and let him know what's going on. Was that ok?"

"Sure, I imagine Mark is having to do the same thing, only Richard knows it's me, he won't have to answer so many questions."

"Really, how is that?"

"Richard was in the office when I killed Beta Carlson. He was there when I used my Alpha power. I was so upset I couldn't hold onto my ruse, but he was less upset than I thought he would be. He was more upset about me commanding him to keep my secret."

"I can only imagine, Jay, and I hate to be you when you reveal to my old Alpha."

"I hate to be there, as well, but let's eat and then get to work. Wait till you see the security offices. You're going to love it. We also must get the company organization updated. I originally had Olivia Parker on there, so that must be changed, but I think we still need another person. We must decide who that should be. We have a lot to decide over the next few weeks. I need to know all that was to happen by the time my Alphas arrive. We have to start thinking out of the box."

I take my seat and begin filling my plate with cheesy scrambled eggs, bacon, sausage, and toast. I obviously was a lot hungrier than I thought. Once I fill my belly, I head to the front of the room, "Excuse me everyone, from this room there's a hallway that leads to the security room. You will have to set up your own security passcode. This will give you access to the first door. However, you'll have to have your eyes scanned and your fingerprint taken simultaneously to enter the next door. The same fingerprint and passcode you set up will give you access to your computer terminal.

The security team members have already set this up, so they can enter first. Then the rest of you can go through. Samuel, Lisa, Samantha and Pete, we have to decide how long you're going to be here because you're all in the system for temporary access. When you each step up, I'll input how long so the system will allow you access based on that time frame." Samuel and Lisa move forward, and say they both will be here until my Alphas arrive, maybe a month. I enter the date, and they move forward.

Samantha chooses sixty days, she wants to stay until her born day, which is in fifty or so days. She won't know if Mark is her mate until then, and if he's not, she's going back to her pack. Pete is still trying to figure out what he's going to do about his Beta position at home, we just enter ninety days for now. Once everyone is logged in, I enter and head to the security room, and I'm not surprised to see the biggest smile on Jane's face as she peruses through the system. Also, not surprisingly, she booted one of the security guys from the largest terminal, taking it over for herself.

I pull out my laptop and connect to the system from the seat originally set up for Jane. Not everyone in this room cares about the electronic shit, so there are desks they can work at without terminals. "Jane, can you please update everyone on what we're trying to determine. Maybe someone here will see something we didn't. Edmond, you should be prepared because one of our theories is going to be upsetting to you."

"Really, Jay, more than my father being involved?"

"Yes, more than that, Jane please, Jane."

"Yes, sorry, this system is amazing."

"That's great. So can you begin?" As she gives everyone the run-down, I concentrate on watching each person, trying to gauge their responses. Unfortunately I'm not sensing anything out of the ordinary. Edmond is seething with disbelief, anger, hurt, sadness, anger, mostly anger, which I can understand. I would feel that way if I found out my mother survived and chose to leave me. Chose to not be a part of my life. He rises from his seat and I rise to follow him, but he puts up his hands.

"You were right, this is upsetting, I can't be of help right now, I need to get out of here. If I think of anything besides wanting to kill someone, I'll come back."

"Edmond, you don't know what she was thinking, and this theory might not be true."

"Based on what you found, Jay, it's the most logical explanation. I also have to deal with the fact that the woman who birthed me is also trying to kill one of the closest people to me."

He turns and hugs me, then moves away. "Edmond."

"No, Jay, I need to think and be gone from here."

Edmond walks out and Samuel walks up, saying he will go talk to him since he doesn't see anything that changes my perspective. "Thank you, Samuel."

I walk over to Alpha Lisa; she grabs my hand, saying how brave I am to take on this task because she's not sure she could. "Yes you could, Alpha Lisa, you're doing it for your boys." I love them and they give me the courage, she says. "I had a Nanna who I loved and told me everyday I could do anything. I also had Samuel, Edmond, and Mark training me, teaching me, preparing me. I love our kind and know we can be better than we are. I'm going to try it, but believe me, I wasn't sure in the beginning.

I actually have a separate life set up for myself, just in case I needed to get away and be someone else." At least you had a backup plan, she responds. I look her in the face. "What is it, Alpha Lisa?" I want to thank you, she says, for giving Alpha Samuel the freedom to be with me. "You don't have to thank me for anything, Alpha Samuel was never mine to free. Any limitations he put on himself were self-inflicted, I only helped him realize that. Besides I'll have my hands full with my three mates."

"What?"

She looks at me. "Yes, three." Then she looks upset. Don't worry, I will love them equally and individually. Richard already knows he may be one of three, and they're already used to sharing their bed partners." She responds, doubtfully,

"I'm aware of this, but sharing a mate, I'm not sure Alphas can do that."

"I think mine will, but I knew all along Samuel would not. I just think he didn't realize he wouldn't."

"He told me it's because his mate rejected him for being a second son. He didn't really feel the rejection as hard as his wolf and his wolf wants his own mate."

She continues, telling me that they've decided to be chosen mates. They will wait until her boys are eighteen so they don't have any pups who could challenge them. I look at her. "Are you good with that?" She tells me that she's nervous about it. "You know, Lisa, you'll only get pregnant if you're marked and mated, there is nothing that says you can't mark him to keep the she-wolves away. Once the females know he's on the market he'll be food for the she-wolf mommas. Especially with his connection to me."

"You know, I didn't consider that, but I'm concerned I mark him, would it be fair to him, that he can't mark me."

"There's only one way to find out, and I suggest you find out before the Luna party that's being prepared. Once they arrive and see I'm a female who has all my mates, who are the three Regional Alphas at that, there are going to be some very upset she-wolves." She agrees with me saying she would give it more thought. I leave Alpha Lisa to join Jane, hoping to discuss the connection we found with Beta Matt and Beta Shaw.

She was completely caught up with learning the new system that she didn't even acknowledge me. I returned to going over the company organization and setting her up as my new partner. I send out updated emails to our clients, and updating the banking information. With getting all my personal company data logged onto the new network, the day flew by. For dinner we move to the dining hall. While everyone is talking and enjoying themselves it makes me feel like I finally have the pack life I wish I would have had growing up.

Edmond is missing, but Samuel informs me he's doing as best he can, so I take his word for it and eventually we called it a night. I was happy, and at least tonight I wasn't as tired. I spend some time admiring the work I had done on the pack house as a whole, and it looks great. I finally go to my suite, which looks like me with bright countertops, dark cabinetry, dark floors, white walls, and a lot of light from large windows. I'm more than happy with the end results. I remove my shoes near the front door and move to the living area, taking a seat on the couch, pulling my phone out to call Richard.

"Jay, how are you?"

"Things are going well, we're going to have to decide what to do about Pete. I've made Mark my Ruling Gamma and Jane my Ruling Beta, and I can't imagine he would want to be away from his mate. Since you're probably my mate, it only makes sense for him to continue as your Beta from here."

"That all sounds well, but who will be the Regional Alpha for this pack? I have no children, as you know, what's the plan, Jay?"

"There was no plan, Richard, I had no idea you all would be my mates, but after speaking with Alpha Small today, I think a solution is developing. How about we hold those positions for our future pups?"

"How will we determine which of our pups hold the ruling Alpha position?"

"No, Richard, remember that's not how this position works. This position is filled by a Ruler being born when prophesied. Any pups born with my mates will continue to become the Alpha of the pack they came from. That's how it has happened in the past, no reason it should change now."

"That sounds like how it should be done, do we divide our time, Jay?"

"No, you put in place stewards for our pups when they're born to hold their place. With technology these days, you don't have to be at your packs full time to run, them and I'm sure your parents can step in to help, based on this unique situation."

"You seem to have figured it all out."

"Yep, with my Mighty Man's help."

"Have you told Jarrod and Tony about this plan?"

"Nope, planning on telling them when they arrive with you."

"You're expecting me to keep this secret for that long?"

"Absolutely, Richard, and thank you. I have to go,Tony's freaking out about losing his best Beta to the Ruler."

"At least he's not losing his pack Beta, that honor is mine. Night, Jay."

"Night, Richard." I hang up and call Tony.

"What the hell, Jay, who does he think he is to just scoop up my pack member without at least discussing it with me?"

"It was discussed with me, Tony. And remember when I was in New York, we discussed Jane coming to work for my company, and you were alright with that. Well for her to do that she was always going to be leaving your pack; she made that decision."

"But Jay, if you're my Luna aren't you coming back to my pack? Where will that leave Jane?"

"In the capable hands of the Ruler, I presume, but for now, you know she's alive and safe with me, right?"

"I guess you're right, but something just doesn't make sense to me, Jay."

"Did you receive my package?"

"Yes, Jay."

"And, Tony?

"And, what Jay?"

"Don't you have something to say, Tony?

"Thank you, Jay."

"You don't sound very happy, Tony. "

"I'm not. You stole my Beta, and if you think returning my bike makes up for it, you're wrong."

"I could have kept your bike, and I would have been within my rights to keep it, and then I would have had them both. You act like you'll never see Beta Jamison again, you will, I promise. And when you arrive at Haven, you can see for yourself, you know she found her mate right?"

"*Yes, I heard.*"

"You were probably going to lose her to Richard's pack anyway because he's the Beta of his pack."

"*At least I know Richard.*"

"You know me, and I represent the Ruler."

"*What else is going on, Jay? Have you figured out who's trying to kill you?*"

"Not exactly. We think we know who's involved, but we're missing one key person. Beta Matt from your pack is involved as well as your uncle, but we need them to come to Haven. Any tip to them that we're onto them will not be good, so don't let on we know anything."

"*I can't believe my uncle would have anything to do with this, Jay.*"

"And you, Jarrod and Richard meeting in Miami makes you believe that."

"*Oohh, you know about that.*"

"I do, we have to consider everyone."

"*Very well, I have to go, Jay. I have a lot to put in place now that you've stolen the head of my security, and the next best person had to be relocated to my DC offices.*"

"Since Jane is working for the Ruler from here, why not make her the head of all the Regional Security Offices and make everyone at each office you trust be second in command under her? Your guy in DC can take on her role and be the head of the firm just from his DC location."

"That actually sounds like a great idea, Jay. I'll get that set up, I miss you and can't wait to see you."

"You'll be here before you know it and I miss you, too."

"You'll have your born day soon and then that sexy little body of yours will be all mine."

"You do know Jarrod or Richard might be my mate, or you all might be my mates?"

"I'm aware, Jay, I don't care about that, just as long as I can get my hands on you. I'm not a selfish wolf when it comes to Jarrod and Richard only.

"Good to know. Night, Alpha."

"Night, Jay."

Chapter 17

ALPHA JAIDAN

B<u>*irthday Surprise*</u>

I hang up the phone, tired and ready to get some sleep. I contemplate calling Jarrod, but as I go up the stairs, I get a text from him. He's in meetings and will call me in the morning, I was a little relieved. I rushed into the bathroom to shower and change into my night shirt. My mind is reeling over the decisions made today, but they've been good ones. Tomorrow, we begin training bright and early in the morning, and six o'clock will arrive before I know it. I crawl into bed, glad for the cool comfy covers, but wishing I had a warm Alpha to snuggle up next to. Night, Jewel. *"Night, Jay."*

The next morning, I wake early, hoping to get to the training field before Mark. I throw on my leggings, training bra and socks, then grab my phone and run downstairs. I put on my Nikes from the closet and head out. I requested a cooler with bottled water be provided for every training morning. I head out the back of the pack house, exiting through the garage, jogging the quarter mile to get to the training field, passing by some of the casitas on the way. I notice a couple of people leaving them, Jane jogs to join me.

"You ready for this, Jay?"

"I'm excited to begin." When we finally hit the field, I see I'm not the only one who wanted to get here early. I see Mark in the front, jumping up and down, his form of warming up his legs. "Alright, Jane, you do your best to stay out of the Alpha's way. If anyone give you shit for not being an Alpha, you tell me. With the increased power boost, you should be alright, though." I move forward, standing next to Mark. He looks to me, asking if I will be leading this training now.

"Not at all, but I do want to say something. Good morning, listen up everyone! When I was at the California pack, they had a training system that was set up where everyone starts off as equals. We started out in the groups that we fell into from our run time. The security team will know this part already. There's a five-mile path circling this training field that will automatically track your run time once you begin, no one will keep your time for you. I've provided a watch for each of you in the box on the bench behind me.

The one you take is yours moving forward, and it will keep up with your training starting from today. I don't care if you're female or male, Alpha or Beta, the system determines which group you fall into. The system determines which group you train with, and the system determines if or when you improve to move up, if that's what you want to do or need to do. Don't come to me to complain about the system. I won't change anything in the system. I'll also tell you the system was set up to compare you to me. So, if you ever get to the point in the system where you beat it, you are more than welcome to challenge me.

I welcome you to. Like in the past, every Alpha must hold his or her Alpha-hood. Lastly, Gamma Mark will run this training. What he says, I say, I know that might be difficult for some of the Alphas in this group. My advice to you is to get over it. Gamma Mark, the field is yours." I move to join the rest of the crowd.

"Thank you. As Alpha Jaidan said, I'm here to help and guide you in any way I can. I'll set your training schedule based off the recommendations from the system that's monitoring you. You will learn I take training seriously; I believe if you slack off, you die. I've taken Alpha Jaidan competing in various forms of combat for the last ten years. We've won most, if not all of those in the last eight years.

So, Let's get this started. If you'll come and choose your watch, you will see behind you the starting line for the running course. It takes you through the pack grounds, which will lead you around to exit to the left of me there." He points, then continues. "I will tell you I ran this track yesterday, so you will have to pay attention. I always believe in training. This is how I trained Alpha Jaidan on the island, this is how I will train you here. As you can see, I have my watch on, I completed my run this morning.

When you come up to grab yours, you're welcome to see my time, it's not a secret. You'll be able to login and see where you are regarding everyone until you're placed in a group. Once you're placed, then you will only see your group placing until you move into another group. Take notice I don't say move up because if you don't train harder you can move down in grouping. With that being said, there is no competition. It depends on you and where you want your training to be. The only ones required to maintain a high-level placement is the security team who provide protection for Alpha Jaidan, myself, and Beta Jane. Other than that it's only the minimum training required in case the pack grounds need to be protected. The weakest wolf is always the weakest link in our security."

After Mark finishes talking, we all move forward and grab our watches. I didn't care which color I got, they're identical in function, but I ended up with a gray one. I put it on, setting it up so it can record my run. I start walking to the route with the rest of the group. When Mark shoots the flare gun and we all take off.

I'm familiar with this type of course as are most of us here. I pace myself, but Jewel is fired up and wants to move, I lower my hold and let her go. Within minutes we're in the front of the line, leaving everyone behind. The crazy thing is I don't even feel like I've exerted much energy. Jewel, this is amazing. When I finally run into the clearing, even Mark's surprised to see me this soon.

"Jay, that's crazy how fast you finished that course. I don't think any Ruler in the past has been as fast as you. I don't think you're going to be in any group."

"That's fine, I'll train with you." I turn and see Jane, Samuel, Lisa and a couple of the security team enter the field. I need to start learning their names. I know that one of them who has entered is one who hasn't bent the neck. He's watching me and I feel his confusion. He walks up to me saying, Alpha Scott, can I see your watch? "Absolutely." I provide my arm, he looks at it. "You did see me pass you on the course though, right?" Yes, he responds, but I wasn't sure exactly, you're fast. "Yes, I am."

He walks away and after the rest of the group arrives, Mark sends everyone their groupings and a couple of the Alphas weren't happy with Jane being in their group. Her mate wanted to kick ass for them being that way, but he didn't make it into their group and that settled it for now. If he becomes Richard's Beta, he'll get his increased power as well. All the other Betas in the group are training together, and even though Samantha is a Gamma she is placed in the group with the Betas.

I imagine that's due to her training with Mark most of the time. Once everyone is separated into their groups, we start hand to hand combat, alternating between human and wolf forms to shake it up whenever Mark blows the whistle. Since I placed above this group, I just watch. We decided I would help and advise where needed, and eventually took on the training of just Jane because the Alphas in the groups were letting her Beta blood get in the way.

It wasn't a challenge for me, but I was happy to teach her some new techniques like I did with Olivia. After two hours, Mark calls it a day. We head in for breakfast and when it's done, Alpha Leo from the security team comes up to me and bends the neck. I accept him and welcome him privately like I did the rest. Now I only have one hold out and I feel like I've made great progress. I was sad the one holdout was a female Alpha. I thought her being a female she'd be more open, but you never know about these things.

After Alpha Leo walks away, she looks at me annoyed, I'm not sure why she's annoyed but I'll deal with her at the end of the week. For now she's allowed to feel how she wants. I did notice she did well in her training, she was in the group with Alpha Lisa and she wasn't happy about it. I walked over to Lisa saying, "Hey, what did you think about the other female Alpha in your group?"

"I don't like her." And I can't wait to get Samuel away from here. She kept smiling at him with those damn blue eyes. He was ignoring her but still. She fights well, though. Why?"

"She hasn't chosen to bend the neck, but she has until the end of the week to make a decision." You're more generous than I would be, she responds. "Lisa, you need to get on with thinking about that marking we talked about." She's still not sure, but I tell her to remember what I warned her about. I walk away and head to my suite to get showered and dressed for the workday. "Jane, I'll meet you in the security room. I might have thought of something to help us figure out the who and why of the California Omega."

"Sounds good, Jay, but I'm going to be late. My mate is having some issues after training this morning."

"Is he ok, Jane? Does he need to go to the clinic? I have a full staff on board."

"No, it's more like his bruised ego on the inside."

"Oh, I understand, I'll see you when you get there." I head out to go to my room, waving to Samuel and Lisa who are talking to the caretakers with the twins as they are leaving the pack house. They are taking them to go running around outside. I decided that I want to have a playground put in for them but haven't figured it all out yet. I wasn't aware they were coming, but they seem to love to just run around in the woods.

The next few week's flew by, training went well, and a couple of the members moved up. The last remaining security member decided she didn't want to be a part of the new kind of pack and left the compound. I think it had less to do with me being a female and more with Samuel showing up the next morning for training marked by Alpha Lisa. The following day she was gone, it didn't even take her the rest of the week. I had Jane disable all her access and set up a security watch on her for the next ten years. I also want to make sure Samuel and Lisa are safe.

I was happy about them and laughed my ass off when I saw the tattoo on Lisa's neck that read POS, property of Samuel. They wanted to get a smell infused with her tattoo but weren't able to. Lisa agreed to have a special perfume created that smells like Samuel's favorite cologne. That way she's wearing his scent on her even if it doesn't permeate from her skin like it would if she was marked.

I haven't figured out the where of the California Omega, but we figured out she's the one who's behind everything. We had the cemetery of Beta Matts mother dug up and confirmed she was indeed dead. This was done secretly to not alert her daughter. We realize they're going to use the Alpha meeting to get access to me for revenge. She used Alpha Edward to give her niece access to his pack's security company so she can get into Haven. We think she'll come in with her niece or one of the other packs. Any other pack who bring any older female wolves with them after my Alphas arrive will be held separate from the rest. We'll take samples of their DNA to check it against what we have from the dead excavated Omega.

We're confident that will be our California Omega. With this plan in place, we relax and train. I work on pinpointing my power so I can feel who is feeling what. Once my Alphas arrive, I'll have my born-day celebration and get my mates boost which will make me more than ready to protect myself when the rest of the Alphas arrive. I'll stop this damn Omega and whoever is supporting her. I'm excited to see my Alphas, I just want a small affair with my favorite people, enjoying good food, great desserts, and good conversation and we plan to do just that. And in two days my favorite men will arrive, and the following day it will be my twenty-fifth born day.

I join Jane in the security room, and she tells me the wipes we created to retrieve the DNA are ready. I grab one, wipe my hands and drop it in the bin, a few minutes later the report on the screen says zero percent match. She tries it after me to see it works as well, with the same result. We have one of the female security members named Rose use one, and again zero percent match. I'm satisfied now. We just need to decide where to set it up and what ruse to use that will require them all to use it upon entering the room.

Samantha walks in the room eating a chocolate candy bar, sees the wipes and grabs one cleaning her hands and tosses it in the bin, not even paying attention to us. We all start laughing, she looks at us, asking what she did. "You just helped us figure something out." Well, whatever it was your welcome, she says, right before her results come up zero percent match. We'll have someone offer them chocolates to taste, saying it's the Ruler's favorite treat, which is the truth. Then offer them the wipe to clean their hands and require them to put the wipe in the bin.

Once it passes the lid, it's scanned for any DNA, then the wipe is disintegrated in seconds. Whoever is responsible for this will have to be one of us, so that they wait the required five seconds between each wipe entering the bin. Samantha volunteers to do it, because it will give her something to do while Mark is doing his security shit. "Great, Samantha, thank you." I need to leave so I can figure out which outfit to wear for my born day.

"Hey, Jay, how about we have a girls' night, and we can help you pick something new from your wardrobe?"

"Sounds like fun, Jane, we'll meet in my suite around seven tonight. I have a couple of bottles of California sangria. I'll also have some snacks delivered, see y'all then." Later that night when they arrive, I yell for them to join me in my closet. When they enter with all their favorite snacks, I'm chewing on a chocolate bar sitting on my ottoman seat, having had no luck in choosing anything. When Jane enters, she sits in the corner on the floor, only Jane would arrive with chewy candy and her laptop. I can tell she will be of no help. "I'll sit here, and you all tell me what to wear."

Rose, Samantha, Lisa, and Jane occasionally, go through almost all my options before they settle on a sleeveless thigh high silver dress. It's simple but sexy, and my added curves make it work. Plus, this color represents perfectly, it being my twenty-fifth born day, which is the color for that year. I'll pair it with silver strap sandals, my hair in a loose bun on the top of my head revealing my mark, and appropriately matched jewelry. I'm happy with their selection and wonder why I didn't think of it myself.

We spend the rest of the night laughing and speculating on which of the three Alphas will be my mate or how I will handle it if it's all three. Or which one would I want it to be and would I be disappointed if it's not. But over all, it was a fun night, and I was exhausted by the time everyone left. I put on my night shirt and crawl into bed. Jewel, what do you think about our Alphas? "*I think they all belong to us, and they'll be here tomorrow.*" Really, Jewel? "*Yes, it's after twelve and I can feel the mate power building in me and I'm ready for it, Jay, are you?*" "I believe so, Jewel. "*Night, Jay, you are going to need your rest once they arrive.*" Night, Jewel.

I spend the next day pampering myself, taking care of all the places that needed extra shaving, cleansing and softening the places that needed softening. I start feeling like a prune after hours of soaking in a tub full of jasmine oils. I rub myself down with my special jasmine infused shea butter and dress in a grey pair of cotton lounge pants with a matching short sleeve top that's paired with a short robe. Samantha painted my toes silver and I love it, I don't put on socks.

I had lunch in my suite and was surprised when the Alphas began arriving earlier than planned. I had security escort them to their rooms that are connected to my suite through their closets but they're not aware of it now. I send a group text once I know they're in residence requesting they join me for dinner in my suite with directions on how to locate me at seven tonight as secretly as they can. I'm excited to see them all, especially because I haven't seen Jarrod in the longest time and I miss him terribly.

I order dinner for us, as well as Vodka for Richard, Bourbon for Tony, and Whiskey for Jarrod, and of course I have bottles of my favorite Sangria. When the meal arrives, I set the table and put the bottles with tumblers for them each. I turn the fireplace on and sit at the head of the table to wait, nerves tingling in my belly. I know Jarrod and Richard will be on time, Tony will be late because he'll take extra time to get ready. But I'm not opening the door until I sense them all out there.

To my surprise they must've decided to descend on me together, because promptly at seven, a knock came on my door. When I opened it, there stood my mates. And yes, I can feel the tingles running amok on my skin and I haven't even touched them yet. "Hello Jarrod, Tony, and Richard, please come in." As they pile in, I peruse them all. All six feet four of Jarrod's tanned slender muscles bulging from his short sleeve shirt. I missed his face and his man-bun. He's clean shaven tonight, showing off his sexy square jaw. I step up smiling, looking into his beautiful gray eyes. I hug him tightly, loving his minty chocolate scent. "I've missed you, my Alpha man, glad you made it here safely." He's hugging me tight.

"I missed you too, Jay, and these tingles are filling me with joy, babe."

I release him, pointing to the table, asking him to have a seat. I look over at Tony, his soulful dark eyes smiling down at me. He's not quite as tall as Jarrod but built thicker in all the right places, from what I remember. I step into his open arms, breathing in his coco-mocha scent and loving the feel of him around me. I reach up, rubbing his bald head, running my fingers through his soft beard. I enjoy his fingers smoothing along the back of my neck. I sense him taking in my scent as well.

"I've missed you, my sweet Jay."

"I've missed you, to, my mocha Alpha. Please have a seat." And finally, I turn to Richard. He's the shorter, bulkier one of my Alphas, sporting a short crew cut and clean-shaven face today. His brown eyes are smiling back at me and I step into his open arms as well. "I know I saw you recently, but I've still missed you, Mighty Man." He smiles down, pulling me close and hugging me tight. His chocolate honey goodness scent overloads my senses. "Ok, let's join the others at the table" And as we move to join Jarrod and Tony, I take in how great it feels to finally be in the same room with them all at once.

"I've ordered your favorites for dinner while we catch up. You know we all feel the tingles, and I'm pretty sure you're all my mates. We will have to decide how it'll go if it's something you all want to do. I've come up with a way it can work, but you're the ones who must ultimately decide, and I'll accept whatever you decide, since it's your life as well as mine. First, I'll start with sharing that I'm the Ruler, which I'm sure you know based on the fact that none of you are surprised."

"We all guessed it based on pieces of information we had after spending time with you babe."

"You are correct, Jarrod. How do you feel about it? Oh, by the way Richard, I rescind my command."

"Thank you, Jay."

Jarrod looks at Richard.

"What's that about?"

"Jay revealed herself to me about two weeks before she left my pack."

"And you didn't tell us?"

"I didn't because of the command, Jarrod."

"Oh, that must have been shitty."

"It wasn't fun, Jarrod, but I understood it because that same night I wanted to call and talk to you guys about it, and I couldn't."

"Tony, do you have anything to say, you seem quiet?"

"I'm just wondering, Jay, how it would work with all of us being your mates?"

"Yes, Tony, let me explain. I thought, like in the past, the pups of the current Ruler would continue to be the Alpha of whichever pack the Luna of the pack came from. This way her family didn't lose their Alpha-hood if there already wasn't one. I thought we could do the same in our situation. The position of Ruler is prophesied, not regionally birthed, and most of the time the Luna comes from one of the regional packs. I suggest when we have pups, we have them become the Regional Alphas of the perspective packs of their father. This way the Regional Alpha-hood is continued."

"Sounds like a good plan, but what do we do about who holds those positions until then."

"You hold those positions for them, Jarrod, until they are old enough to take them. It will be hard for us in the beginning, but not impossible, and with technology we can manage when you're all here with me. Or we can rotate and travel from one pack to the other throughout the year. There's no reason I must be held up at Haven the whole time. I'm the Ruler; I can make the rules I want to follow. So, what do you think? Tony, Jarrod, Richard, do you want to be my mates? If not, whichever one of you doesn't, you'll hold your pack, and I'll make it work with the other, and know I will miss you being a part of my life. With that being said, I'll not force this life on any of you. I care too much for each of you to do that." Richard smiles at me.

"I'm in, Jay."

I smile at him, Jarrod says he's in, as well."Tony?"

"I'm not sure, Jay, I never thought I would share my mate. At first, I thought I would accept you any way that I can have you, but now I'm not sure. I always thought it would be only what we did as musketeers but when it came to pups and family life, I would have mine, you both would have yours, and we would laugh about the good old days."

I walk over to him without touching, as badly as I want to. "You're more than welcome to make that decision." He looks at me, a sad smile in his eyes and on his lips. "How about we enjoy this dinner and have a couple of drinks." I return to my seat and begin putting food on plates, pouring myself a large glass of sangria. It never occurred to me that one of my Alphas wouldn't choose me, and I'm beginning to feel the pain just from the thought of it. I quietly serve them, smiling as I take a gulp from my glass.

I see Jarrod watching me over his tumbler, smiling, trying to make me feel better. I look over to Richard and he's stuffing his face, not a care in the world, while sipping on his vodka every now and then. I fill my plate with fried chicken and collard greens. Surprisingly, it's some of the meal I had when I was in New York with Tony and a lot of what he now put on his plate. I can tell he's distracted; he's probably having a not-so-happy discussion with Asher. I start eating, and though the food is good, it's like sawdust in my mouth. Richard calls out, getting my attention.

"Jay, how is Star settling in?"

I look at him. "She's fine, I've ridden her quite a bit since she's been here. My stallions are excited to get at her but she's a boss bitch, and until she goes in season they're shit out of luck. I admit I'm excited to see which of the two she lets get at her first. Whichever one it is she's going to have a beautiful foal,"

"That's nice."

"Jay, who is Star?"

"She's the mare Richard bought me, Tony, and she's beautiful."

"Wait, let me get this straight, he bought you a horse?"

"Yes, it was very sweet of him, too."

"Yes it was."

Tony looks to Richard.

"You're a suck up, Rich."

Richard looks at Tony and smiles.

"You're right I am."

We all start laughing, I'm grabbing my belly, it's hurting me really bad. I finally feel the tension in the room dissipate.

"I needed to even the odds with you guys. You, Jarrod, with your damn surfing, and you, Tony with that damn monster bike of yours, she was gushing about. And since she missed my ski season, and sucks at it masterfully by the way, I needed something to put me on equal footing. Mark told me about the two horses, I bought her one and I think it was a great idea."

"You were right, Richard, it was, and I wish I would have thought of it."

"Me too, Jarrod, I spent the first couple of weeks complaining about her taking my bike. When she left, she gave it back and I actually wanted it back."

"You, Tony, are a selfish ass, taking a gift back."

"It wasn't a gift, Rich, she asked for it as a way of forgiving me for a mistake I made. I wish I could've given something else like a horse."

We start laughing again, except Tony wasn't laughing as hard as the rest of us. I look over at him. "I never planned on keeping your bike."

"I know, Jay, that's why I wish I would have come up with a different gift, but I do have something for your birthday."

"Really, aww, I love gifts."

"We all brought you something. We actually planned a special evening for you before your dinner party and before your born day. That way, if we're not your mates, we get to have our time with you, what do you think?"

"If you weren't my mates you weren't getting anywhere near me, I think. Since that's not the case, I love that idea, Jarrod, even though I'm sure, according to Jewel, you are all our mates. So I'm going to listen to my wolf, knowing I kept my promise to my mate."

"Let's grab our drinks, bottles included, and head up to your room."

"Sounds like fun to me," I get overflowing tingles in my belly, the excitement and anticipation makes me skip up the stairs, sashaying my ass every couple of steps. This to remind them of the treat I plan to provide while thinking, I'm about to have the night of my life. I turn left at the top of the stairs, and once I reach my room, I push open my door, feeling the excited anticipation coming from my Alphas. I hear the door close behind me, and even though the lights automatically come on with movement, I see them dim.

Chapter 18

THE QUEEN'S MATES

Tony walks in, taking a seat in the corner and placing items from his pocket on the floor. Jarrod and Richard move to the massive bed I had custom made to accommodate us. Once I knew I had more than one mate, I changed out my king size for this and I love it. It's made low to the ground with large wooden posts of mahogany wood on each corner with one gold and three black wolves engraved. I love the symbolism. As I stand closer to the door leading to my closet I turn watching my Alphas. Tony, sitting in the chair, removes his shirt, stands and removes his pants, no boxers on letting me know they were prepared for me.

I watch him intently, remembering his coco-mocha goodness very well, and the excitement in my lower belly is taking notice as my juices start to flow. I hear a sound from the other side of my bed, and look over to see Richard is already undressed and I missed the reveal. But his more than seven-inch Mighty Man is raring to go as he watches me with lustful eyes. Whatever he has on the end table wasn't more interesting than what's standing at attention from his nether regions, dancing past the second row on his eight pack. I look over to Jarrod, equally as undressed, beach tanned and smooth, and I can't wait to touch him. His bun is still intact and I'm anxious to run my hands through its softness, releasing it from its bundle. My Alpha looks at me with smoldering eyes.

"You, Jay, seem to be the only one not ready to enjoy her born-day gift."

I walk towards the front of my bed, slowly pulling my shirt over my head. I, too, was prepared, hoping for this night. I toss it at Tony who catches it, inhaling my scent before placing it on the floor next to him. I do the same with my bottoms, knowing my juices have flowed because we can all smell me in the air. These he holds onto a little bit longer, eyes closed. Watching the excitement on his face increases mine even more. Watching his member grow even larger while he smells me on my bottoms sends more juices flowing from me. I hear Richard and Jarrod breathing heavily behind me, then Jarrod commands lowly.

"Get that sweet ass over here, Jay."

I sit on my bed, pushing to the middle. I use my feet to lift myself, spreading my legs and providing my undecided Mocha Alpha the view of the delights he might not want to claim. He moves further down in his seat, grabbing himself, fisting to control his excitement. I watch him, smiling because I know how hard this is going to be for him. I lay down, resting my head as I feel Jarrod on my right and Richard on my left, rubbing my arms and my chest. Both hands feel warm and silky with oil. Something that smells like jasmine with gardenia and I like it.

It's soothing to the nose and relaxes my muscles. They start massaging my breasts, focusing around my nipple but not touching it. They're spreading the oil throughout my chest and belly. They start placing soft open mouthed kisses along my arms, and all I keep thinking is I would rather those lips kiss other pointy things on my body. I'm sure they can read my mind because they look at me, smiling, and start teasing my nipples with their tongue. Each giving one a thorough licking before devouring fully, sending tingling sparks shooting into my belly.

While sucking on my nipples they're rubbing up and down my belly, pulling as much of my breast they can fit into their mouths. My breathing is rapidly increasing and shallow, and the sucking and rubbing slows, letting me catch my breath. I don't want it to end; it feels so good. They continue slowly massaging, rubbing my sides, moving further down on each including my legs. Rubbing the inside of my thighs, pushing each open wider and down. I'm spread eagle on the bed, feeling the cool air on my lady parts for only Tony to see, he's the one watching.

As Jarrod and Richard continue to pleasure my breasts, heating my skin, massaging my body, I feel more relaxed, which is surprising considering the electric tingles I feel with each rub. Each suck sends pleasurable sparks into me before I feel it, I feel him. Tony's hands, those huge hands, those long magical fingers. One perfectly long finger touches the inside arch of my foot sending sparks running in and up the inside of my spread open legs. My instinct is to close them but Jarrod and Richard prevent it, massaging them back down and open now for Tony's attention.

His finger runs further up, touching lightly, barely, softly inside my knee. Again, I jerk, again, they massage, again I relax. Trying to concentrate on where his finger is going to touch me next and the sucking, biting, and flicking happening at my breast has my mind reeling. His finger grazes around the outer parts of my lower lips, causing tingles to shoot into me. More of my juices flow out, with my pleasurable groans. His legs touching up against my skin, that too is another point of excited sparks. Jarrod and Richard start moaning, adding vibrations to my nipples.

I can sense their enjoyment pressing into my mind. I reach out, grabbing their penises, filling my hands with hard warmth that's pulsing, vibrating in my palms, increasing the moaning and sucking increased with all our breathing. I forgot about those beautiful fingers of Tony's until I feel them rubbing around the head of my clit. I'm over stimulated at this point, the slightest touch to my sensitive part sends me shivering, close to coming. But no, he wasn't ready to let that happen.

He removes his finger, making me groan in protest. I try to raise my head to look past my fog of pleasure into his dark smoldering eyes. Seeing him lean down towards me, I smile, staring at him trying to concentrate. Tony's sleek tongue takes the place of his finger, but just the tip slithers and touches just the tip of my clit, teasing lightly. He twirls it around causing me to push myself closer to him, wanting more, yet not knowing how much more I can take.

Jarrod and Richard start rubbing a finger gently along the sides of my pussy lips, massaging them open further and further, making it easy for Tony to massage me with his amazing tongue. He starts steadily rotating his tongue around and around and around my clit then sucking me into his mouth, making me scream out in pleasure. And if I didn't know better, I would swear they planned the sucking on my clit to the sucking on my nipples. And so it went on, twirling and twirling, on my clit, on my right nipple, and on my left nipple.

Then hard sucking on each simultaneously, and when I'm about to come they release me and blow on my pleasure tortured organs. And it begins again, twirling, twirling, twirling, on my clit, on my right nipple, on my left nipple, and then hard, hard, and harder sucking on each of my nipples and on my clit. Only this time they don't stop until I screamed and creamed, breathing hard I felt like my heart was going to burst from my chest. Back bowed off the bed not realizing I had continued rubbing and massaging both my Alphas and they too joined me in my mind-blowing release.

I fall back as Jarrod and Richard continue to massage and kiss my body, soothing me through my orgasm. I look up at Tony, who's staring down at me. He walks away, while we continue trying to catch our breath, not moving a muscle. I smile, loving my birthday gift so far. When Tony returns, he passes a hand towel to both Jarrod and Richard who both stand and clean themselves. Tony leans forward, cleaning me, careful of the parts of me that are tender. I pull myself up and start knee walking to Tony, who's watching me intently. "You, my Mocha Alpha, haven't had the opportunity to enjoy yourself yet this evening."

"It's your born-day, Jay, besides I enjoyed you and that was enjoyable enough for me."

"But I didn't get to enjoy you, and like you said it's my born day, come here." He moves onto the bed, and I pull him closer pushing him onto his back. I crawl between his legs pushing his knees slightly open, making room for me to explore. I start massaging his thighs, loving having him laid out at my mercy. "Relax Alpha, I got you." Taking his warm steel in my hands sends power into me. Sparks shoot wherever I touch him, and I know he's more than I can manage, but I'll take all I can.

I gently blow on his tip, before running my tongue around it, giving the tease as well as I took it from him. The jumping excitement makes me grab on a little tighter, and before I realize it, I've surrounded him like my favorite chocolate lollipop, trying to find the secret cream in the middle. Tony's gut tightening moans tell that he's getting close and a few seconds later I feel Jarrod and Richard rubbing my back. Again, the oils that relax me, Jarrod starts pulling my hair that's come loose of its binding, tying it in a messy bun.

My hair bun expert. While he's over me rubbing my back and shoulders, I can feel Richard massaging my butt cheeks open, warm oil spilling down my crack and a nice warmth settles in my ass. Whatever this oil is, I like it, and I can feel myself relaxing. Even more when his finger begins massaging my ass hole. Every time I come up on Tony to catch my breath, I push back further wanting his finger to enter and bring the pleasure I know it can. Releasing Tony only prolongs his release, but I can tell he's not complaining. Finally without me even pushing back Richard pushes his finger in me and hits my pleasure point I shoot forward on Tony, gagging and causing him to jerk.

I'm losing my ability to concentrate on what I'm doing, I release him from my mouth and smile up at him. I begin massaging him with my hand as I slowly begin crawling further up his body. He's watching me, barely breathing, I feel Richard starting to come out and I stop moving. I turn to look at him shaking my head squeezing my asscheeks on his amazing feeling finger. He pushes in creating pleasure again as I continue traveling up over Tony. I grab him, placing him at my opening, rubbing his tip around me, and pressing him into my clit, sending sparks of pleasure there as well.

Tony relaxes back on the bed breathing heavily from his anticipation. I look up and see Jarrod watching me, as he nods his head yes, with the decision I'm about to make. I lean down, grabbing Tony's face, kissing him softly while still feeling Richard slowly moving in and out of my ass hitting my spot. I slowly lower onto his warm steel, stopping when needed to give myself time to adjust to having something this huge pulsing inside of me. I'm taking numerous deep breaths before he's fully inside.

I wait, not sure if I can move with him this deep in me and Richard pushing two maybe three fingers in my ass. All this time Tony has been sucking on a breast and Jarrod has been sucking on the other. And the extreme overstimulation and moving is short circuiting my brain's ability to function. I can't move but I need to move. Richard rubs my back and leans towards me whispering don't move, just relax. He pushes my knees up further on each side of Tony making him slide further up into me.

I begin chewing on my bottom lip, the pleasure is bordering on unbearable. Jarrod releases my breast and even though it gives me a moment to breathe, I miss his touch. I feel Richard remove his fingers and I miss the added pleasure, groaning my complaint. Then I see his smiling brown eyes looking at me, his face coming at me licking his tongue out to tease my nipple sending sparks into it. "My Alpha man, what are you doing over here?" Then I feel it more of the warm oil pooling in the crack of my ass.

Jarrod begins squeezing my ass cheeks while pushing them open, ensuring the warm oil pools in my hole. He pushes his finger in my ass quickly with no problem hitting my spot making me moan loudly.

"There you are, my little pleasure spot, I've missed you all these months."

Hearing him say that I know what's coming, but with Tony in me pulsating over and over, I've no way of moving and not sure I want to. If memory serves me, I thoroughly enjoyed myself the last time Jarrod entered me back there. And then I feel him as he starts rubbing my back.

"Remember, my strawberry love, relax your back, relax and breathe, Tony?"

"I got her."

Soon Jarrod starts pushing his penis in my ass, but to his surprise I don't tense, I didn't squeeze, I pushed back at him, and he slid all the way in causing pleasurable moans and uncontrollable shivering. I can tell it surprises the hell out of Jarrod because I can hear him chanting shit, shit, shit, shit, as he pushes into my spot over and over and over. I look down at Tony, and mouth, move, and he does. When Jarrod pulls out he pushes up and in. When Jarrod pushes in he pulls back and halfway out. Jarrod pulls out, Tony pushes up and in. Jarrod pushes in, Tony pulls back and halfway out, and this rotation went on for long slow strokes in me, out, up and in, in, back and out, out, up and in, in, back and out, over and over.

While Richard and Tony suck on my breasts they all rub every inch of my body whereever their hands can reach. I feel my orgasm building, I'm close to coming, I whisper to Tony and Jarrod quietly in their heads harder, faster, harder, faster, I'm so close, and they listen, Jarrod starts pushing in and out of my ass harder and faster. Tony starts pushing up and in, down and out, with my knees raised up in this position every time he pushes back into me his pelvic bone hits my clit. With every move faster and harder I get closer and closer, faster and harder, from both of my Alphas until I come screaming my pleasure.

I sense them coming within seconds of me, increasing my pleasure and prolonging my orgasm. Right then Richard leans up and begins kissing me capturing my pleasure in his mouth. I collapse on Tony, desperate to catch my breath. Still being stimulated with both Tony and Jarrod still inside of me. I feel Jarrod relax in my ass, pull out, and head to the bathroom. I know I need to move, and I feel Tony get slightly soft and I take this opportunity to rise and roll to the side still trying to catch my breath. Jarrod returns with multiple hand cloths and a large bowl full of warm scented water.

He hands one to Tony as he starts cleaning me, causing me to hiss from the discomfort. I open my eyes to see them all watching me closely. I'm not sure what's happening when Jewel says "Jay, *do you smell that?*" No, what is it, Jewel? "*Chocolate, lots and lots of chocolate and mint and honey, seeping into our senses.*" I smell that all the time, Jewel, why? "*Look at the Alphas, Jay.*" I look again and they're looking at me intensely, I get a little worried. What is happening, Jewel?

"*It's after midnight, you're twenty-five, and they can smell you now, they know you're their mate for real.*" Why does that change any-thing? "*Well, for one, Jay, you were mating with Tony and Jarrod when it happened, so they have tasted you already, and now their wolves are pushing to get at you again.*" What do we do now, Jewel? "*You phase, quickly.*" I jump up and they all jump up as well. I put my hand up screaming "WAIT," they stop. "I'm not going anywhere, Alphas," I phase into my wolf letting them all see her for the first time and smell her as well.

I can tell their wolves are fighting them, but they can hear Jewel talking to them now. I phase back. "WAIT, so I know we're officially mates, and Tony I think you've made a decision you weren't sure you were going to make."

"I'm not upset with how things have turned out, Jay, but I need you right now."

"Well, there's a problem with that."

"And that is?"

"You have to wait until Richard has me, you both had me when I turned twenty-five." Richard steps forward.

"It's a good thing you phased because you will be hard pressed to handle me the way I feel right now."

He lays on the bed.

"You climb on, Jay, because you're gonna need to be able to control me if I get too stron,g and remember, Bryce is bossy as hell when he wants something."

I can see his member pulsating and he's drastically fatter than the other two. I look into his eyes as I start to crawl on his lap. "First, we're accepting each other as mates?"

"Yes, Jay, I accept you as my mate, now get that ass over here."

I do as he says, lowering on him and hissing with the width of him but damn, he feels good. I slap his hands. "Slow your shit, it's huge and my vajajay is delicate."

"Sorry, babe, but you feel tight and fucking good."

I start to rotate my hips, enjoying the friction this causes while he starts twirling his tongue around my nipple. I start moaning and can sense Tony losing it behind me, he's going to have to just wait. I continue rotating faster because I know the other two Alphas are not going to last long before they pounce, and he knows it as well. He increases his pumps up in me countering, the friction caused by my rotating, and within minutes I can feel my pleasure building.

Richard reaches around and grabs my ass cheeks, massaging and spreading them open, which is a teaser he shouldn't be doing. I suddenly feel us being pulled down, they must have grabbed his legs, giving them access to my ass for whoever is there and to my delight, or maybe not, it's Tony. I see Jarrod passing him the special oil and I feel it spilling on my ass as Richard continues slowly pushing up in me while holding my ass cheeks open wide. I can only imagine how I look, but I don't care because my Alphas are making me feel damn good.

Jarrod starts rubbing on my back, on my shoulders and I realize I don't need much preparation when Tony pushes his finger in my ass, spreading the oil inside. By now they know which way to go for my pleasure spot and he hits it immediately. He pulls out and I push out at him, but he slaps my butt.

"Don't be greedy, babe, I'll give you what you want very soon."

He leans down and kisses the middle of my back and the top crack of my ass, pushing his finger in again. He's hitting my spot, making me clench my ass in pleasure. He's making me want it, making me beg for it. I don't want to but every time he puts his finger in and hits my spot I really do want it, and the slow pulsating pushes from Richard while him and Jarrod are slowly sucking on my nipples is driving me crazy. Well, I have something for his ass, I've pretty much mastered the control over my powers. I close my eyes trying to concentrate through the pleasure rolling through me.

I think of only Tony, while mentally whispering "grab yourself softly, easy don't cause him pain. Massage the tip making sure it's nice and slick and covered in oil, I love this oil baby. Now place that hard chocolatey goodness at the entrance to my ass, now slowly, very slowly push into me slightly to the right like you know I like it until you hit my spot. Very good, yes, yes, goddess yes, that's it, now slowly pull out, but not all the way, leave just the tip in. Now again very slowly push into me again, slightly to the right until you hit my spot, very good my mocha Alpha. Now I want you to continue doing this until I tell you to do something different."

I hear Tony groaning and moaning behind me, filling me deliciously. I open my eyes looking down, once again struggling to concentrate on Richard. He must sense something because he releases my right nipple looking up at me saying don't you dare. I smile seductively down at him. "Then stop teasing me and move, Mighty Man." He smiles saying he aims to please, and sure enough he starts pushing up into me still slow but with more force behind, it going deeper and deeper sending pleasure shooting throughout my insides.

I release Tony of my command, and he keeps it up slowly pushing forward hitting my spot and barely pulling out and then in again. I feel pleasurable electricity flowing throughout my body from Tony behind me laying close to my back kissing the back of my neck, to Jarrod to the left of me kissing and sucking on the left side of my neck. I feel his pleasure traveling up my left arm. I must have grabbed him sometime to include him in our circle of pleasure, to Richard under me, licking and sucking on the right side of my neck.

I feel pressure from inside my head, my body, my heart, mingled with the overwhelming sense of right, Jewel? "*I know, Jay, I feel it,*" I open my eyes looking down at Richard seeing his eyes bright with a smirk on his lips. I can see Bryce clear as day and a sense of excited apprehension washes over me before I see his canines drop and he bites down on my shoulder, a sharp pain shoots through my neck but is quickly replaced by pleasure, then warmth as I feel his bond snap in.

I hear Jewel calling Jarrod and Tony's wolves, Jake and Asher, and seconds later I feel their bond almost simultaneously. The pleasure is so intense I never even felt them bite down on me. My teeth start to tingle right before my canines drop and I lean down biting my Mighty Man and suck deeply from him. My bond slides around him settling in place and I release him licking my bite to heal it. I lean up to see Jarrod has made himself available for my mark, so I bite down equally, taking deep gulps until I feel our bonds intertwine. I release him, licking his bite to heal and seal my mark.

The added pleasure from Richard reaching his release and still pulsating inside of me while Tony pushes into me is mind blowing but I feel incomplete. I hear Jarrod moan and feel him shuddering through his release. Afterwards, I let him go, push up on Richard's chest and turn to look at my Mocha Alpha. He presents his neck to me without hesitation and when I bite down on him I feel him coming inside of me, pushing me over the edge joining him. I feel my bond forcefully tangle with Tony's like it wants to ensure it never separates. I release him, licking and sealing my mark before collapsing on Richard's chest.

Tony relaxes and removes himself from my ass and I'm afraid to look at him thinking he's going to be upset. Richard is smiling up at me and once I feel him get smaller, I roll over on the side. I'm an Alpha damn it, so I look at Tony to see him smiling at me.

"You have some temper, Jay."

"I do, Alpha."

"I'll have to remember that."

"You will, Alpha."

"What you had me do felt a hell of a lot better than what I was going to do."

"You're glad I did it then?"

"Yes, I was surprised and the Alpha in me was pissed at first, but, then when the pleasure started shooting up my nut sacks, how could I be mad about it? I'll have to remember you can also have a mean streak in you as well."

Jarrod hands me a towel to clean myself. I phase into my wolf, giving them each a chance to meet Jewel and rub her fur. I phase back, walk up to Tony pushing him onto the bed. "I accept you, Tony, as my mate." He responds, saying he accepts me as his mate, even though I thought the whole biting each other made it clear. I kiss him again for his obstinance and move over to Jarrod. "I accept you, Jarrod, as my mate." He also responds that he accepts me as his mate.

I kiss him softly, running my hands through his messy hair, man bun all gone for the moment. I move over to Richard, and we already said this part. I kiss him just because he's mine and I want to and I finally feel whole, like I have my family.

"Jay, I think your idea about us passing the Regional Alpha-Hoods onto our pups is a great one."

"I'm glad you agree, Tony."

"Yeah, we can hold it for them until they're old enough."

I quietly ask them will they bend the neck? They all stand, and say.

"I, Alpha Jarrod Jacobs, accept you, Alpha Jaidan Emerald Scott, as my Ruling Alpha Queen. I promise to Loyally Defend, Protect and Serve you with my life."

"I, Alpha Anthony Mathews, accept you, Alpha Jaidan Emerald Scott, as my Ruling Alpha Queen. I promise to Loyally Defend, Protect and Serve you with my life."

"I, Alpha Richard Peterson, accept you, Alpha Jaidan Emerald Scott, as my Ruling Alpha Queen. I promise to Loyally Defend, Protect, and Serve you with my life."

I step forward, turning over each of their hands, I extend my claw and slice first Jarrod and hold his hand so my blood can bond with him. I release Jarrods hand, reaching for Tony and grab his hand, and finally grab Richard's hand. I then respond, "I, Alpha Jaidan Emerald Scott, Ruling Alpha Queen accept you, Alpha Jarrod Jacobs, and you, Alpha Anthony Mathews, and you, Alpha Richard Peterson, as my Ruling mates. I promise to Loyally Defend, Protect and Serve you with my life." I whisper into each of their heads. "I promise to learn from and love you all." I couldn't imagine or put words to the power surge that rises in me from just finishing those words. I can sense it in my mates, as well, as I turn and head to the door.

I hear Jarrod behind me asking where I'm going. "Oh, this isn't finished, you have to run and mate your wolves with Jewel. I can tell you she's very excited to get her chance to play with her boys as much as I was." They hurry after me and when we get downstairs I head towards the kitchen. I have a door that leads to the back of the pack, heading to where we train. It's early morning but the moon is still high in the night sky. I quickly phase to Jewel, barely thinking about it and my Alphas join me. We take off into the night and I let Jewel have fun with her Alphas as I had mine. I think what a great way to start my twenty- fifth born day.

Chapter 19

ALPHA JAIDAN

F<u>iguring It Out</u>

I wake feeling happy and yet overwhelmingly suffocated. I can only describe it as being smothered in a muscle sandwich. In front of me, wrapped in my arms, is the back of Jarrod's torso and I'm sure I have a mouth full of his hair. Behind me I can feel my mocha Alpha spooning me with his arm under my head. Below me, hugging my belly like he's trying to dislodge Jarrod from being spooned by me, is my Richard. I smile only imagining what he had to do to maneuver himself into that spot.

Then I think about if we are wearing clothes because if not, Jarrod's ass is glued to the back of Richard's shoulders and Richard's face will see Tony's junk first thing when he opens his eyes. I then remember before we fell asleep making a no naked sleeping rule for all male mates for that exact reason. I'm sure they're all at least wearing underwear. I smile remembering our late-night shower and my birthday gifts, they actually bought me a gift. My very own motorcycle with matching accessories, I can't wait to take her for a spin.

I'm happy they showed up early to celebrate with me. I sent Jane

287

a text to let her know to send out notices to the regional packs that their Alphas were fine, just in case they felt something when they joined my pack. I tried to prevent it when I joined them but wasn't sure. I'm going to meet with her to see how things went, and I know we've been held up in my room most of the morning. I can hear some activity going on around the pack house. I move and start stretching my limbs with protest. "Alphas, I have to get up, I have a meeting with Jane. I know you're awake as I can hear you." I start pushing them off and Jarrod sits up first.

"We're about to make the walk of shame to our suites."

"No need for that. Your rooms all connect through my closet."

"That was great forethought, Jay."

"Yes it was, Jarrod, a small change and a little loss of closet space for all of us." Richard sits up.

"I'm still sleepy, I'm going to rest, Jewel took us for the run of our lives. She's beautiful and damn feisty too, Bryce is head over heels. I had to fight for control back."

"Yes, I remember, and Jewel is still complaining about the bite on her tail; she'll get him back for that, trust me, Richard."

I push Tony. "Wake up, sleepy head."

"I'm awake; just enjoying the noise."

"Nice, but you all have to get to your rooms and pretend you arrived early this morning. I want to surprise my family with you all being my mates, so cover them up." Ok, Alpha, they say at the same time. I jump up, rushing in my closet with them following close behind. I move clothing out the way and start pointing to the panels, "I was going to have your initials put on them but decided against it. You'll know which one leads to your rooms soon enough."

I grab a pair of loose-fitting sweats, a sweater, and leave my hair down to cover up my mark. Jewel, can we disguise our scent? "*I can try.*" Just until our dinner. I pull on a pair of socks, head into the bathroom to take care of business, grab my phone and then head out. Once I leave my suite, I turn immediately towards the security wing. I don't sense many people moving around now. Luckily I didn't run into anyone. I rush to the security door and punch in my code. Once I enter, I quickly rush down the hall and stairs and see Jane sitting at her terminal. She looks at me and smiles.

"You look satisfied."

"I am. How are things?"

"All set up for next week, how was last night?"

"Great. Are things ready for the born day celebration?"

"Yes they are, and happy born day, Jay."

She gives me a hug. "Thank you, Jane."

"I figured out the best room to set up the wipes and trash bin."

"Really, where?"

"The receiving room."

"I don't have a receiving room, Jane."

"You do now, the room that is the informal dining room. We're going to use it as the receiving room and set it up to serve chocolates and tea to the older ladies who attend the event. There's a location that has a planter in it in which I was able to sit the scanning bin in."

"Oh, so you did it already, Jane? Is it safe?"

"Of course. It just looks like a waste bin. Besides, anything that gets put in it will fall past the lid, get scanned for DNA, then fall to the bottom to disintegrate."

"You're correct. Now the only thing we have to do is have Samantha in there passing out our special wipe. It'll compare the DNA to our dead Omega. Very good."

"Tell me, where are your Alphas? I thought they would have marked and mated you by now."

I reach up and pull my sweater down so she can see, and she yells.

"Why can't I tell?"

"I'm masking it so I can keep it a secret till later." She jumps up and hugs me again.

"I'm happy for you, Jay, now we have to keep you safe. And I didn't feel anything, you masked it well with the packs also."

We hear the outer door open, and I adjust my sweater. I want it to be a surprise for my born day celebration. When the next door opens, Samantha walks in all smiling and proud of herself. "Why are you so happy?" She informs us that she has the receiving room all set up nicely, chairs and tables in place. She also hopes I don't mind that she asked Glenda to get her some cleaning supplies to wipe some things down and Glenda volunteered to do it for her. "Yes, it's fine, she's helpful that way."

Samantha continues, saying that Glenda said to tell me that everything is ready for my party, and that we're just waiting for the Alphas to arrive, but Samantha says she told Glenda they arrived early this morning. "How did you know that, Samantha?" She said from Mark because he felt their Alpha yesterday. Still no announcement was made, so they figured we wanted our alone time. She just let her know they arrived early this morning and she wanted to know if that was a problem. "No, that's what we were going to tell everyone, but I wonder why she was waiting for them."

Something about having a personal gift for them, Samantha responds. I scrunch my nose up at that, trying to remember if Glenda ever mentioned any gifts to me that she was getting for the Regional Alphas. Now that I think about it, we've never even talked about them. At that exact moment I get a very bad feeling in the pit of my stomach, and then the DNA alarm goes off.

"What the hell is that?"

"It's the alarm on the DNA, Jane."

"But there are no wipes up there."

"Maybe someone put another type of napkin or something in it and it read it and got rid of it." But as we pull up the screen it reads one hundred percent match, and then we know, Glenda. She was right under my nose. I take off running and Jane takes off behind me. I've never regretted the heavy ass security doors, the fifty-thousand damn stairs and the long ass hallway in my life as much as I do right now. I hit the door, exiting into the pack house, panic setting in my gut.

I reach out to my Alphas. "Guys, where are you?" An Immediate response from Jarrod, saying he's in the shower, asking if I want to join him? "Not now, stay in your room please." He asks why. "Richard, where are you?" He responds, in my room talking to Mark and he, too, wants to know why. "Can you stay there? I will explain later." I feel like my legs can't move fast enough, "Tony, Tony, Tony, where are you?" He finally responds that he's in his room talking with Edmond. "Good, stay there and please, guys don't open your doors." He asks why but says it's too late, and then I hear it.

The clicking sound of a gun, but louder, more powerful and I quietly scream *NO* because I'm going to be late again. My legs aren't moving me fast enough and when I reach the top step and turn the corner, I see her standing at the door pointing the gun. I scream no and she turns to fire again but is tackled from the inside, but I still hear the gun fire. All I can think about is my mocha man, I don't see him. I rush forward into his room to see him lying on the floor holding his chest.

I rush to him, pressing my hand over the hole seeping blood, and I know where this ends. I flash back to that snowy day on the mountain, holding Olivia's dead body in my arms. I start screaming "NO, NO, NO, NO, NO, not again," Jewel, not again. "*Jay, listen to me, he is not Olivia, he is our mate, he is not Olivia, he is our mate.*" I think, he's not Olivia, he's our mate, he's not Olivia, he's our mate, he's, our mate. I look down and see his dark shining eyes looking up at me.

"My sweet,"

"No, Tony, don't talk, this is going to hurt." I extend my claw, cutting around his wound then pressing my two fingers into his chest. I feel the burn from the wolfsbane, but I don't care, I'll give my fingers to save him. I feel it, but it's slippery with his blood. I try again, and it slips, and again, but it's slippery, damn it. I take a deep breath, the burning is painful, but the loss will be unbearable. I use my forearm to wipe the tears from my eyes and grab for it again. I can feel Tony's breathing getting shallow, finally I have it and pull it free, tossing it away.

I want to suck the poison out but there's too much, and it's too deep in him now. Someone was smart enough to call the clinic. I continue to hold him, rocking him; I whisper in his head, "Please fight for me, mocha man, please fight for me, fight for us, please, please, please. I can't lose you, not now. I just got you." I get no response. They try to take him from me, but I can't let go, I won't let him go. Jarrod grabs me saying, Jay, you must let them give him the medicine to fight off the wolfsbane so he can have a chance.

That makes sense. "*Jay, let them save our mate.*" Jewel makes sense, and I let them take him, but I'm close on their heels as we leave his room, heading to the pack clinic. I follow with Jarrod and Richard close behind. I can feel them, sense them, I can sense him. He's still with me, but his breathing is shallow, but he's a fighter, I know it. We get to the clinic, and they get to work, the doctor tells me they'll do all they can to save the Alpha. I look at him. "You'll do all you can to save one of your Ruling Alphas." I reveal my mark and point to the mark on his neck.

I can see the surprise on all their faces, then they say yes My Queen, and they get to work. I step back watching, thinking, swearing that, "Anyone who slacks off will die before he does." Within the hour, he's cleaned up and the fluid line is being administered, but he is still in critical condition. Still not stable, still not giving me any type of response when I call to him, to Asher, but still alive. I hold on to that. I'm so tired, I go in the bathroom to get sort of cleaned up and look at myself in the mirror. I look a mess;

I wash the blood from my hands and then my face.

This is a familiar look for me lately, hopefully this one ends with a win for me. When I come back into his room, I see the nurses setting up a bed for me to rest next to Tony's. I thank them, laying down and grabbing his hand that is closest to me. I start thinking that I wish I could send him some of my quick healing abilities, then he would be better in no time, super fast, wouldn't that be great, Jewel? This is what I think when exhaustion takes over and I pass out. I wake up to something softly, no, someone softly calling my name.

"Jay, Jay, Jay."

"Yes."

"How are you feeling?"

"I'm fine, you're the one that was shot in the chest, how are you feeling?"

"Because of you I'm better, but should you be giving me slack when I'm still recovering from a bullet wound in the chest?"

And then it sinks in, that I'm speaking to Tony. I open my eyes and look over at him, he's smiling at me, I smile back. "You're ok?

"I'm alive thanks to you. You saved my life."

"You would have done the same for me."

"Absolutely I would, sweetness."

"How do you feel, really?"

"Tired, weak as a babe, it hurts to breathe, but I'm breathing."

"Don't speak then."

"Ok, I won't."

"Do you want me to get the doctors?"

"No just keep holding my hand, whatever you're doing is helping me."

"What am I doing?"

"I don't know. When I was hurting badly and trying to heal myself faster, I couldn't. I think the poison was preventing it, actually slowing it down. Suddenly I could feel this warmth seeping into my hand and then my healing started increasing, and I started getting better really quick."

"I have increased healing abilities; all I did was wish I could give it to you."

"Well, your wish came true, Jay."

"I'm glad. I don't think I could have survived without you."

"You would have, you're the Queen Alpha."

"Maybe, but it would have been hard."

"Yes, I'm pretty hard to get over."

I smile at him.

"What, no funny retort?"

"I can't make you laugh right now; it might hurt your wound and you need to heal more." We lay there smiling at each other for a couple more hours. The nurse checks on him and notes his vitals are improving, and gives him another bag of fluids to flush the wolfsbane, just in case. Finally, he is able to speak and releases my hand even though I don't want to let go. Not just yet, so he grabs my hand again.

"Soon Jay, I'm going to have to use the toilet and you're going to have to let my hand go."

I think about this for a moment, and while keeping his hand, I grab a bedpan with the other and hand it to him. He looks at me with that 'are-you-fucking-serious' expression, and I smile.

"Absolutely not, Jay, I will not piss in a bed pan, I'm an Alpha, damn it."

He snatches his hand away and gets up, barely able to walk to the bathroom, while I'm laughing at him so hard I was going to need the bedpan myself. This is the sound Jarrod and Richard walk in on.

"What's so funny? I thought he was dying."

"Well he's not, Rich, the only thing he's dying to do is use the toilet." Tony comes out looking not very happy with me.

"Why are you upset with Jay? She saved your life."

"She knows, Jarrod, and that's all I'm going to say about it."

He climbs back in the bed, still frowning at me and refusing to give me his hand. "You might need more of my healing powers, Tony."

"I'm fine enough to heal on my own for now, thank you."

"Jay, what did you do?"

"Nothing, I promise, Jarrod."

"Right, on to more important things, can someone tell me why your Moon-Ma tried to kill Tony?"

I sober up quickly, looking around at each of them. "She wanted to make her son Regional Alpha of Anneleot-Sky Pack."

"What? How would that be possible?" Tony said it first.

"You're talking about Edmond?"

"Yes, Beta Edmond, he is her son, and if things would have gone her way, she would have been Luna and he would have been Regional Alpha. But it didn't, and he isn't."

"You know, it's funny, Jay, we were talking about him being Alpha while I was here with you, holding it as steward until we have pups. Since he doesn't want pups of his of own, according to him, but he still said no, he doesn't want to be Regional Alpha."

"I know that, but Glenda didn't believe that. It's what she wanted for him, and I didn't figure it out until it was too late, and it almost got you killed. I'm so sorry, Tony, she was right under my nose the whole time. I was so vain I thought the person was trying to kill me."

"Don't beat yourself up, Jay, we all thought they were trying to kill you."

"Where is she now, Rich?"

"In a security holding cell, not doing very well."

"Why is that?"

"She not only shot Tony, she also shot Edmond, as well, and no one will tell her how he's doing. She thinks she killed him."

I jumped up. "How is he?"

"He's fine. The bullet went through his shoulder. They have him next door getting the same meds, but since the bullet didn't stay in, it didn't cause much damage."

"But how did you realize it was her? You started screaming in our head before he was shot?"

"Samantha set up the trap in the receiving room and Glenda volunteered to wipe it down for her. She must have put the dirty napkin in the bin because it scanned and came back with a one hundred percent match. We had just discussed that she was in the room, and it all fell into place. Why I couldn't find her, what she would gain, why I then knew I wasn't the target. I was moving as fast as I could, I promise, Tony."

"I know you were, just think if you wouldn't have gotten there, I surely would have died."

"Was anyone else hurt?"

"No, Richard. Can you have Beta Pete set it up so I can talk to her? But I want to talk to Edmond first."

"Will do, Jay,"

I lean forward and kiss Tony on the forehead. "You rest, you still have some healing to do." As I leave, I kiss both my other Alphas, "I'll see you all soon."

"Jay, please don't do anything that you'll regret."

I look at Richard, "I've never done anything I regretted." I turn and walk out the room, asking the first nurse I see if she can lead me to the room where Beta Edmond is. She walks me two doors down from Tony's room, I knock on the door then enter.

"You never wait for permission to enter."

"I knew you were going to tell me I could come in." He looks well, physically but I can feel the sadness in him.

"Well, it seems that Glenda's my mother?"

I nod my head yes.

"When did you figure it out?"

"Not that long before she shot you and Tony, sorry it took me so long."

"Yeah, how is my Alpha?"

"He's alive, he's healing."

"Thanks to you, Jay."

"And thanks to you for stopping her from shooting him twice."

"I couldn't believe what I was seeing when she shot him the first time."

"I know, I couldn't either, Edmond."

"Why did she want him dead?"

I know I am about to cause him more pain. "She wanted you to be the Regional Alpha you would have been."

"I never wanted to be the Regional Alpha."

"I know that, but she didn't. I think it was more about what she didn't get to be more than what you wanted. She was supposed to be Regional Pack Luna, which meant her son was going to be Regional Pack Alpha. When that didn't happen, she was, needless to say, very upset."

"All this was about making me something I wasn't. All these years I wished for my mother, yet she was in my life for half my life and didn't care enough to acknowledge me. She had the opportunity to get to know me and love me and find out what I wanted, and she didn't."

"Edmond, this wasn't ever about you; you have to remember that."

"Then why did she try to kill Olivia?"

"Because she thought Olivia saw her when she met with her co-conspirators in Miami. Only, Olivia never saw her, or didn't realize she saw her, but for her plan to be successful she needed to make sure. The only way to make sure was to get rid of the nobody female Beta from her old pack. She blamed Beta Shaw because Olivia went there to surprise him, even though he didn't know she was coming, but he was tasked with getting rid of her."

"What about my father? What was his role in all this?"

"Oh, he knew she saw him, but he never saw Glenda. We found footage of him meeting with Gloria. Jane found an old email where he made a promise to your aunt, the Omega from New York, who he had real feelings for that he would always help her in the future. So, when her daughter contacted him about wanting to transfer back to her mother's original pack after her passing, he made it happen for her and her father. He got her a job at the security firm, which let her handle the computer work for Glenda."

"He was meeting in Miami with Beta Shaw because he convinced him he was going to meet his old Omega, but she never showed up, we're not exactly sure why. Glenda was very smart; she kept all the working pieces separate, the only ones who ever knew of each other was her. She knew and met with Beta Curtis, who met with Beta Gloria, and Alpha Edward who met with Beta Gloria, who then met with Beta Carlson. But the only one who ever met with Glenda was Beta Curtis. She was his babysitter when he was young, and his mother was the nurse who helped her fake her death and leave the California pack."

"It all sounds convoluted to me, Jay."

"Yes, it does, Edmond."

"What are you going to do with her? She did try to kill a Ruling Alpha."

"Tony told you he's one of my mates?"

"Yes, we were discussing it when the knock came, and you know what happened after that."

"What would you like me to do with her?"

"Why are you asking me?"

"She is your mother, Edmond."

"It's not like she cares about being my mother, Jay. I say you turn her into the tribunal and let them decide."

"Do you think she'll try this again?"

"Yes, I do, Jay."

"You have no care for what I do to her?"

"Nope, she had no care for me, and she tried to kill the person who is a brother to me. Do you know, Tony would have stepped away and let me be Alpha if I had wanted it. He says I'm probably Andrew's son and older than him, but the headaches he must deal with, I say hell no. I just want to teach at my university, spend my money like I want, and not deal with that shit. Maybe find me a chosen mate who won't care about all that other shit, either."

I smiled at him. "So, then, you picked a university?"

"Yes, Boston University."

"That's great, Edmond."

"Yeah, I need a change of scenery. Now tell me, how long are they holding me hostage in this clinic?"

"Until that bag is complete, then they'll let you leave. Get some rest, Edmond."

"Yes, Alpha. Wait, Jay, I would like to request one thing for taking a bullet for your mate."

"Really, what's that?"

"I would like my Alpha classification back. I was born an Alpha, I would like to live and eventually die as one."

"You got it, Edmond, I'll set it up immediately."

"Thank you, Jay."

"You're more than welcome, Edmond, but you know you could have had that at any time. Tony would have done it."

"Yeah, but my father's mate would have caused bloody hell for it. But with the order coming from the Ruler, she can't say a thing without jeopardizing the family by going against your orders."

"That's very smart of you, and that's what you were waiting for all this time."

"Sure was, as soon as you were Ruler it was going to be my only request. I can't have my family suffering her mouth every day because of me. I knew only you would have the ability to silence someone."

"You're right about that, Edmond." I smile as I turn and leave the room.

Chapter 20

ALPHA JAIDAN

Questions Answered

I was going to take a shower, but I'm stopped by Jane as I leave the clinic. "What's up?"

"I hear you're going to talk to Glenda. Considering your history, do you think it should be you?"

"Why, who do you think it should be?"

"I think you're too close to her. Too close to the whole situation. Maybe let someone else have that conversation. Maybe put it off until you feel better, until your mate is better, when it's not your born day."

I stop at that statement. "You know what, Jane, you're right." I turn around and head back to the clinic and to Tony's room. I enter and see my mates all sitting, talking, laughing with each other, asking if I had spoken to Glenda. "Nope, I decided today is my born day and we should celebrate it and you being alive. Once the doctors say you can leave this room, which I hope is sometime before seven tonight, which is when my celebration begins. We're all going to get dressed in our nice clothes, enjoy some very good food and drinks with very good family and friends and not worry about her until it's not my born day, how about that?"

They all agree, and I join Tony on his bed, sitting between his legs. I grab his hand and think heal, heal, heal faster. He smiles down at me, and whispers, that's definitely helping me, sweetness. The doctors agree to let Tony leave the clinic around five twenty, giving us just enough time to get showered and dressed up for our dinner party. I didn't have the time I thought I would to do something fabulous with my hair, so I chose a sleeked back ponytail with two braids coming down the center front falling to the side, with the back up in a hair clamp hanging down.

I put my silver dress on after getting all jasmine shea buttered up and I'm ready to go. I slip on my strapped silver sandals on the way out and head to the dining hall. I can hear the low music and people talking already, but I don't smell my Alphas. Soon as I near the stairs, I smell them, and I can tell they smell me as I hear them call my name in my head, calling for me before they see me.

I turn to watch as they descend the steps. Jarrod in a dark charcoal suit with a silver shirt and black shoes, clean shaven hair up in his man bun, gray eyes shining at me. Tony, in a light gray suit, charcoal shirt underneath, charcoal shoes, head clean shaven, beard trimmed, and smooth, dark shimmering eyes looking at me. I look him over, checking for signs of pain, I hear him say, I'm fine, sweety, just a little tired, but I'm good. I smile up at him. "Good to know, mocha man." Then there's Richard, in a silver suit like the color I'm wearing, with a white shirt underneath, black shoes, crew cut not as short as usual, shadow beard, brown eyes smiling at me.

They all say simultaneous, Happy Born Day again, Baby. "Thank you" and they each join me, leaning in and kissing my cheek. We turn, heading into my celebration, and as I enter the room it erupts with born day greetings and congratulations, because now everyone knows we're mates based on our smell and the obvious marks I have revealed by my strapless dress. We head to our table and take our seats. I stand thanking everyone for their well wishes and for attending this special day.

"Let's eat, drink, and enjoy ourselves." I'm happy to say that's exactly what we did. I look around the room, seeing all the happy faces of the friends who have become family. Mark and Samantha, who it turns out are mates, Jane and Pete, mates I couldn't have imagined would be. Now I rarely see Jane with her hair up in a bun. Samuel and Lisa with her little twins, her making sure they stay around their table and him watching her like a hawk with love shining from his eyes. He feels me watching him, looks over, and smiles, and I smile back.

Edmond sits at the table with the Security team members. One Alpha in particular I've noticed him training with and talking to a lot lately, but I'm not going to speculate on that at this moment. Only the future will tell. The only one missing is Olivia and I feel sadness from Jewel. We miss her, and she would have loved to see what I'm seeing now. I feel my mates begin rubbing on me asking if I'm ok. "Yes, just looking around, appreciating who is here and missing those who are not."

"We will add to this group in the future, and we will need a larger pack house when we do."

"I'm sure of it, Jarrod, and I think we need to build something closer to the Ocean on the back end of the property."

"That's pretty far from where the pack house is now, Jay."

"I know, Richard, but I want a new beginning in a new location. A brand new everything, that way I can ride my horses on the beach like I did on my island. Jarrod can surf and I can get even better at it, and we can teach you and Tony."

"Sounds like a great plan, Jay."

"Ones we'll tackle after today, Tony. Tonight I want to celebrate, starting with food, I need food." So, I eat, and believe me, I eat more food than I've ever eaten in a twenty-four hour period, but avoid my favorite double chocolate cake. I'm not sure if I'll ever be able to eat it again without it bringing back bad memories of Glenda. Hopefully soon because it tastes good, and this will be my first born day not having a taste, that I can remember. Then I dance and I'm sure my feet will hurt for days, especially after I decide to kick my shoes off. But I have to dance with all my Alphas equally, making sure I save most of the slow ones for Tony since he is still healing.

Jarrod thinks he's milking it, but I didn't care, he was breathing and he could milk all he wanted for a little while, at least. Jarrod came with cases of my favorite sangria, one of my born day gifts, and boy was I happy. My girls and I enjoy quite a few bottles of our favorite drink. I actually drank so much sangria it required all my mates to carry me to bed many, many, many hours later. From what little I can remember, it was a great born day. One of the best ones since my Nanna Grace left me.

I decide to let Jane conduct the interrogation of Glenda, and I no longer refer to her as my Moon-Ma. I, along with my mates, watch from the viewing room attached to the interrogation room. At first, she would answer no questions, but after Jane agrees to give her information on Beta Edmond, she quickly agrees to talk, saying first, she would like to say, 'I love you. Jaidan, I know you're watching, you were never my target, I just wanted my son to have the future that was supposed to be his. I'm sorry I took it from him, I hope he can forgive me if he survived. I hope the goddess saves him. I never meant to hurt him. I don't know where things went wrong.'

Jane asks her why she had to kill Beta Olivia Parker. I could see the pain on Jane's face. She continues saying Olivia saw her in Miami. No, she didn't, Jane responds, she didn't even remember seeing Alpha Edward until she saw his picture, so she wouldn't have told anyone. She looks up at where I imagine she thinks the camera is, saying,

"Jay, she saw me at the airport. I didn't know who she was, but she was very helpful with getting my luggage for me and directing me around in Miami. I had never been there, you see. When we were talking, we figured out we were going to the same hotel and decided we would share a cab together, and while standing, waiting for our cab, I was nervous, and she asked me about it. I spoke on how I was meeting my pup's father for the first time since he was conceived, and she wished me luck. She then tells me she was nervous about how her boyfriend, Curtis, was going to react to her surprising him while he was in town for his computer work."

"When I heard that, I knew the mistake I had made had jeopardized everything I had put in place for my son's future. What was the chance she would not remember me? I couldn't take that chance. I sadly made up an excuse about forgetting one of my bags, and told her I would hopefully see her at the hotel. I left her standing there, went back in the airport, and changed my flight."

After I heard that, I knew there was never a situation where she would have thought it wasn't required to kill Olivia. Or to cancel her plans all together because that was never an option for her. There was never a likelihood we would have figured out some random older lady Olivia helped with her luggage at the airport was the person we were looking for. I stand and walk into the room; she stands up looking at me with pleading eyes. I thought I would be angrier, that I would want her dead, but I feel mostly pity. I was angry, yes, but mostly pity, she says please forgive her.

"No, Glenda, I won't. You know, the crazy part is Edmond didn't want to be the Alpha. If you would have taken any time to really know him while on the island you would have known that. Even the day you shot him, he was talking to Alpha Tony, who was asking him to take the position, since he's one of my mates." I see the surprise shock on her face before she asks me if Edmond really said no. "Yes, Glenda, he did, then you shot them both." She drops back down to her seat and starts sobbing loudly. I turn to leave the room. "Jane, we're done here." Then I walk out.

When I exit, I walk into the open arms of my Alphas, silent tears for the loss of the woman who was like a mother to me for half my life, but more for the woman who was like a sister to me and her short life. Jane exits the room

"I'm sorry, Jay."

I compose of myself. "It's fine, Jane, please have her transferred to the prison for our kind for attempted murder of both Alpha Edmond Mathews and Ruling Alpha Anthony Mathews."

"Yes, Alpha."

We turn and leave the viewing room. Glenda never made it to the prison, she died thinking she killed her son, because no one told her differently, that I'm aware of. She was found the following day in her holding room dead from wolfsbane poisoning. Apparently, she had it in a heart shaped pendant vial she wore around her neck. She left no note, no apology, nothing, she just didn't want to pay for what she did in Edmond's name. I know this upset him, but I told him I would leave her things for him to go through, and maybe in there he would find something. He said not now, but maybe later.

I had her casita locked up with instructions to never be opened, and gave Edmond the key for him to use whenever he was ready.

The rest of the weekend was spent preparing for the Alphas from the packs and their attendants to arrive to bend the neck. The additional security arrived just in time, but from what Jane and I had set up in advance, things moved as smoothly as could be. We chose to reveal who I was along with my mates via large screen in the theater hall located on the west section of the property.

We secured Beta Matt and her father upon their arrival informing them of what we knew. Beta Matt eventually admitted she was the one who shot Olivia for her aunt, who she believed should have been the Ruling Luna of her mother's pack. She wishes she would have known that day in the woods who I really was, and she would have shot us both. We determined her father had nothing to do with his daughter's plans so we released him with a warning.

The announcement that the next Ruler was a Queen went over as well as could be expected in twenty twenty-three. But after hearing and seeing I was also mated to all three Regional Alphas, most bent the neck out of respect and thoughts of safety for their families. Some left, not enough for us to feel threatened over, but evidently concerned about.

The plan moving forward is to travel to those packs, give them the opportunity to accept me or be replaced by an Alpha that will. If the head of the pack doesn't accept the Ruler, the pack doesn't, and there are about four or five packs now whose Alpha walked out of the ceremony, refusing. It was a small number, but still a number. Jane is compiling who those Alphas are, their locations, and their pack sizes. Jewel is under the belief that once the Regional Alphas accept me that those Alphas under them, are all under me, but that's never been tested in the past. No Alpha has ever not bent the neck to the new Ruler. We'll have to see what happens. But we're up to the challenge, regardless.

The paperwork was issued to re-instate Beta Edmond Mathews back to Alpha Edmond Mathews, and there was noise made at first until said unhappy she-wolf was informed it was by decree of the new Ruling Alpha Queen. Who was now mated to Alpha Anthony Mathews, who is her Regional Alpha. That shut her up very quickly and made Edmond very happy.

I'm excited about all the plans my little ruling pack has put in place for our family and the wolf kind, and it feels like the next adventure will be a lot more fun.

In the beginning I wasn't too happy with some damn prophecy ruling my life. Now when I think of who I have in my life because of that damn Prophecy, it turned out to be the best thing that ever happened to me!

The End

Special Acknowledgements

MY DEN TEAM

I would like to give *Special Thanks* by acknowledging the people in my life who provided productive advice, creative feedback, and well needed encouragement which moved me to publishing my books. To my Sister~Friends Kima YB. and Tracy Dk. and to my Siblings Tori S., Kyle S. and Robin L. for being my own personal cheering squad and always showing support.

To my Brother~Friend Garrick C. for being the best everything but mostly my Editor-In-Chief, To my new friend April W. for being the best line editor I know. I couldn't have gone to print without you both. Finally, to my amazing Beta Den Readers, you know who you are. Thanks for helping me realize I wasn't crazy to write my story and that there are those who will read it, or they're just crazy too.

Authors Bio

I spend most of my time reading all forms of romance genre, paranormal werewolf shifters being my favorite even though dragon, fae, and witches are not far behind. I'm a big lover of all animals, from horses, cats, and dogs, but currently my Maine Coon is capturing my heart and taking up anytime left after writing.

Growing up my grandmother had a library of historical romance novels which introduced me to this genre and helped me escape into all forms of romance that I've expounded on over the years. My love for those books sparked my love of reading, imagining, writing, and dreaming, that one day I would see my imaginings on the pages of my own novel. I'm excited the day is finally here, I finally had the courage to pursue being a published author, and hope the readers enjoy reading as much as I have enjoyed writing.

I hope you enjoyed the Finale of "A Jaiden's Prophecy Duology ~ The Alpha Queen's mate." I hope you will continue along with me on my next paranormal romance. "Destiny Be Damned." A dragon shifter romance with a morally gray protagonist, who will keep you on your toes more than Jaidan did!

If you would like to follow me and find out more about what's coming out next or which author signing event I will be at you can visit my website at http://www.magnoliaxen.com